MICHAEL LAWRENCE

Michael Lawrence

Killarney Traynor

Original Thirteen Publishing

For Terry,
who said: "Remember that old script of yours?
Let's make a movie!"

and for Dan,
who brought my Michael to life.

Prologue

Samantha Harris decided to take Amtrak instead of flying from California to New Hampshire. It was a decision that she made on a whim, but once her mind was made up no amount of arguing would change it.

Her husband, Jonathan St. Jean, tried. It was Thursday night, date night. They were at home enjoying dinner for two with their cells phones left in the bedroom where they could not hear them. He offered her round-trip, first class airline tickets, something that she could have easily afforded on her own, but he could not persuade her. The romance of the idea had got hold of her and she would not budge.

"I've never taken the train before," she explained to him over a dinner of vegetarian lasagna and white wine. "It'll be an experience. I might even be able to use it in my next novel. It'll be a homage to Agatha Christie."

He laughed at that and Samantha warmed to the deep rumbling sound. They had been married a year now but being around Jonathan still made her feel like a teenager with a first crush. He was tall, fit, with a full head of dark hair and the polished manners that came easily to those born well-off.

I got lucky this time around, she thought as she watched him over her wineglass. *I only had to marry a few frogs before I landed my prince.*

"I'm not sure if I'd be so willing to reenact *Murder on the Orient Express*," Jonathan was saying, still grinning. "But honey, a train will really extend your travel time by what, at least another day?"

"Oh, at least a week. I want to do it properly."

"I'm not sure there is a *proper* way to do the Amtrak," he grunted. "What does Matt have to say about it?"

"I haven't told him yet."

His dark eyes glimmered at her as he took a slow sip of his wine. "Waiting until you've bought the tickets? Probably wise."

It was gently said, but nevertheless, Samantha felt like she needed to defend her son. "He'll be game. Matt's a good boy."

"That he is."

It was a generous admission on Jonathan's part. Matt had not been thrilled when Samantha married Jonathan and a year of living together had done little to soften his opinion. Now that he was fifteen and suffering from the usual, hormonal, teenager drama, he had become even more withdrawn and sullen.

"He always needs some time to get used to new things," she explained, "But once he gets into it, he'll be fine."

Hearing the words aloud made her wonder whether she was, in fact, speaking the truth. Matthew *was* a good boy, that much was true, but she was not going to New Hampshire for the impressive mountain peaks or the pristine lakes. She had been hired as a guest lecturer to teach a summer course at a college where she'd once been a student. In between the days of trying to convince weary, and often inattentive, students of the importance of properly using the passive tense, the correct placement of commas, and how to plug plot holes, she was also scheduled to outline and begin the latest novel in her mystery/thriller series. It was more than enough to keep anyone busy. She was not entirely sure how she would manage to keep a teenage boy occupied as well.

Jonathan got up from his chair and took her empty plate along with his own and set off for the kitchen. Samantha followed. While he loaded the dishwasher silently, his forehead pinched in thought, Samantha pulled a plate of fruit from the fridge and carried it out onto the back patio.

A warm breeze met her at the door, caressing her skin with a soft touch. Overhead, palm trees swayed to the gentle rhythm of the wind and the comforting chorus of the Pacific, beating against the rapidly darkening beach. From Samantha's vantage point, she could see a handful of couples, strolling hand in hand on the edge of the surf, at peace with the world and themselves.

It was simply another gorgeous Californian night and Samantha Harris was about as lucky as any woman could hope to be. She was blessed with good health, a good man, a good son, and a thriving literary career. Only three books into her *Cromwell* series and already critics were comparing her with Patterson, Gerritsen, and Cornwell. She had earned enough money to live here on the beautiful, California coastline and to drive a custom Mercedes. Her mother was now happily situated far enough away so that she could not cause too much trouble, and though she was a few years past forty, Samantha was frequently, pleasantly reminded that she could still pass for at least thirty-five.

Despite her marital status, Samantha was in no way short of admirers. She was trim with a curvy, feminine figure and large eyes the deep brown color of melted chocolate, trimmed with long eyelashes.

Then there was this lecture series. It was an honor really. The dean of the college, a man she vaguely remembered from her student years, had called her personally to make the request. Of course, she had been flattered, albeit hesitant. When her agent heard about the offer, however, she had gone mental with excitement.

"Of course you'll go," she had said. "You need more exposure on the East Coast and this gig will lend you an academic air. It'll look terrific on your bio. You *have* to do it."

So here she was, several months later, making plans for a trip to the other side of the country. Samantha looked out over the ocean, listening to the seagulls and breathing in the ever-present scent of flowers and palms. Despite everything, she could not help feeling some regret over her decision. An entire summer was a long time to be away and the nervous butterflies in her stomach would not stop their fluttering.

It'll be all right, Sam, she told herself. *You can do this. It's been a long time since you've seen Portsmouth or Noble College. Things change: people age, memories dissipate, and we move on. There's nothing to be worried about.*

She was relieved when she heard Jonathan come up behind her. There was a container of brownies in his hand and she smiled when she saw it. It was a game they played every date night. She would bring the sophisticated, healthy snack outside and he would follow with the one she really wanted.

He put the container onto the table, but instead of settling into his usual chair, he came up behind her and wrapped his arms around her waist. She leaned back into his embrace and felt his chin rest on her shoulder. She lifted her hand and cupped his face and he nuzzled her neck tenderly. Her tension melted away at his touch.

"How does a girl get so lucky?" she murmured.

"Hmmm." He lifted his head to look out over the ocean. "I was just thinking the same thing, babe."

"It's going to be hard, leaving you behind."

He let go of her and stepped around her so that he was looking into her eyes. He placed a hand under her chin and lifted it. "Are you sure you want to go?"

She blinked, startled. "Do I want to go?"

"You seem to be dragging your heels about this whole thing." His hand slid up to caress her cheek. "If you don't want to do this, don't. No one can make you."

She laughed. "Except Carol."

"Carol's your agent, of course she's going to push. But you're the star, babe. You don't have to do anything you don't want to do."

Samantha leaned into his hand and looked out towards the sea. He was right. She had signed the contract and the arrangements had all been made, but even so, she could certainly find a way out of the obligation. But that would be messy, unprofessional, and, worst still, there would be questions raised. She simply could not afford that.

If only Daddy were still here.

Jonathan was a rock, but Samantha's father had been an earthmover and one word from him would have set

Samantha's doubts to rest at one. But even the indomitable will of Jasper Brown could not force the cancer from his system and so here she was, stuck in the middle of a situation she did not want to face.

Why did I say yes?

The answer to that was simple. It was a flattering proposal, one made by Professor Charles Stewart, a well-respected man of boundless energy and charm and on the face of it, there had been simply no reason to say no.

You're just nervous, she told herself. *It's been a while and no one likes a class reunion. But it'll be fine when you get there. There's nothing to fear.*

So she laughed as she squeezed Jonathan's arm reassuringly. "I guess I just don't like the idea of leaving you alone in this great big house." She looked up adoringly at his blue eyes, so reminiscent of the ocean below. "Say you'll come and visit while we're out there."

Jonathan Harris returned her smile. "Just try and keep me away."

Tuesday

1

P ure notes echoed in the empty hall.

"Ici bas, tous les lilas meurent,

"Tous les chants des oiseaux sont courts...

"Je reve aux ete, qui demeurent toujours..."

Even the poor acoustics could not take away from the artistry of the song and the elegance of the performer. Professor Emma Gagnon sat up straight in her uncomfortably stiff, folding chair. Her hands rested on her knees. Her eyes were closed, blocking out every other sense as she drank in the sound. She had heard the song many times over the course of her career – it was a sweet, wistful song, easily learned but harder to interpret - yet she never tired of it. She spoke little French, but she knew the translation by heart.

"...I dream of summers that remain forever..."

The pianist took advantage of the brief interlude between verses to improvise. Arlene Chase was a talented pianist who could read music as well as any practiced musician, but she always preferred to interpret.

It was no matter: Rose Chancellor would be the accompanist at the concert on Friday night, a good, steady, reliable player who never deviated from the written notes. Even so, it would take more than Arlene's spirited interpretation to detract from Bridget Madden's exquisite soprano.

Bridget's voice came on cue, soft, tender, heartbreaking,

"Ice-bas les levres effleurent,

"Sans rien laisser de leur velours..."

It was masterfully delivered. Emma smiled, in spite of herself, and Harry came to mind. Harry, her husband of twenty-two years; the man she had loved for far longer than that, the man who was insisting upon her retirement. "You've been teaching for almost forty years now, Emma," he had said. "It's time for other things, time to look after yourself for a change."

"Je reve aux baisers qui demeur-rent toujours..."

Poor Harry. He simply could not understand that Emma loved what she did, that she taught as much for herself as she did for others. Then again, how could she expect him to understand what it was like for a woman who wanted children so badly and never could bear any of her own to full term? How could he understand the kind of emotional suffering that came from such grief?

It was what society often described as an old fashioned desire, one not really considered worthy or necessary for a woman with a career. Yet ever since she was a small girl Emma had yearned for children of her own. Harry had been willing. Four times they had tried. Only once did the pregnancy last through eight months. Finally, the callous doctor made a painful diagnosis: "You simply weren't made for children..."

That was twenty years ago and the memory was still raw enough to make her eyes moisten. Teaching the young was a way to express that nurturing part of herself which had no other outlet. Teaching, looking after Harry... and Bridget.

She opened her eyes then. Arlene was building to the final verse, her hands spread wide across the keys, her red hair glinting in the shaft of sun that fell through the wide old window panes.

Bridget was watching Arlene, the sheet music held loosely in her hands. She had been Emma's ward since she was orphaned at age fifteen, a slim, small slip of a girl with big brown eyes, black hair, dusky skin, and ambition that very nearly matched her spirit. She was indomitable, strong-minded, and assertive, about as different from Emma's temperament as you could get, yet she stood quietly now, as though mesmerized by the music. Music was what they shared and that love of song and melody had gotten them through many a rough patch.

The cue came and Bridget began sing the final verse. This time, Emma did not hear the French, all she focused on was the meaning of the words:

"Here below, all men weep

"For their friendships or their loves...

"I dream of couple who remain...

"Who remains... forever."

Such a beautiful, ethereal song. Some dismissed it as blatantly sentimental, but Emma had never been one among that crowd. She was, as Harry often said, too old-fashioned and romantic for the world as it now was. She could not help it any more than she could help the fact that her eyes were blue or that she had grown into a younger version of her mother. Some things simply were.

The last notes drifted away. The rehearsal was over and only just in time. Bridget and Arlene went over the last few bars quickly while Emma reluctantly got to her feet and checked her watch. It was nearly two, almost time for her Musical History and Theory 101.

It was a good class, even if it was beneath her usual grade and contained some of the more troublesome students in the college. She waited for Bridget and when the conference was done her ward reluctantly turned towards her. Emma did not notice the look of weariness in her ward's eyes – she clapped her hands with gushing pride in her student.

"That was wonderful, dear, just wonderful. It's going to be beautiful this Friday."

Bridget shrugged uncomfortably, "It'll be all right." She looked anxious, as though she wanted nothing more than to run from the room.

Emma touched her cheek tenderly.

"I am so proud of you," she whispered.

The interaction was interrupted by a buzzing sound that brought Bridget's head down to her phone. Emma's hand fell limp at her side. She suddenly became conscious again of the expanding rift between her and her ward. Many times she had tried to convince herself that this was normal and temporary in any relationship, but no matter what she told herself, each rebuff of affection, however mild, was painful.

Bridget's fingers flew across the face of her phone. She held it angled so that Emma was unable to see who she was texting. She took a half-step towards the door with her eyes still locked on the screen.

"You'll be home for dinner tonight?" Emma asked. "It'll be late, I have the Dean's party tonight."

It was a party for which she had tried her hardest to get an invitation extended to Bridget. It wasn't every day that a famous author, one with an intimate connection to Emma and Bridget, came to Noble College.

Emma had hoped to introduce Bridget to Samantha Harris but the Dean's assistant had been unmoving – faculty only, as alcohol would be served.

Bridget barely lifted her head. "Can't," she said. "I'm busy."

She turned and hurried off, only remembering to say goodbye as if it were an afterthought.

Emma watched her go.

Poor girl, she thought. *You poor, poor girl.*

She said goodbye to Arlene and left the hall humming to herself: *"Here below, all men weep..."*

2

She was immediately recognizable, even from the behind; the curvy figure draped in expertly cut, well chosen, fashionable clothing. The long, dark, wavy hair, the laughing eyes, the bow-shaped mouth. She moved gracefully, sinuously, just like the girl he had known twenty years ago as Samantha Brown. One look at her now and you could understand why it was that she'd left a trail of broken hearts behind her when she transferred out of Portsmouth.

Samantha Brown Harris, he thought. *It's been a long time.*

Much had changed. Much had not.

He had changed. Then he had been merely Charles Stewart, a man who had been made immune to her particular charm by a merciful creator. Now he was Professor Stewart, Dean and President of Noble College. He was a little older, a little wiser, a little heavier, and with much more on his plate than he had had in his younger days.

Harris stood at the bottom of the stairs, talking to a tall, lanky teenager with a sullen expression. The long walk from the car to the station had winded Stewart. He was not as young as he used to be and diabetes had slowed him down even more. He waited a moment, catching his breath and watching them.

Samantha Harris. If only you knew the hopes we've pinned on you.

Noble College was in a poor state, not that you could tell from looking at the buildings or its president. Recently, three years ago to be exact, the committee had recognized that something needed to change. Attendance was down, grants were getting harder to secure, and last year's particularly harsh winter had further impacted the need for repairs now sorely necessary to keep the buildings up to code. The committee, which he had chaired, had put together an ambitious plan that combined fundraising, advertising, and high-visibility events to draw attention to the school's stellar reputation for quality education and it's gorgeous New England locale.

The guest lecture series had been Stewart's idea. At first the committee had balked at the idea of paying appearance fees and room and board for high-rollers who were used to the finer things in life. He had insisted and then persisted and made use of his legendary charm. Samantha's offer to halve her usual fee, in recognition of her own student days, was the final incentive that won the committee's approval.

Though Stewart may have won the battle, he was keenly aware that the war was far from over. Much was riding on this lecture series, his own reputation included. If this plan failed, it was very likely that he would be the last president of Noble College. The thought was depressing even for a man who was not the type to entertain melancholy. He forced the worry to the back of his mind, put on his most welcoming smile, and called Samantha's name.

Samantha turned and her cheerful smile faded into shock when she saw who it was that had come to pick her up. She tapped her son's arm and the pair charged forward, carry-ons in hand, to greet him. Fifteen minutes later, they were outside, Samantha tipping the porters while Stewart hauled the last of the suitcases into the trunk of his car. They had brought very little luggage despite their planned two month stay and he mentioned this to Matt.

The boy did not look up from his phone. "Mom brought tons of junk. She just sent it on ahead. You know, to the address she got or something."

"Very sensible."

Matt shrugged. "She's got a lot of papers and books. Probably didn't want to pay the train fees for the extra."

"I'm surprised you came by train. I prefer flying myself."

The boy grimaced. "So do I."

Samantha turned to them, smiling as she returned her wallet to her purse. Though her eyes showed obvious signs of weariness she was in an exuberant mood and beamed.

"I feel like a real celebrity!" she exclaimed. "I didn't expect the committee to send the dean to pick us up."

Stewart made a gracious little bow. "Well, with everything it took to get you here, I guess I just wanted to make sure we had the real you."

She laughed, a bell-like sound, and Matt rolled his eyes.

Stewart took Samantha's arm and led her to the passenger seat. "We're just so glad you both are here. There's been so much excitement about your classes – far beyond our expectations."

That last comment was an exaggeration, but if there was one thing Stewart knew, it was that egos needed petting. He opened the door for her.

"I hope you like the house. Emma helped me pick it out. You remember Emma Gagnon, don't you?" he asked.

Samantha hesitated, trying to recall the name, then recognition lit her face. "Oh, yes, of course I remember her." She slipped into the car and beamed up at him. "You look wonderful. How is Miles, by the way? I'm so looking forward to meeting him in person."

Miles.

Even the mention of his name was like a knife driven into his heart.

He answered carefully, "We decided to call it off. We weren't suited for each other."

He shut the door so that Samantha could not see the emotion on his face. By the time he had worked his way around to the driver's seat, his cheerful expression and easy manners were firmly back in place. His next intended statement choked in his throat when he turned and found Samantha with her hand to her mouth and her eyes closed.

"Are you okay?" he asked with alarm.

She held up an ornate little box with a cameo on the cover. "Just another one of my headaches," she said, sheepishly. "I don't travel well, I'm afraid."

"Well, who does?" he replied. "We've arranged a little welcome party for you tonight, at my house. It's just a gathering of old friends to welcome you back and wish us luck. But if you aren't feeling well…"

Samantha shook her head vigorously as she struggled to down the pills.

"Oh," she said, when she was once more able to speak. "I wouldn't want you to cancel your party! I'll be fine, honest. I get these all the time, but a couple of pills and I'm okay. I'd be delighted to meet everyone."

For a moment, Stewart dropped his façade. He was no longer the dean of the college, a man trying to impress a pretty woman – he was a man relieved.

"I'm just so glad you've come," he said.

Samantha Brown Harris smiled at him through pain-rimmed eyes.

3

———

It was never Sarah's fault.

This was something that Thomas Atkinson learned early on about his employee. She could be late for work for three days in a row, spill coffee on a rare second printing of *The Fellowship of the Rings,* accidentally ring up a five dollar book as fifty dollars, or get a parking ticket for leaving her bike in the street and her reaction to all of these offenses would be the same: *"It isn't my fault, okay? If such-and-such hadn't done this-and-that, it would have been fine."*

In all the months that Sarah Hopper had worked at Atkinson's Books, Thomas Atkinson had hardly heard more than a slight variant of the same refrain. Take today for instance; Thomas opened his shop at ten in the morning on Tuesdays, and required his employees to arrive ten minutes beforehand. His apartment was over the store and he was loath to have his morning peace disturbed by fledgling adults messing about in the shop below. This seemed to him a reasonable expectation, even for college kids. To their credit, most of the staff over the years had managed to drag their weary, hung-over selves in by ten, if not earlier. Max Griffin, his other employee, who was even less interested in the book business than Sarah, managed it regularly and he was a totally hopeless human being otherwise.

Sarah, however, would be late, because Sarah was always late. You could set your watch by her tardiness. Sometimes Thomas wondered why he put up with the Sarah Hoppers of the world. His standard reply, when asked by one of the few people whom he was friendly with, was that he had once been a college student himself and he understood the type. When he was being honest with himself, he knew better. The Sarah Hoppers and Max Griffins of the world came cheap and they never stayed around long enough for one to become friendly with them.

Thomas Atkinson had always considered himself someone who lived outside of the norm of society. Where once he was an outsider by popular decree, he had come to embrace the role.

His shop was a reflection of this. The quirky store was housed in a small building, just off the main road. His business model attracted wealthy tourists and locals who wanted not just a copy of *Waiting for Godot*, but a specific *edition* of the same. This resulted in a comfortable lifestyle: lonely, perhaps, but quiet, tranquil, and self-sufficient. Thomas Atkinson was, in the end, his own man.

So it came as something of a shock to him when he heard frantic banging on the glass of the shop's front door at nine forty-five in the morning. Thomas was upstairs in his apartment washing dishes with a franticness that spoke to great personal excitement. He listened for a moment, wondering if the intruder would pass. When the pounding continued, he dropped the dish rag, grabbed his glasses from the shelf, and hurried downstairs.

The door's window was almost completely covered with advertisement pages that announced the various plays, shows, and live music performances that were going on around town. At first, Atkinson could not see who it was on the opposite side of the door. He was reaching for the handle when a face suddenly appeared within the one spot free of advertisements.

It was Sarah, fifteen minutes early. He almost choked.

Atkinson unlocked the door and opened it. Sarah, a thin, pretty girl with stick-straight brown hair, pushed past him, a warm breeze and the scent of the ocean following in her wake. She was weighed down as usual; a camera case with its nylon strap crossed over her chest, her purse clutched in one hand, and, of course, the ever-present yellow backpack, packed so solidly that it seemed that it might burst at the seams. For a girl who showed no interest in any of the volumes that she sorted, stacked, and sold in Atkinson's shop, she was always conscientious of her studies.

"Thanks," she said brusquely as she passed.

Her incivility nettled Atkinson and he called after her, "Hey!"

Sarah stopped and turned half-way with an air of reluctance.

He gestured to the door, "Where's your key?"

Few of Atkinson's employees had a key. Max certainly did not, but Max was never willing to work the late shift, unlike Sarah, who did on occasion. Once or twice Atkinson had left her the responsibility of closing up the shop. True, she was a hair-brained, perpetually late person, but she was also scrupulously honest, another personal quirk of hers that Atkinson could not quite reconcile.

She stood there, her dark eyes flashing and a guilty flush stealing across her face. The expression struck Atkinson.

What are you running from, Sarah? he wondered silently.

Sarah shrugged. "I lost it."

She hitched the backpack strap farther up her shoulder. Then she turned and hurried towards the backroom, her ponytail bouncing.

Atkinson grunted. *Trying to outrun your landlord again?*

He wanted to shout his thoughts out to her but there was no point. It was not his business whether she could pay the landlord or not. He knew that she was frequently behind in her rent and often had to rely on the good graces of her land-lady to keep the roof over her head. It was not Atkinson's fault that Sarah chose boyfriends badly, or had eating issues, or was keeping her grades up only by God's blessings. These were all things that she confided to Max and, doubtless, her girlfriends. They were her problems, not Thomas Atkinson's. He was just her employer, and was in no way looking to change that relationship status.

All that mattered to Thomas was that Sarah was here, meaning that he could open the shop now rather than later. He flipped the open sign over and went back up to his apart-ment to finish with the dishes. He had his own problems to work out.

4

Professor Stewart lived only a mile from Noble College in a large, rambling, renovated New England farmhouse. It had a long driveway and a lovely shaded patio that overlooked the well-tended gardens. It was, Samantha Harris thought, as she got out of her rented steel-gray Volvo and straightened her black dress, just the sort of house that one could turn into a gentile bed and breakfast.

The thought of Professor Stewart turning into an innkeeper made her smile. The professor lived to host events, but he was the quintessential small college dean: verbose, well read, and as content as anyone could reasonably expect to be. She thought again, as she had thought when she first laid eyes on the man at the train station, that she had never met anyone so particularly suited to his profession.

Lucky Professor, she thought, as she followed the stone path around to the front of the house. *Not everyone is so fortunate to find their perfect position in life.*

Samantha had been careful to arrive fifteen minutes after the party had already started. She did not want to be the first person there nor did she not want to stay very late. The trip had been long and exhausting and she disliked leaving Matt alone in the rented house on his first night here, not that he had seemed at all disturbed by the idea.

Just a few hours to pay my dues, then home to bed, she promised herself.

It would not be hard to tear herself away. New England faculty cocktail parties might be useful in their own right but they paled in comparison to the excitement of a West Coast parties with all the pomp and circumstance. One never knew who they might meet at those parties… or who one might happen to bring home.

Not that I'm into that sort of thing, anymore, she reminded herself. *I'm perfectly content with Jonathan.*

Just the thought of her husband and the distance between them was enough to evoke a pang of regret. It was a feeling that she knew she had to put aside so that she could attend to the business at hand.

The patio was already alive with sound and movement. Faculty members mingled about, wine glasses in hand and dressed in the standard variety of blacks and blues. The college and art patrons dressed with a little more color, generally in the form of patterns or bright colors. They spoke with privileged student teachers, who responded with the nervous pasted on smiles of those who had been elevated beyond their usual station in life.

There was no obvious wait staff. Samantha recognized the man behind the outdoor bar who was pouring drinks and holding up glasses of wine for playful inspection as Stewart's own assistant, Cumberbatch.

This is *supposed to be a small gathering,* she thought and it was, by her usual standards. Though Samantha Harris was no wilting, introverted, flower, she found herself hesitating at the edge of the scene. Aside from Cumberbatch, she spotted no one that she recognized. To her own surprise, she found herself wishing to be anywhere but here.

Don't be a goose, Sam!

"Samantha!"

The professor's resonant tone rang out over the din of the party. He was at her side in a moment, taking her wrap and purse, his voice and hands gentle. His very presence instilled her with warmth and a sense of homecoming. She relaxed and even worked up some enthusiasm when he introduced her to a tall, slightly disheveled, man who headed the Language Department at Noble College.

The professor disappeared to attend to his hosting duties and when the conversation with the Language Department director dried up, a woman introduced herself to Samantha as a fan of her work. Soon there were others. A half an hour passed before Samantha realized that she had worked her way through half the room without having been offered a drink.

She managed to slip out of a conversation between Millicent Hayes, who ran a gallery in town, and Jessica Monarch, a local poet, discussing the merits of Ivy League versus smaller, more focused schools, and found her way to the bar. To her disappointment, Cumberbatch was no longer at his station. She was wondering whether it would be polite to go around to the back of the bar and find her own glass, when she caught sight of a framed picture sitting at one end of the bar. It was a photograph of the professor and another man.

It was not a particularly remarkable picture. The two men were on the beach, arm-in-arm, dressed in tropical shirts, swim trunks, and Santa hats, toasting the photographer with enormous glasses of slushy alcohol. She stared at it, unblinking, still absently wondering about the propriety of pouring her own drink, when she was startled by a gentle voice at her side.

"That's Miles," the voice chimed.

An older woman stood next to Samantha, smiling in a way that was vaguely familiar. She was dressed in a powder-blue dress with a navy sweater and held a glass of Sauvignon Blanc loosely in her hand.

When Samantha did not reply, the woman continued, "We thought we might have a college wedding, but..." She shrugged and sighed. "Sometimes things just don't work out the way we plan. Poor Charles."

It was then that Samantha recognized her.

"It's Mrs. Gagnon, isn't it?" she asked, hoping that the sinking feeling in her stomach was not reflected in her expression. "Mrs. Emma Gagnon, music department, class of-"

Emma Gagnon laughed and put her hand up, "Oh, please!" she said. "Let's avoid going there, shall we? Oh, Samantha! It's been such a long time!"

She embraced Samantha, a natural motherly motion that revived all the old feelings that Samantha had hoped were past: security and anxiety, love and loss, the mixture of bittersweet memories that even the passing of time could not completely dispel.

Samantha received the embrace stiffly and pulled back as soon as decorum would allow.

"I think," Emma said, "that you'd better call me Emma now."

Samantha nodded while taking a closer look at the woman. Twenty years was a long time and they had left their mark, but gently. Emma had always been motherly – now she was grandmotherly, with silver-laced hair and brush strokes of creases grown deeper around her eyes and mouth. Her motions were gentle and her eyes as penetrating and soft as always, though with a greater depth of memory in them now. The eyes searched Samantha's face, probing, and Samantha almost blushed at the absurd idea that Emma Gagnon might actually see what was hidden behind the smooth, carefully cultivated façade of S. J. Harris.

We all change. We all have things we'd rather not speak of.

That being said, it was impossible to think that Emma Gagnon was anything more than a motherly romantic who occasionally allowed herself to become too involved in her student's lives.

"You look absolutely stunning, Emma," she said with sincerity.

Emma beamed. "This is just so wonderful, Sam. I haven't seen you in... twenty years, I think. A lot has happened since then."

Samantha laughed. "Well, my son, for one."

"Oh, yes, of course. Charles told me about Matthew. I'm so glad you brought him with you. We're all excited to meet him."

"He'll be pleased to meet you, too. I've told him all about you."

There was a measure of truth in that. Samantha had told Matt some stories of her days in college and Emma was featured in a few of them. But Matt was at the age now where nothing excited him all that much. Even this trip East evinced little more than passivity and too-cool-for-this nonchalance. He was a teenager, though, it was to be expected. Samantha had been the same when she was his age.

Mrs. Gagnon was speaking. "I'm sure he'll enjoy Portsmouth – there is so much to do around here, plus we're close to Boston. He'll certainly enjoy meeting my ward. There's a few years difference, but I'm sure they'll get along." Her expression changed and she looked quizzically at Samantha. "I suppose you've heard that Bridget Madden is my ward now."

Here it comes...

Samantha's response was careless, "Bridget Madden... Oh, yes, Professor Stewart told me about her mother. Very sad."

Her throat was so dry it felt as though it were closing and she thought furiously, *Will no one offer me a drink?*

Emma did not notice her discomfort. "Your family was so generous towards her scholarship fund and Bridget is so grateful."

"My parents were generous people," Samantha replied. "My mother still is."

Her throat constricted when she thought of her father. Three years and his passing still had the power to reduce her to tears. She shoved the memories back forcefully and felt an even greater desire to have a glass in her hand.

"It is such a pity that they haven't been able to see what their generosity has wrought," Emma was saying. "You should come and meet her, Sam. Bridget has grown into such a beautiful young woman…and what a voice." She placed her hand on Samantha's arm, a gentle pressure that made Samantha flinch involuntarily. "She has an early morning rehearsal tomorrow. We can do breakfast and catch up. Won't you come and see her?"

Samantha hesitated. There was any number of reasons that she could give as an excuse. She had just arrived in town and was exhausted. She had her son with her and did not want to leave him on her first day. She was supposed to get in touch with her editor to go over some of the necessary rewrites for her next book. She could even fake a migraine tomorrow. That would be an easy enough task, given that she had no shortage of experience with the real thing.

Of course, reasonably thinking, there was really very little point in doing so. She had come to Portsmouth knowing that Emma would be there. It was a poorly kept secret that the Brown family had been chief contributors to the trust which had been established when Bridget's father had met a tragic death. Samantha had known that there was no way she could avoid Bridget and the complications that tied her unwillingly to the young girl's future. Facing this tangle was better done sooner rather than later.

Some things you just can't get away from.

Emma was watching her with steady eyes. She was a sweet motherly woman, for sure, but Samantha Harris had known many other motherly types who were barracudas where their own plans were concerned.

"All right," she said reluctantly. "I'll come."

5

If there was one place that Portsmouth police detective Michael Lawrence really hated, it was Meadowbrook Hospice. He hated the size and the smell of it. He hated the too-cheery décor and the blend of intense fluorescent lighting coupled with the warmth of the silly lamps that the staff insisted on placing by the bedsides. He hated the food. It tasted like it came from a hospital kitchen, and he hated the cheap plastic chairs that were used in the waiting room. Most of all, he hated the fact that he had a reason to visit every night.

It used to be hospitals that he hated most. They were septic, impersonal places where you went ostensibly to be healed, but from which some occasionally never left. It was a childish fear that probably stemmed from the day when his father went in, suffering from a heart condition. The doctor on call misdiagnosed the case. It happens. The man was only human, but the mistake cost Lawrence his father and he had never reconciled himself with the institution since. Hospices were worse, because the mask was off. You came here to die or to visit the dying. It was that simple.

Michael Lawrence sat in the parking lot of Meadowbrook, drumming his fingers on the steering wheel of his truck, waiting. It was evening, a little before nine, and the parking lot was empty. That meant that there were no other visitors, yet still he waited. He wanted to be certain to have the place to himself and he would at nine.

There were carnations on the seat next to him, their clean scent filling the cab. Until a few months ago, he would not have been able to tell the difference between the perfume of a rose and that of a carnation. He preferred the latter. It was less cloying and roses seemed somehow inappropriate for the circumstances.

He drummed and he thought. The court appearance went well today, but then, he had done so many of those in the past twenty-odd years on the force that he could sleepwalk through them now. Joshua Flynn was arraigned as was right and proper. He had beaten an elderly woman to death while robbing her apartment and the judge didn't hesitate to bind him over. Lawrence would not have to deal with him again, at least until the trial. Small comfort, that.

"Another one off the streets," his junior partner, Sohm, had commented as they left the courtroom.

He sounded satisfied, but Lawrence was not.

"Until the trial," Lawrence grunted.

"With all the evidence stacked against him, he'll need a miracle to get off."

"Yeah, well, miracles seem to happen to the wrong people." Embarrassed by bitterness in his own tone, Lawrence changed the subject by nodding towards the phone in Sohm's hand. "Good game?"

He already knew it was. Sohm was, as Janine liked to say, an old man in a young man's body. He dressed too well for a millennial, knew too much about classical subjects, and too little about modern culture. He talked a little too well, smirked a little too often, and he had two weaknesses; he had a temper (seldom seen, but impressive when expressed) and he loved chess to the point of distraction. When he had a good game going, his phone hardly left his hand. Even in the courtroom, where decorum was expected and cell phone usage discouraged, Lawrence had looked up from the witness box to see his partner bent over his tiny screen, frowning in contented puzzlement.

Sohm was looking at the phone during their conversation. Though he was too smart to miss the defensive conversational shift, he was polite enough answer the question. "Started off with the Sicilian and moved into the Yugoslav defense. Now she's doing something that I can't identify."

"Sicilian?"

"A classic, but still effective opening move. It was first recorded by Giulio Polerio in 1594, but the move predates him, of course."

Sometimes Lawrence was not sure if Sohm was trying to show off or whether he simply did not realize how annoying his casual date dropping habit was.

He answered flippantly, "Of course. Still, I suppose chess is a better game than Dungeons and Dragons or Chutes and Ladders."

He meant to be sarcastic. Sohm, putting his phone away in his jacket pocket, said quietly, "'Life is a kind of chess, with struggle, competition, good and ill events.'"

"Shakespeare?"

Sohm looked up at his superior, unblinking behind the oversized glasses that he wore. "Ben Franklin."

It was little things like that which gave Sohm a bit of a reputation in the office. Most of the senior officers, and probably the junior ones too, didn't know what to make of Sohm. Most preferred not to work with him; inferiority complexes are as common among the men in blue as they are anywhere else but Sohm never bothered Lawrence. For all his quirkiness and his occasional moments of showing off, Sohm was a good partner; he was smart and knew when to be silent, something that most men his age had a difficult time with. Over the past year and a half, he and Lawrence had built up something of a rapport. Between Lawrence's expansive knowledge of sports and classic rock and Sohm's knowledge of, well, everything else, they absolutely crushed the other teams in the annual Portsmouth Police Trivial Pursuit competition.

Sohm's a good man, Lawrence thought, rubbing his chin as time crept slowly by. *He'll work out his kinks out eventually.*

Lawrence relied on him. He trusted him, and the… 'event' back in February had only solidified their relationship. Lawrence did not talk about February with Sohm any more than he talked to anyone else about what had happened, about what was happening. Of the people in his life, Sohm was one of the few that understood that he couldn't speak of it. Sohm did not ask. For that, Lawrence was grateful.

He checked the clock on the dash again. 8:55 p.m. The last vestiges of light and color clung to the late spring night sky.

The days were lengthening and Lawrence was glad for it. It did not look as though you were trying to work overtime or avoid leaving the office when daylight lasted until eight.

He caught a glimpse of himself in the rearview mirror and grimaced. He had visibly lost weight this year, the result of a combination of loss of appetite and increased time at the gym, working off excess anxiety on the punching bag or the basketball court. His face had narrowed and lengthened. Though his blue eyes were as vivid as ever, there were dark stains underneath and a haunted, almost defeated glint in them.

Janine would have something to say about that, he thought. He quickly pushed the thought away and looked at the clock again: 8:57 p.m. Close enough. He pushed open the door, grabbed the flowers, and went out into the clean, brisk air.

***

There was always a hushed atmosphere of calm at Meadowbrook Hospice and Long Term Care Facility with an underlying sense of anticipation: whether of release or sorrow or sorrow from release, it didn't matter. People did not come here to have appendixes taken out or to welcome new children into the world. They came here as an anticlimax – an accident, a disease, a surgery, a terminal diagnosis. It was a hushed place because the balancing act between life and death was so tenuous at times that an unrestrained giggle might decide the matter.

At least that was how it always appeared to Lawrence. Meadowbrook's staff clearly did not see it that way. They were always cheerful despite being overworked in a tough profession and they impressed all visitors with their tenacity and optimism. Lawrence had been impressed too at first. Now that he was more experienced, more worn, he could not see the cheer and actively resented the attempts to instill hope. It had been too many months since February for him to have much hope or optimism left.

Still, he dutifully and politely greeted the nurse on staff by name as he signed himself in. Nurse Candace McNeil was a forcibly cheerful woman with colorful taste in clothing, bright blonde hair, and a permanently oversized smile on her face. She had been a nurse for her entire adult life and she loved her work almost as much as she loved the three kids she was putting or had already put through college. She returned Lawrence's greeting as she welcomed everyone who came into her waiting room; as though they were a long-anticipated visiting friend.

She complimented Lawrence's choice of flowers and her smile grew knowingly when he asked if Lizzy was available.

"Lizzy is *always* happy to see you, Michael. Go right in."

Lawrence turned from her quickly, schooling his face to keep the grimace from showing. She always answered in the same way and if the irony of the statement was lost on her, it never failed to hit him like a roundhouse strike to the jaw. He moved for the hallway, but not before hearing Candace call after him:

"I'm afraid you missed your wife – she just left."

He had been a detective far too long to miss the probing note behind the statement.

"I know," he said and continued down the hall. *Let her think about that for a while.*

Lizzy's room was indistinguishable from any other room which lined the broad hallway, except for the tiny, change-able sign on the door which read *E. Lawrence,* not that he needed the sign to find her. He had been down this hallway enough times to know where to go; third door on the left - no need to knock before entering.

The light went on automatically when he entered, an-other intimation of the kind of crisis that had brought his daughter to Meadowbrook. The room was large and fairly empty, dwarfing the bed and the girl that lay in it. It was oversized because the staff needed room for moveable equip-ment, equipment that was not present tonight.

The room was light blue and had a peaceful ambiance. Lizzy's old stuffed bear sat next to a collection of her books on the chest of drawers. A 'Happy Birthday' sign was tacked up to the corkboard over the bed and a cluster of balloons had been tied to the bed post. Someone had scrawled '*Happy Birth-day!*' on the dry-erase board by the door with a succession of smiley faces following the exclamation point. Colorful cards with scribbled sentiments were propped up on the side table next to the framed photo of Lawrence and a six-year-old Lizzy at the Big E Fair. There was a gift bag on the table, too, unopened and waiting for the birthday girl to wake up.

Lawrence noted these things mechanically – years of observational training and practice could not be undone in a scant few months. He kept his eyes on his daughter, refusing to dwell on the items that surrounded him and their implied promise.

"Hey, baby," he called softly from the doorway.

Elizabeth Lawrence lay unmoving on the bed. Her slender frame was almost lost in the layer of thick, sanitary coverings. Her long, dark hair, so much like Janine's when she was seventeen, lay fanned out around her, a dark halo on the pillow. Her eyes were closed, her expression peaceful.

She did not stir. She would not stir.

Lawrence knew this, but hope stubbornly arose anyway, as it did every time he saw her. She did not look like the victim of a driving accident. She looked as though she might wake at any moment, gaze at him with her big, dark eyes and ask in her wheedling voice, "Dad, have you got the Fenway tickets yet?"

"Don't be afraid to speak to her," nurses and doctors had told them repeatedly. "We don't know how much they can hear, but they do hear us."

They.

As though Lizzy had ceased to be a person and had become a case.

Oh, Lizzy, girl...

He forced himself to speak. "Pretty flowers for a pretty birthday girl." He held up the carnations as he walked forward, taking pride in the fact that there were no other flowers in the room. "Happy birthday, sweetheart."

There was an upholstered rocking chair on the far side of the bed. He sank into it and took Lizzy's hand. Her hand felt small and cool and he squeezed it impulsively.

"Want to say hello, honey? Let Daddy know you're there?"

Hope was a stubborn thing, after all.

There was nothing. No answering pressure on his palm, no change in expression, not even a twitch. Lizzy breathed, her chest rising and falling in a comforting rhythm. She was in there, somewhere, trapped in the prison of her broken body, as alone in herself as he was alone in that oversized room.

Only Lawrence could leave and Lizzy could not.

Michael Lawrence should have been immune to disappointment by this time, but this night, on his daughter's sixteenth birthday, the emotion almost overwhelmed him. Her hand fell from his. He pressed his hand against his eyes and fell back into the rocking chair.

"Oh, Lizzy…"

There was no answer. There never was.

6

—————

Emma did not realize that she had left her cell phone behind until she arrived home. Harry, her husband, was waiting for her in the living room. Her cellphone was on the coffee table beside him, blinking impatiently with unheard messages.

Emma was feeling overheated and too weary to deal with much more than a cup of tea and bed. She came over and dutifully kissed Harry on the forehead.

"You didn't have to wait up for me, dear," she said.

"Of course I did." Harry looked up at her fondly, the aviation magazine on his lap forgotten. "Anyway, I didn't want to sleep."

There was a story behind that remark but Emma was too tired to inquire. If he was having nightmares again he would tell her, hopefully later, when she had less on her plate.

She took the cellphone and sank into the side of the couch opposite him. She pulled her hair out of its bun with a sigh. "It was a nice party. You should have come."

Harry grunted and took up his magazine again. "I don't mix well with swells, you know that."

"I was thinking more that they'd benefit from knowing you."

He looked over the top of the magazine and winked at her. "Flatterer." Then he gestured to the phone in her hand. "You're a popular woman tonight."

Her stomach clenched and suddenly Emma became alert. She swiped to open the phone, praying that her features were schooled enough so that Harry could not see the fear.

Harry can't know. He'd never understand and he wouldn't stand for it.

But it had to be done. Of that, Emma was sure.

It was as she had suspected; eight calls and a barrage of text messages, each one more insistent and panicky. They were all from the same person, all starting from early this evening, all doubtless about the same subject.

So, Emma thought. *She got my message. Maybe this will work out after all.*

She looked at her watch. It was too late for conversations tonight, even if she could manage it without catching Harry's attention. Tomorrow would be soon enough.

She started typing, *We'll discuss it when I see you tomorrow...*

She willed herself to be calm and reasonable in her response but she could not shake the feeling that she was getting in way over her head.

Wednesday

7

Thomas Atkinson was at the front desk minding the store when Max Griffin wandered in holding a latte in one hand and his clunky flip-phone in the other.

"So, like, that shipment arrived." Max said, his eyes on his tiny screen. "The books for that signing, I think. They're by the back door."

Naturally, it had not occurred to Max that he might carry them inside himself. It took a suggestion from his boss to enlighten him.

There were four boxes by the back steps, all of which were labeled *heavy* in bright orange tape. Atkinson could handle two at a time, but Max, a tall, slim boy with a head of thick hair that nearly rivaled Atkinson's own, opted to carry only one. They brought them into the back room, which was already crammed with boxes of books, and set them down before the workstation. Max went for the last box while Atkinson, with uncharacteristic eagerness, ripped open the top box.

Nestled among the cardboard and thick packing paper were layers of the same book: S. J. Harris' new thriller, *Truth or Dare.* He lifted one of the top copies and weighed it in his hand. It was a heavy novel with a stark cover depicting a tiny boat in the middle of a dark ocean. The tagline was *Sometimes we go too far...*

Better than playing it too safe, he thought ruefully.

He flipped the book over to find her picture on the back. Dark eyes coyly looked up from under a mane of thick, black hair. The hairstyle was different now - he remembered bangs and highlights - but that smile... knowing and playful, full of illusions and promises. Twenty years had left the smile untouched.

It's been a long time, Sam Brown. Welcome home...

Max came crashing in, grunting with the effort of carrying his load. For once, Atkinson was grateful for the gracelessness of his entrance. It gave him time to drop the book before the boy became aware of his fascination.

"Put it by the door, Max," he snapped. "Open it – make sure they aren't damaged."

Max dropped the box carelessly and began to fumble with the tape. "Man, I got my workout for the day," he said. "Are these all the same books?"

By now, Atkinson had the second box open and he pulled out a copy of Harris', *The Lies We Tell.*

"Three boxes of her new book, one box with a few copies of her older ones. Her appearance will sell a few of each."

"*Three* boxes!" Max looked incredulous. "How many people do you think will come to this reading?"

Atkinson shifted uncomfortably. The bookshop was a small place with a smaller clientele. Book signings were a rarity and usually featured minor local talent. Atkinson's Books did not have the clout or the amenities to draw in the big names like the Music Hall did with their 'Evenings with the Author' series. Usually he considered himself lucky if ten people showed for a signing.

Max was still talking. "I mean, like, when you had that local chick here, I think we got three old ladies and her mom to come, and her mom already had a copy of the book."

His shop assistant had an annoying way of stating the obvious in tactless terms.

"This is different," Atkinson said stiffly. "This is S. J. Harris. She's the big leagues and this book only came out last week. The response will be good and what we don't sell when she's actually here, we'll have her sign and we'll keep on hand. It's a good investment."

Max nodded thoughtfully. The idea of holding onto autographed copies obviously had not occurred to him. Nevertheless Max was right; Atkinson *had* ordered too many books, an admission that embarrassed him. He was usually careful about that sort of thing. Then again, he was not usually ordering Sam's books.

"She's, like, an old girlfriend of yours, right?" Max asked.

Atkinson grit his teeth.

"An old friend," he corrected with painful accuracy. "She's doing this store a favor, so I expect you to be on your best behavior when she comes, right?"

Max threw up his hands. "I get it, I get it. Totally professional." He sounded wounded. From behind him a bell rang, alerting them to an entering customer.

Atkinson jerked his thumb at the door.

Max sighed. "I'm on it."

"Remember!" Atkinson said. "Helpful without hovering."

"Yeah, yeah..."

Alone, Atkinson looked at his prized pile and worried. He *had* bought too many. Would he look too... eager?

The old worries descended with a rush. What would she think when she saw him? When she saw the shop? He usually took a perverse sort of pride in its run-down, haphazard style that spoke of his independence of spirit. But would she see it that way? Or would she see beyond the mask of lace-curtain Irish pride and see what he really was, what their other friends already knew him to be, a failure, a might-have-been, a man who's luck always ran in the wrong direction?

He kicked the boxes and swore under his breath.

Stupid, stupid!

"Hey, boss!"

Max's voice startled him. Atkinson spun about. His assistant was in the doorway and there was no telling whether he had witnessed Atkinson's fit of temper. "What *is* it, Max?"

Max seemed unconcerned by the tension in Atkinson's voice.

"Isn't Sarah supposed to be in this morning?" he asked. "She put a copy of *Alice in Wonderland* aside and now I can't find it."

There were, after all, decided drawbacks to hiring only the slowest of the slow.

8

———

Emma sat at her dressing-room table, staring into the mirror. It was seven in the morning and though she had been up for an hour already, she still felt as though she had barely rolled out of bed. Her eyelids were heavy with exhaustion and her body ached and protested as she dressed. If she had run a marathon the day before she could not have felt more tired.

Stress, she thought, as she studied the weary face in the glass. *It can do a real number. Look at what it does to Bridget. But this will be over soon and everything will go back to normal. I just hope we don't have to bring in the...*

Harry appeared in the glass then, bringing her train of thought to an abrupt halt. He looked bright and happy. He had reason to be. He was dressed casually and she heard the sound of sneakers against the tiled bathroom floor.

"Going for your walk, dear?" she asked, as he rested his strong hands on her shoulders.

"On my way now." He gave her shoulders a little squeeze.

"You'll meet us for breakfast? Bridget probably has plans, but you'll like meeting Samantha."

"Yes, I'll meet you at the concert hall and you can drive me to the diner. How's that?"

She smiled. "That's perfect."

Harry was so much better now than he had been. He never really liked winter and this year the snow had been unrelenting. Harry's cabin-fever reached such a pitch that they had actually argued, a rare occurrence that unnerved even Bridget. He spoke constantly of moving south, an idea that Emma, who loved Portsmouth almost as much as she loved her people, could not stomach.

But that was before the warm weather moved in. Now Harry was back in his morning routine of walking five miles every day with their dog, Otis, looping around the parks and sidewalks of Portsmouth. Between these walks and his beloved little motorboat, he spent most of his time outdoors and that was for the best. Harry was never happier or more relaxed than when he was outside in the sun and fresh air. Emma supposed that she would be better off if she went outside more, too, but her talents and interests always lead her back indoors.

To each his own, I suppose, she thought.

She had her music and students. Harry had his boat and his dog, and they both had each other. Harry still spoke occasionally about moving to Florida or South Carolina, but it was without impatience and he knew that they could not move until Bridget was settled. Not that Emma wanted to move even then, but she could not bring herself to put her foot down about it.

Harry was kneading her shoulders lightly. She closed her

eyes and leaned back into the massage, wishing, yet again, that she could confide in him.

It isn't his secret and there's nothing he can do. This is my work. Telling Harry would only cause problems. My poor Harry...

Harry broke into her thoughts. "You won't forget what I asked, will you?"

She held back a sigh of impatience. They had spoken about it only yesterday; his renewed plea that she decide on a year for retirement. She deferred giving him a real answer last night, as she did every time he asked the question. How could she retire when teaching was her life? But how could she tell Harry that when, by deduction, he would know that he was not?

"I won't, dear," she said softly.

"You'll give it some thought?"

"Lots and lots." She earned a kiss on the head for her efforts.

"That's all a man can ask for." Harry sounded like a man who had already won the argument. "I'll see you at the concert hall."

He left, calling for Otis, and Emma slumped onto the counter as though the weight of the world had just been thrown onto her shoulders. In the other room, her cellphone vibrated for the third time that morning.

9

Bridget Madden was having a tough day. She had over-slept, spilled orange juice on her blouse, necessitating a change, then there was the long walk to the hall, during which she got hung up at every crosswalk between home and the hall, eventually making her late for rehearsal. Of course, these were just the physical manifestations of the true cause of her tardiness.

Bridget Madden was scared right down to her toes.

Arlene Chase was waiting for her, sitting by the piano with her sheet music in one hand and her phone in the other. She was unconcerned by the time, probably caught up in some online drama either between her own friends or the celebrities that she so diligently followed.

"Arlene Chase knows everything you didn't want to know about everyone else," Bridget's friend, Rose, liked to say, "And she spreads it to anyone who'll listen."

It was an astute observation, but Bridget genuinely liked Arlene – the older woman was enthusiastic and carelessly kind, with a good deal of knowledge about how to handle those in the artistic world. That and her husband, Peter

Chase, was the arts director for the hall, and so both were good relationships to cultivate.

Bridget waved to Arlene as she hurried past. "Got to use the ladies," she called.

Arlene looked up and smiled broadly. The cream colored blouse she wore highlighted her red hair and dark brown eyes. "I'm here all morning, Madam Star," she said cheerfully and held up her sheet music. "I was practicing last night."

Arlene was not Bridget's normal accompanist – that would be Rose, who would be coming back Friday morning, barely in time for the concert. In any other situation, working with the wrong accompanist would have had Bridget's teeth grinding with nerves. She was a perfectionist and each pianist was different, adding and subtracting subtle tonal differences that could throw her off. Not being able to rehearse right up to the performance with her stage partner, especially when it was an important event like this one, would usually have her in a wreck by now.

Not this time. Friday's concert had shrunk in importance compared to the plans she had for later that day and the days following.

Calm, calm, Bridget. Calm.

She entered the bathroom and yanked out her phone, pulling up Colin's number as she swore under her breath.

Men! They never get back to you, even when it's important.

She sent him a quick, stinging reminder, and slapped the phone impatiently onto the counter. Closing her eyes, she took several deep breaths, then opened them and looked into the mirror. Large, dark eyes stared back at her from beneath long lashes. Her hair, black and glossy, was pulled up in a messy bun. She had dressed with more than her usual care this morning, selecting a salmon colored blouse to highlight her olive skin and high-heeled boots to disguise her short stature. She was slim and delicately featured, with an active mind and a temperament that reminded those who had known him of her father, a man Bridget had never met.

She stared at her reflection and the thought flashed through her mind before she could stop it: *Is this* really *the face of a star?*

The thought snapped her out of her reverie and she shook herself, thinking fiercely, *You can't afford that kind of thinking, Bridget, not today of all days.*

She had to go out and rehearse and she knew that the act of singing would be soothing. Still she lingered in the bathroom, touching up her lipstick, checking her phone. Emma would be coming by the rehearsal today, bringing some woman with her. They'd want to talk and Bridget could not afford that. She had been carefully avoiding Emma for the past few days. All she needed was a few more hours to do what she knew had to be done.

You can't interfere now, Emma. I can't let you.

A string of piano chords rang merrily throughout the hall. Arlene was growing impatient.

Bridget took one last look at herself in the mirror and thought, *This is the face of a woman who knows what she is doing. And no one, especially not Emma, is going to stop me.*

There was great satisfaction in knowing that. Her

newfound confidence was only slightly marred when she saw that her text still had not been answered.

Come on, Colin. Come through for me.

10

Peter Chase was not expecting visitors in the concert hall that morning. Bridget was halfway through her aria, a pretty piece that she sang too well to need his supervision, and his attention had wandered towards the entryway when he spotted her. A woman stood in the entryway, biting her lip as she scanned the auditorium. He recognized her right away of course: S. J. Harris, the novelist that kept his wife up to all hours of the night. Portsmouth had been flooded with announcements of her impending arrival for weeks now. She was as pretty in person as she was in the advertisements.

Just when he was wondering whether Mrs. Harris was lost, Emma Gagnon, who was sitting in a middle row holding two paper cups of steaming liquid, rose to greet her. Harris looked relieved when she saw Emma and took a cup.

So much for the sign prohibiting drinks in the auditorium, Peter thought sourly. Sometimes he wondered why he bothered even trying to keep people from bringing food inside.

Harris sat down with the older woman to listen to Bridget. Emma, who had seemed poorly when Peter spoke to her earlier, was looking perky now. She gestured to Bridget and leaned over to whisper in Harris's ear. Normally, neither Bridget nor Peter would have approved of strangers coming in to listen to the rehearsal; this was a personal time between the conductor, the teacher, and the performing student and corrections were more difficult to make in the presence of others.

Harris was different, though. She was Emma's guest, for one thing, and Bridget was so well rehearsed that any comment from Peter or Emma would be on minor technique. If Bridget did not mind an audience - and judging from the way she powered through her aria, she certainly did not - then Peter would have no objection.

He would not have thrown S. J. Harris out in any case. Her arrival would be instrumental in getting Peter out of the doghouse with his wife. Ever since Arlene learned that they could not go to Stewart's welcome party due to previous plans that Peter had made, she had been sulky and annoyed. A private introduction, especially one that he could initiate himself, would be just the thing to get back into her good graces.

They had a few more songs to run through before the rehearsal came to an end and Peter kept a sharp eye on the audience. Harris and Emma whispered to one another, gesturing and nodding approval of what they heard. When Emma stood up in the middle of *Panis Angelicus,* Peter thought that they were leaving early, that he may have lost his chance. However, Emma merely handed her cup to Harris, excused herself and hurried out of the auditorium with a hand rubbing her forehead. Harris remained where she was, holding the cups and appearing as if she felt out of place.

The rehearsal ended with *Ave Maria*. Bridget finished strong and seemed as anxious as Peter that the rehearsal should not extend any longer than the hour which they had allotted for it. Peter offered her some pointers as well as a verbal slap on the back. If the morning's performance was any indication, the concert would turn out exceptionally well. To his surprise, Bridget barely seemed to notice his affirmation. She gathered her things quickly while glancing at her cell phone repeatedly.

Bridget was a confident young woman by nature but it was Peter's experience that even the most arrogant of students wanted reassurance before their first big solo effort. When Bridget turned her back on him to speak to Arlene, he had to suppress his irritation. As confident as she was, Bridget Madden would do well to pay attention for the sake of risking blowing the concert. Recovering from a poor performance here would take more time and talent than she could muster on ego alone.

She has enough confidence to fill this auditorium but her talent needs maturing, Peter thought, then, *Let it go, Peter. You've done your bit. Let her learn the hard away.*

A babble of feminine chatter drew his attention to his second project. Emma had returned and was talking with Harris. They were both holding their purses as thought ready to leave at any moment. If they did, Peter would lose his chance of introducing his wife to the celebrity.

He came down from the stage and proceeded briskly down the aisle.

He faintly heard Arlene asking, in her low but penetrating voice, "Bridget! Is *that* who I think it is?"

She too had spotted Harris.

Samantha Harris had her back to the stage as Peter came up behind her. He heard her say to the beaming Emma, "I have to say, she is very, very good."

Peter's pride in his student swelled, despite his earlier irritation.

Emma was nodding with motherly pride, her face gray even in the bright morning light. "Isn't she though? You really must meet her before we go…" She spotted Peter over Harris's shoulder. "Oh, Peter! Have you met Samantha yet?"

Emma made the customary introductions and stood by, quietly rubbing her neck as they talked. Samantha Harris was a charming woman with a light handshake, a lovely smile, and a way of looking at a man as though he were the only thing of interest in the room. Peter Chase, who had become immune to the flattery of parents hoping to garner extra attention for their student children, now found himself in danger of falling under her spell.

Samantha was quick to compliment both Bridget's performance and Peter's management. Peter countered with his hope that he would see more of Samantha while she was in town. She thought that would be marvelous as she was working on a new novel and could use an insider's knowledge of the city.

"I'll be in town for a few weeks because of the lecture series," she explained. "As it happens, I was looking for a setting for my next novel. When Professor Stewart called me, I thought, Why not set the plot where I'd gone to school?"

"Why not, indeed?" Peter agreed. In the back of his head, he was already imagining his name heading the thank you list which would appear at end of the novel: '*And to Peter Chase, whose knowledge, good humor, and surprising insights proved instrumental in creating...*'

Emma spoke somewhat distractedly, "How very lucky." She took a sip of her coffee and glanced over her shoulder as though expecting to see someone.

Samantha nodded. "Yes, it was, and you know, I'd forgotten how truly lovely your Portsmouth is."

"You're seeing her at her best," Peter was quick to say. "There is nothing more beautiful than Portsmouth in the spring. It almost makes the winters worthwhile."

There was a pause. Samantha was smiling radiantly. Emma frowned at the doorway while Peter tried to come up with something, anything, more to say. For once, he would not have minded if Arlene barged in on the conversation in her usual, tactless way.

"So..." he said, finally, "you came out this early in the morning just to hear our young star in the making?"

Samantha leaned in, her brown eyes twinkling. "I was bribed with breakfast," she said, in a faux whisper.

"Oh?" Peter turned with raised eyebrows to Emma.

Emma was still fixated on the door and Peter caught a quick glimpse of a brown ponytail and a hoodie crossing the entryway. He was not able to look more closely; Emma distracted him by turning and offering him a pained smile.

"Yes," she said, a little breathless. "Harry's joining us. He should be here any minute."

Emma's eyes darted to the doorway again and it was at that moment that Arlene came hurrying over and grabbed Peter's arm.

"Pe*ter*!" she said, her voice pitched high in excitement. "You didn't tell me that we were having a *celebrity* in to watch our rehearsal today!"

Arlene Chase was a fine woman in many respects but if there was one talent that she lacked it was the ability to contain herself. Her thrill in that moment could not be more palpable if she had been carrying a sign and wearing a shirt proclaiming herself #1 fan girl. Samantha Harris watched her with a wariness that approached alarm.

Peter put his arm around his wife. "Samantha Harris, my wife and your biggest fan, Arlene."

Samantha bowed her head towards the excitable red-head. Arlene leapt forward with her hand out to shake Samantha's and shrugged off Peter's embrace as she began to gush.

"Oh my gosh, oh my gosh, I was *soo* excited when I heard you were coming, Mrs. Harris! Peter's so right, I am your biggest fan – I've read every single one of your books and I just loved them all!" She leaned forward, holding Samantha's hand captive in her own, her eyes glittering. "Any chance you could tell me… What is your next book about? And does it have the *delicious* Martin Cromwell in it again?"

Arlene might have been a schoolgirl asking about her first crush. Samantha Harris, speechless, looked to Peter for help, but he could only shrug. Once Arlene got started, it was best just to let her run at the mouth until she tired.

Poor Samantha, he thought. *Hopefully Bridget will come over here soon, to break this up.*

He was destined to wait for that in vain.

***

Bridget slipped behind the curtain of the stage. Out in the auditorium, Arlene's excited voice rose above the more modulated tones of the others. She had been so excited when she saw Samantha Harris that she barely waited to finish going over the notes for Rose with Bridget before she tore down the aisle to insert herself into the conversation. The notes may have suffered as a consequence but Bridget was pleased, nonetheless, with this turn of events. Arlene's interruption would give her more time to slip away before Emma noticed.

As he had promised in his text, Colin Rideout was waiting for her in the wings. He did not see her at first. He was pacing back and forth, pounding his fist into his hand as he walked. The darkness backstage made his solid frame seem more muscular than usual. Colin had about five inches on Bridget. He was dressed as usual in jeans and a black tee-shirt, the short sleeves revealing the first tattoos in an eventual sleeve. People were often surprised when they learned that Bridget knew Colin. He had a record, after all, and physically they were in no way a match. They had met on campus and though Bridget would not exactly consider Colin a friend, there were certain advantages to knowing him. Colin knew useful people for one and he had a car, for the second. Whether he still had his license was a question Bridget did not think prudent to ask.

He started when she called out to him.

"We're all set then?" she asked softly.

"Yeah, yeah." Colin ran his fingers nervously through his hair. Even in the dim light she could see that his round face looked paler than usual.

"Are you okay, Colin?"

"Yeah." He shrugged and stepped towards the door, almost as impatient as she to leave. "Just got something going on, is all."

She stopped. "It won't…?"

Colin wrenched open the door and turned to her with annoyance. "Nothing will interfere with your plans, don't worry."

At any other time Bridget would have called him out on his tone, but they were already late, so she merely nodded. "Good."

She followed him outside.

***

It was not yet ten and already Samantha's head was beginning to pound in an ominous manner. The red-head who had joined Peter Chase, a nice man with a nice manner, was talking in a steady stream of adjectives and suggestive questions. It was not the first time that Samantha had to face one of her ardent fans, but Arlene was certainly one of the most persistent that she'd ever encountered.

"…and when Martin and Jane had that moment on the yacht?" Arlene sighed and pressed her hand over her heart. "To me, it was the most romantic moment ever captured in print."

Her dark eyes never left Samantha's face and Sam had the fleeting idea that she knew what it was like for a butterfly to be pinned to a collector's board.

"Yes," she replied, feeling increasingly uncomfortable. "It, um, came out rather nicely, I thought."

Arlene jumped on the response. "Nicely! And then Eric came in and spoiled the whole thing!"

I know, Samantha wanted to say. *I wrote the damn thing.*

She glanced at Emma. Emma was looking distractedly at the floor, her face pinched as though she were trying to make her mind up about something.

Save me, Emma!

"Eric?" Peter Chase said. "Who's he again?"

Arlene rolled her eyes, "Oh, Peter, I've told you a dozen times already. He's Jane's husband, a miserable drip who always gets in the way of true love! I've got to tell you, Mrs. Harris," she leaned forward in an alarmingly confidential way. "I've had so many *dreams* about Martin Cromwell…"

Arlene's eyes glittered mischievously. Samantha stood, horror-stricken and tongue-tied, keenly aware of Peter's presence. But when she glanced at him, he merely looked amused.

Poor man, she thought. *Second banana to a piece of fiction.*

Arlene was still talking. "I'm not ashamed to say it, either. Martin Cromwell is just the stuff that dreams are made of and I'm not going to let you go until you give me at least a *hint* of what's going on in your next book!"

Save me, someone! Aren't we ever going to breakfast?

She felt Emma's hand on her arm and thought with relief that the cavalry had finally arrived. She was disappointed when Emma leaned in to whisper, "I'll be right back."

She was gone before Samantha could protest and Arlene had taken her arm before she could follow. Samantha was forced to listen to Arlene's long history of obsession with the Cromwell novels, starting when she was recovering from surgery (she went into explicit and unnecessary detail about that) and ending with Samantha's last book which she, Arlene, had read about a half a dozen times.

"I feel as though I could write them myself!" she crowed.

Be my guest, Samantha wanted to say. In all honesty, she had been growing bored with the Cromwell series but had not been able to successfully pitch a new series to either her agent or her publisher. This encounter with Arlene made her more determined to find a way to end it.

I'd push him off a cliff if I thought that'd do any good.

It would not though. As her editor had pointed out, it would turn into another Reichenbach Falls and she would only make Cromwell's fans more devoted.

"You should be pleased, Sam," the editor had scolded her. "Most people would kill for the kind of following you have."

She was probably right, but her editor had never had to deal with the likes of Arlene Chase. Success had its price.

Samantha glanced covertly at her watch. Ten minutes had gone by since the end of the concert. Emma's husband should have arrived by now. Maybe he was already here. She could just make out the sound of Emma speaking to someone in the entryway, but she couldn't see who it was. A bore though Arlene Chase was, Samantha had not yet reached the stage where she could be rude.

Arlene talked. Peter Chase nodded. Samantha listened and smiled and starved while her headache grew. Arlene, in what Samantha believed to be an attempt to impress her into revealing the plot of the next novel, was going into a detailed analysis of novel seven.

"…and then I thought, 'No, he can't *really* be dead, because we never actually *saw* the body, if you know what I mean.'"

"Oh," Samantha said faintly. "So you figured it out?"

Hardly shocking, really. She had only put that twist in because her editor insisted that act two was dragging.

Arlene beamed. "Oh, *yes*. When you've seen or read as many thrillers and mysteries as I have, you begin to recognize the rules."

"The rules?"

Peter said, "Oh, she knows *all* the rules. What are there, sweetheart? Ten?"

"Thirteen, actually." Arlene lifted her fingers to count. "Number one," she began as Samantha's heart sank, "if you didn't see the body, the person isn't actually dead. Of course, if it's sci-fi, sometimes even if they *are* dead, it doesn't mean that they'll stay that way."

"Like in comic books," Peter offered.

"Especially in those, but comic books," Arlene sniffed, "aren't literature. Anyway, rule two, if the body is burned beyond recognition, then it isn't who they initially thought it was. Three..."

She rattled off two more rules while Samantha took the opportunity to look over her shoulder. She could only see a bit of Emma's back through the doorway, quivering and arguing, but she was too far away to hear what was being said.

"...which is so obvious, it doesn't even need mentioning. Six, the person caught holding the gun at the scene of the crime is never the person who committed the crime." Arlene paused, then amended, "Unless it's an Agatha Christie or Elizabeth George novel. Then it is *definitely* that person."

That one was interesting.

Sam offered up a feeble laugh. "Why, Mrs. Chase," she said, "you *could* write one of these books! I think you've figured out all of my secrets."

Arlene beamed and Peter added, "She's an absolute fanatic, Mrs. Harris. I don't think there's one crime writer that she hasn't read."

"I'm a fast reader, too," she said modestly. "I can finish a book a night, when I'm on a roll."

"Goodness," Samantha said. "I'm lucky if I can finish one in a week."

"Not all novels are created equal," Arlene said. "But you would know that, having won an Edgar. Now, where was I? Oh, yes. Rule Seven, when a murder takes place in front of the protagonist, you always, always, *always-*"

Samantha Harris never learned Rule Seven of the Arlene

Chase Order of Thrillers. As Arlene was saying the third *always,* a scream rent the air, killing the conversation as effectively as any murder weapon.

"*EMMA!*"

It came from the entryway.

Samantha spun about.

A teenaged girl stumbled back from behind the door. Her terror-stricken face had lost all color. She clutched her head and looked around wildly.

Someone groaned in agony.

"Emma!" Peter's voice resonated sharply. He was running towards the door, elbowing Samantha aside in his haste.

The teenager saw him coming, Samantha and Arlene on his heels. She turned sharply and fled down the staircase.

Peter skidded around the corner and Samantha had to step lively to avoid running into him.

The scene which followed came to her in a series of still images; Peter, stopping short at the door. The girl bouncing off an older man who was ascending the stairs as she fled. The man looking up in bewilderment, Samantha seeing his ashen face through the spindles of the banister. But it was his voice that would be permanently imprinted on her mind, his exclamation that would steal away her ability to sleep. It was a terrible, heart-rending cry, a blending of pain and love, terror and disbelief: "*Emma!*"

Emma lay on the floor, writhing in pain. Her back was arched unnaturally and her face was rigid. She looked as if she was about to snap in two. Peter was at her side, trying to cradle her head. Arlene was on her knees beside him, reaching out for Emma's hands. The older man vaulted up the stairs with desperate cries, "Emma, my God, Emma!"

Samantha stood helplessly, frozen in place, staring. Peter's voice brought her back from her trance, "Samantha, call 911! Call them now!"

She reacted automatically, grasping her phone and dialing with a rapid, shaky hand. There was no signal. She raced down the stairs, holding her phone out in front of her, but even as she ran, breathless and shaken, she knew that her efforts would do no good. Even the paramedics, no matter how quickly they got there, would be no help to Emma. Samantha Harris recognized what the others did not: Emma Gagnon was in her death throes.

11

When Lawrence arrived at Noble College Hall, a small crowd had already gathered around the entrance. It was a bright, beautiful day and Prescott Park, just across the way, was busy with joggers and tourists snapping photos. Beyond them, the sun shone brightly on the waters of the Piscataqua, lights dancing like diamonds upon the harbor. After the long winter, the warmth and brightness was welcome.

I wish I'd taken today off, Lawrence thought.

He did not actually feel that way, though, not really. He hadn't taken a day off since the end of February when the doctors had given him the bad news about Lizzy and explained that there was nothing to be done but wait. So he waited and he worked, taking on over-time to distract him from his thoughts. He had lost the ability to occupy himself in his free time and idleness had never sat well with him, even before the accident. It was keep busy or collapse. So he kept busy.

Officer Falk was waiting for him in the doorway. A placid, stocky man with a consistently disheveled appearance, Falk had been promoted from beat-cop to junior detective just last month. Lawrence had worked with him a few times and Falk struck him as a man who was more eager than naturally capable. But eagerness was malleable and so as far as Lawrence was concerned, Falk certainly had a future ahead of him in the department.

"I don't know why they called homicide, sir," Falk said, after his usual, cheery greeting. "Looks like an allergy attack or something."

He followed Lawrence inside. The entryway had a white-and-wood interior that appeared as though it had not been updated since 1916, when the building had first been built.

Seeing that Falk was expecting a reply, Lawrence shrugged. "Or something."

The dispatch had not been informative and for all Lawrence knew, Falk was right.

He rubbed his head with a wince. He had not slept well last night and his early morning coffee had only aggravated his growing headache. "Where's Sohm?" he asked.

As if on cue, Sohm came trotting down the stairs, looking neatly pressed and refreshed, as though he had had a healthy breakfast after a good night's sleep in a luxury hotel. But then, he always looked well.

"Morning, sir!" he said.

"What have we got here?" Lawrence asked, with another wince. His allergies were kicking in, adding pressure to his skull. *This is going to be a banner day...*

"Death by undetermined means, sir." Sohm leaned on the heavy wooden banister, his glasses glinting in the morning light. "A woman collapsed this morning and died in a spasm.

Witnesses thought it was an allergy or a stroke, only her husband insists that she didn't have any allergies. They all reported seeing a young woman fleeing the scene as they approached to try to help. The paramedics got suspicious and called us in."

"Poison?" Lawrence asked. It was the one word in the dispatch that had got his attention.

"The paramedics reported that the symptoms were similar to strychnine."

"Strychnine!" Falk repeated. "No one said anything about that to me."

Lawrence let that go, musing as he turned back to Sohm. "Strychnine, Sohm? This isn't an Agatha Christie novel."

Lawrence had only encountered one case of strychnine poisoning in his career: a disgruntled dealer who'd laced his rival's heroin with a solution of rat poisoning. Unfortunately for the enterprising dealer, his rival survived the attack. As the victim in this case was sixty-nine, it seemed unlikely that she was the victim of drug violence.

Not that it's entirely impossible, he thought, as they began the slow climb up the staircase. While drugs were usually reserved for the young, who rarely carried the habit into old age, he had heard of at least one case of dealings occurring within a nursing home.

People are amazing...

Sohm was rattling through the facts: "According to what I've learned so far, our victim skipped breakfast this morning to go Mass, then came straight here to listen to her ward's rehearsal. She was going to breakfast with a friend afterwards and had nothing but coffee before. Her companion also had coffee from the same restaurant, but showed no symptoms. The victim's husband insists that she has no allergies, so we've ruled out anaphylactic shock for the moment."

They were half way up the stairs now and Lawrence stopped short as a horrifying thought struck him. "Her husband - did he see it?"

"Yes, I'm afraid so."

Lawrence uttered a deep sigh and rubbed his face, marshaling his thoughts. Neither Falk nor Sohm were married and they were young, though Sohm seldom acted like he was. They could not possibly imagine what something like that could do to a man...

Facts, Michael, concentrate on the facts.

The facts were that a woman collapsed without apparent warning and died shortly after. That did not necessarily mean that there was foul play. Elderly women were fragile and her husband's information might be incomplete. She may not have told her husband about allergies or refused to admit the truth to herself. Lawrence had known people who had gone blind rather than admit that they needed glasses or refused help for disorders out of an inability to admit weakness. The victim's death might have been caused by any number of natural reasons.

Something that Sohm had said earlier stuck out at him: a young woman had fled the scene when the others had come forward to help. Why had she done that?

"Did he recognize her?" Lawrence inquired.

Sohm and Falk exchanged glances and Falk said, "It's his wife."

Lawrence shook his head. "I *meant* the woman who fled the scene." His tone was unjustifiably testy. "Did the husband recognize her?"

"Yes," Sohm answered promptly. Naturally, he would have already asked that. "But he doesn't know her name. He says it was one of his wife's students. Mrs. Gagnon – that's our victim – was a music teacher and counselor at Noble College. According to the witnesses, Mrs. Gagnon and this mysterious woman were only talking for a few minutes, approximately ten, and then the deceased collapsed. The husband gave me a description of the other woman – I can have it circulating in minutes."

The last thing that Lawrence wanted to do was cause a panic over something which, most likely, was a simple case of a heart-attack.

"Don't rush," he said. "We still don't know what we're dealing with here. It could have been a heart attack and this other woman just panicked. Find her for questioning, of course, but until we're sure this is murder, let's keep this quiet. Where are the other witnesses?"

"In the auditorium." Sohm gestured towards the top of the staircase.

Lawrence followed Sohm and Falk to the landing. An officer stood at the top of the stairs. He nodded as they passed. Half of the area was cordoned off with caution tape and markers. A woman's body lay stretched out on the floor, back arched, body twisted, and a grimace of pain frozen upon the face. She had white hair and wore a teal shirt. One of her shoes lay nearby, kicked off mid-seizure. Her vacant eyes were wide and her hand extended outward as though searching for the aid which had come too late. She looked, Lawrence thought, as though she could have been anyone's grandmother.

Lawrence crouched down to examine the body. From the corner of his eye, he saw Sohm gesture to Falk. Falk nodded and entered into the auditorium through the closed double doors. He shut them gently behind him.

Lawrence studied the dead woman. Fine clothes, expensive but not showy. The shoes were high quality, but several years old. Simple jewelry, not gems, probably handcrafted and collected on travels. Her face was hard to read, rigid and stressed as it was. She had drooled or foamed at the mouth during her dying spasms and the vestiges remained on the floor and on her lips. Her shirt had been torn, probably by the medics, and then modestly arranged to cover her again. There were no other outward signs of trauma or struggle, no bruises, no lacerations, no blood. Her eyes were bulging and Lawrence avoided looking at them.

Watching her die must have been hell. Her husband must be awfully sure about her allergies to have the strength to insist after watching this...

The coroner was sitting on one of the five chairs that lined the wall, a clipboard in hand.

"Lawrence!" he called, when Lawrence lifted his head from his examination. "You look like something the cat dragged in."

Dr. Louie Klugman had worked in the state coroner's office almost as long as Lawrence had been a cop and his signature caustic wit was legendary among his peers. He was a big man, with a large head and a shelf full of awards achieved through various martial arts competitions. He was thorough, competent, and unflappable, though his humor was not always in the best of taste. Lawrence often thought that his tactless front was Klugman's way of keeping sane in what had to be an emotionally trying job.

Lawrence nodded wearily and rose to his feet. "I feel like it, too." He gestured. "What have we got?"

"A dead woman."

"I can see that."

Klugman grinned, then turned to the victim, placing his hands on his widespread knees. "It's impossible to determine what she died of here, but whatever it was, it wasn't a pleasant way to go. You can see here, where her back is arched and the distension of the jaw line. Horrendous agony." He grinned when Lawrence shuddered. "We *are* feeling skittish today."

Lawrence ignored the comment. "Was it poison?"

"It's possible, I guess. According to the witnesses, she had the first spasm little over an hour ago. She died about twenty minutes after that, in the middle of her second, just after the paramedics arrived. They had to drag the husband away from her body..." He paused, then reluctantly added, "It *could* be poison, but with a woman of her age, it could be stroke, tetanus, meningitis, anaphylactic shock - anything really."

"Was she on any medications?"

Sohm supplied the answer. "Her husband is providing us

a list – mostly vitamins and blood pressure medication. She carried no pills in her purse."

"If this were strychnine, how long after she ingested it would she have felt the effects?"

Klugman gave him a look. "Come on, Mikey."

"I know, but humor me for a moment."

Klugman sighed and looked at the victim as though sizing her up. "Twenty to thirty minutes, depending on height, weight, and whether she'd eaten recently."

"Which she hadn't," Lawrence said, frowning down at the woman. "Twenty minutes makes it very unlikely that our mysterious young woman forced anything down her throat."

"We haven't found any signs of assault or evidence of puncture wounds, yet," Klugman said. "But, again, a woman of her age…"

Lawrence nodded and turned back to Sohm. "She was here for a rehearsal? Isn't it a little early in the morning?"

"According to Peter Chase, the director, it was the only time they could manage." Sohm reflexively pulled out his phone which served as his notebook, though with his excellent memory, he had little use for it. "The singer was Bridget Madden, practicing for a charity event which is being held on Friday night. Mrs. Gagnon invited Mrs. Harris to listen."

"Where is this ward, Bridget?"

"She left immediately after rehearsal."

"You said they were drinking coffee?"

"Yes." Unlike Falk, Sohm was used to Lawrence's quick conversational shifts. "They bought them at a drive through. She didn't drink much and we have the cups for analysis."

Lawrence nodded and turned back to Klugman. "How soon until you know exactly what killed her?"

Klugman shrugged. "I'll let you know as soon as I can. If I have to do a tox screening it'll take a couple of days." He smirked. "You know how those boys in tox can be…"

He was about to make another joke, but Lawrence suddenly wasn't in the mood. "I know all about it," he interrupted and gestured to Sohm. "Come on."

They crossed the landing and went through the double doors into the auditorium.

The design of the auditorium was simple, almost stark. Built in an age when the colonial look was all the rage, the pine wood and the white paint made the hall look more like a country church rather than the launch pad used by aspiring Carnegie Hall and Boston Symphony players. The hushed, mournful atmosphere added to the ambiance.

Lawrence stopped upon entry and peered around to get his bearings. Despite having lived for over twenty years either in Portsmouth or in the surrounding area, he had only been in the auditorium twice; once to attend his niece's play and once more for a lecture given by a local author of police procedurals. It had been Janine's idea to attend and one she quickly regretted – he spent the whole of the lecture pointing out the inaccuracies in the author's findings to her in whispers.

Now the hall was nearly empty.

A well-dressed man and an attractive brunette, who seemed somehow familiar, were talking earnestly to Falk. The woman's hands moved animatedly as if she was trying to convince him of something. Lawrence noticed a cell phone clutched in her right hand. On the opposite side of the aisle, a red-headed woman was talking in rapid-fire whispers to a man sitting hunched over, silent and motionless. The brunette was angry, the red-head concerned.

"Is that the husband there?" Lawrence gestured towards the man who sat near to the red-head.

Sohm nodded. "Yes. He's in shock, I think."

No kidding.

Lawrence rubbed his face again, suppressing a sigh.

"You all right, sir?"

Sohm could be embarrassingly formal, but his concern was sincere. Lawrence nodded, brushing it off. "Fine, fine. Just haven't been sleeping well, is all."

Sohm gestured towards the group gathered around Falk. "The man in the suit is the director, Peter Chase," he said. "He was in here when the incident occurred, but he didn't really notice the woman who ran away. The woman with the cell phone is a friend of the victim, a writer named Samantha Harris."

"*Samantha* Harris?" Lawrence frowned. The name sounded familiar, but he could not place her.

"Pen-name S. J. Harris," Sohm supplied quickly. "Mystery novels, best sellers."

Now Lawrence had it. S. J. Harris, the author who specialized in gruesome thrillers, the type that his previous partner, Ed Flynn, used to read. Recently one of the boys in the department had put up a flier announcing something to do with her coming to the area.

Of course, Sohm had all those details, too. "She's in from California to give a lecture series at Noble. Turns out she attended the college about twenty years ago, back when Mrs. Gagnon first started teaching. According to Samantha, she was going to breakfast with Emma and her husband after the rehearsal. They were waiting for him here when Emma collapsed."

"Nasty welcome back to the area, " Lawrence remarked, watching the woman's motions closely. Clearly she thought so, too. She was giving Falk a pretty bad time of it while Chase, the director, stood by watching helplessly. "Let's get started, then."

12

Samantha was nearing the end of her rope. The... incident this morning had been horrendous. Watching Emma thrash about on the floor, hearing her husband's anguished cries and being able to do nothing but watch the horrific scene unfold - it had been a nightmare that would likely haunt her for the rest of her life.

Whatever had killed Emma, stroke or heart attack or something else, it had been beyond human ability to stop. That much Samantha had determined, even before she saw the helpless expressions on the faces of the paramedics.

Watching Emma die had been bad enough. The aftermath was sheer torture. Police procedure demanded that they give their statements to an authority figure and forced them all to stand around in the awful silence of the auditorium with nothing but the sound of Emma's death rattle echoing in their ears. The double doors were shut, mercifully blocking their view of Emma's body, but it did not help much.

There was no cellphone signal, no way to reach the outside. Over and over again, the death scene played out in Samantha's head, with a complete soundtrack of every horrific sound until she felt the walls closing in on her. Even the would-be soothing presence of Peter Chase failed to help.

"It'll be over soon," he continued to repeat. "We can go as soon as that detective arrives."

Peter did not understand. He could not understand. She had to get out of that room. She had to leave before she lost it completely, before...

The door to the hall opened and Samantha turned with a wild surge of hope. But it wasn't someone new, just the officer that they'd spoken to before, a self-effacing man in a rumpled suit who seemed to be mildly confused most of the time. He had already told them that he did not have the authority to release them. Samantha did not care. She jumped up from her seat and rushed over to meet him.

He held up his hands, anticipating her questions.

"Just a little while longer," he said kindly. "My superior..."

She did not give him a chance to finish. She had to call her husband – he watched the news and would be worried, naturally. She had to call her son and let him know that she was alright. She needed to talk to her agent, her publicist, her mother, Professor Stewart, the college board. She threw everyone she could think of at him, but it made no difference. He would not budge. She could feel Peter's growing unease at her side. She saw Arlene lift her head to watch the argument. She paid no attention to either of them. The man in the rumpled suit was beginning to wear down and she *had* to get out of that auditorium.

"Matt is only fifteen." She waved the cell phone. "He's going to be terrified. I just want to reassure him, that's all.

I'm his *mother* for God's sake. I think you could have a little consideration. Five minutes, outside where there is service, so I can talk, that's all, just to let him know I'm all right!"

In her frantic state, Samantha did not notice the double doors opening again. All she could see was Emma's writhing body and the look of horror on that girl's face as she backed away. All she could hear was Emma's gasping cries, setting off again the body jerking nausea that she'd felt when she realized that Emma was really dying...

She felt growing dizziness. It was spinning into a full-blown panic attack.

I have to get out of here, I can't breathe...

"There's no service in here," Chase was saying, as though Samantha had not already explained this. "Surely you can let her outside for just a minute."

I'm going to be sick. They're going to ask me why...

"I'm sorry, I can't let anyone leave until..."

The voice was professional, apologetic, but she could not handle any more of it. She turned on him, nearly screaming into his face, "This is ridiculous! You can't deny me five minutes –*five minutes* to -!"

"Something the matter, Mrs. Harris?"

The voice was close, practically at her elbow. Samantha jumped and found herself looking up into the face of a man who she had never met before.

He was tall, taller than Jonathan, with broad shoulders and a head of thick, white hair. His worn expression told her he was a cop and had been one for a long time and from the way he stood she knew that this was the man whom they had been waiting for, the man who could release her from this imprisonment.

She found herself answering his question hotly, "You mean *besides* Emma..." It was sarcasm, but her throat caught and she found herself fighting back tears instead. The woman had *died* right in front of her, after all. It was not the first time that she had seen death, but...

The man's piercing blue eyes were unsettling. She had to look away, fighting back tears. She wanted control of herself and tears were only useful when they were not prompted by her own emotions.

Hold it together, Samantha, hold it together.

The young man with the glasses was back, too – Sohm, she thought his name was. She heard him say, "Detective Lawrence, these are Mrs. Samantha Harris and Peter Chase. The detective has a few questions to ask you."

Samantha lost her temper then. "Questions, questions! I'm *done* with questions. I-I need to call my husband!"

Detective Lawrence did not react to her outburst. He was still watching her intently, interested, but it wasn't the kind of interest that Samantha was used to receiving from a man. It was as though he were studying her, analyzing her. The thought that he might be capable of that brought her to a full stop.

Don't look at me! she wanted to say. *Stop looking at me – you have no right to look at me!*

It was silly, of course. He could not read minds and even if he did...

This isn't about me, it's about Emma.

He opened his mouth and Samantha cringed. Peter Chase interrupted by putting a hand on her arm. At any other time, his paternal attitude would have been offensive. Today, however, she was grateful for his support.

"She's really not well right now," Peter said apologetically as he patted her arm. He turned to Sohm. "Can't the questions wait, Nick?"

Samantha was not the only one surprised by Peter's casual use of a nick-name. The big detective turned to Sohm, raising his eyebrow in amusement. The younger man looked sheepish.

"Me, sir," he said, unnecessarily. "We, uh, know each other from wine tasting."

To Samantha's surprise and relief, Lawrence grinned.

"Naturally," he said, and from the look on the younger detective's face, there was a great deal of ribbing awaiting him in the near future.

Samantha watched the exchange and thought, *Oh good, they're human.*

Humans were workable. She had this.

Lawrence turned back to her and graced her with a smile. A professional, frosty smile, but she did not care so long as they got down to business. He was rather good looking, too. For a cop, anyway.

"Just a few questions, then you can make your phone call, Mrs. Harris," he said. "Did Mrs. Gagnon show any signs of distress or upset this morning?"

Peter answered quickly, "No, not that I noticed."

The detective nodded. He looked directly at Samantha. "You, ma'am?"

She looked up at him from under her long lashes and stuttered, "N-no. I mean, she had a headache…"

Damn! What are you doing? Are you trying to prolong this?

Her answer upset Sohm. She had not mentioned it before and from the way he snapped out the question that followed, "Did she take anything for it?", she got the impression that he did not like to look like he did not have all of the answers for his boss.

Stick to the truth. Just the truth, Samantha. It'll be over soon.

"No," she said firmly. "I offered her an – an aspirin, but she said it was going away."

"Was she nervous or upset about anything?" Lawrence asked.

"No, not at all. She was excited about the concert and that I was going to see Tommy's shop."

"Tommy?"

She shook her head dismissively. "An old college friend of mine runs a bookshop. I'm doing a signing there in a few days. She was…" The tears were gathering fast. She struggled to keep control of herself. "She was going to come along and…"

"I see," Lawrence cut in. "And the young woman she was talking to in the entryway, did you recognize her?"

Samantha looked up at him, startled. The icy blue eyes met hers, unmoving, unmoved. She had no sway over him. He was weighing her answers, trying to decide… what?

Samantha stammered, her protest a little too firm. "I didn't even see her."

It was the truth, the unvarnished truth, but she could not get any satisfaction out of it. Why was he watching her like that?

Calm down, calm down, he doesn't know anything about you...

Peter interrupted. "I've never seen her before, either. Detective, why are you asking all these questions? Surely it was... well, an allergic reaction or something, right?"

He sounded hopeful. He wanted to get this whole mess out of the hall and off his hands. To that aim, they were united. She wanted nothing more than to get the hell out of there herself.

She was old and she died. It's terrible, but it happens.

There was no need for this. There was no need for any of this and surely Detective Lawrence could see...

Lawrence answered carefully, "At this point, we aren't sure of anything."

It was like a death knell. Samantha reeled inside and fought desperately to keep herself together, to keep the fear from showing. Peter was gaping too, as surprised as she, but he had not been relieved by Emma's death. Most likely, he could not recognize the symptoms. He probably did not know what strychnine even looked like...

Peter opened his mouth to speak, but Lawrence cut him off, his eyes boring into Samantha.

"Sohm says that you and Mrs. Gagnon had coffee together this morning, Mrs. Harris."

Her body went rigid. "Yes. But there couldn't have been anything wrong with it. I'm fine."

Aside from a near panic attack, that is.

"Yes. Can you think of any reason why someone would want to kill Mrs. Gagnon?"

"No! No, she was the dearest, the gentlest…" She paused to swallow hard and finished with a resentful, "It's just a ridiculous idea."

"Someone thought it likely," Lawrence said, lightly, "or we wouldn't be here."

"It was an overreaction," Peter said loudly. "Her husband was in shock and made all kinds of accusations."

Suddenly, it occurred to Peter that the husband in question was only several yards away and that his voice carried. With a wince, he dropped the volume, but not the irritated tone. "I don't blame him, of course, but I'm surprised anyone took it seriously."

"He was just babbling," Samantha agreed.

Peter nodded fervently. "I have to agree. Emma Gagnon was a kind, gentle soul, a mother to everyone. And she was… well, of a certain age. It had to be a medical condition or something."

"Very likely, but we like to be absolutely certain in these cases." Lawrence turned to Samantha again. "And you can think of no one who'd like her dead?"

Damn him. Why is he pushing? Samantha was starting to wonder how she could have ever thought him handsome.

"I already said no!" Her voice, though not loud, pierced through the haunted atmosphere of the hall as though she had screamed. "Look, can't I go now, please? I have a son here and I need to see him. I *really* need to see him."

It was less a request than a demand. As Lawrence contemplated it, Sohm said, "Sir, we've got their contact information and they've both been cautioned about leaving the city limits."

Lawrence searched over her again, his eyes calculating, cold, and unrelenting. She held his gaze, glaring. In the end, he relented...to a point.

"You can go, Mrs. Harris. Just make sure you stay where we can find you, is all."

Samantha snapped, "Thanks," before stalking down the aisle with her dark hair flying and her heels beating an angry tune on the hardwood floor. She felt the detective's gaze on her back as she went and barely restrained her desire to run.

She hurried through the doorway and was relieved to find that the body had already been removed. She made her way quickly down the stairs to the entrance. The ambulance was blocking the exit. The paramedics huddled over the gurney while a big man in white overalls issued orders.

She nearly lost it then. Her stomach bucked wildly and she turned, fleeing towards the back of the building. Someone called her name, but she did not stop until she was in the back room, beyond sight of the body.

"You can think of no one who wanted her dead?"

He had said it as though he had *known*...

Peter came through the doors after her, all concern and solicitation. He was worried. She did not have to ask if there was a back way out. He volunteered it and she followed him gratefully. At her car, he offered to drive her if she needed it, but she turned him down.

"I need to call my son," she said. "I'm fine, really. Shaken, of course, but once I talk to him, I'll be fine."

He left her then, his face pinched, but relieved to have one less person on his hands. He would have been surprised had he stayed to overhear her call, for she did not call Matt, nor Jonathan, nor anyone on the list that she had given the officer in auditorium.

13

══

"You were a little tough on Mrs. Harris," Sohm remarked.

Lawrence watched Peter Chase hurry after Samantha Harris, desperate, no doubt, to try to smooth the waters that he had so carefully stirred. Falk was a short distance away, arguing with the red-headed woman who was gesturing towards Emma's husband. The woman was obviously upset about something and Falk's responses were not satisfying her.

Sohm's question had been respectfully put. Lawrence turned to him.

"I don't believe her."

"Don't believe her about what?"

It was a valid question. *Instinct* did not seem to be a good enough answer so Lawrence shrugged. "I don't know." He shoved his hands in his pockets and glanced around, dissatisfied. "Honestly, Sohm, there doesn't seem to be grounds for a murder inquiry here, but Samantha Harris…" He shook his head. "She's holding something back. I know it."

Sohm was quiet and Lawrence could guess what he was thinking. There could be a plethora of reasons why Samantha

Harris was reluctant to talk to them and any number of those reasons could be perfectly innocent. Most people resented being questioned, even those with clean consciences, and resentment could be mistaken for fear.

Lawrence's attempts to reason with himself were drowned out by his better instincts. He knew what he was looking at. Samantha Harris was not resentful. She was frightened. She *was* holding something back, but until they had a case, there was no basis to push her farther.

Behind him, the red-head was growing louder, her clipped tones conveying her discontent. "...making him sit there for *hours* at a time when *someone* should be getting him home. Do you have any *humanity* in you at all? What are we waiting for? We've told you everything and you can't think..."

Glancing over his shoulder, Lawrence saw Falk, hands raised with his back against the piano, retreating from the woman's wild gestures. He looked completely out of his depth and the red-head was just getting warmed up.

"Who *is* that?" Lawrence muttered to Sohm.

Sohm resolutely kept his back to the unfolding drama. "Another witness – Arlene Chase, Peter's wife. She'll talk your ear off if you let her."

"Did she see anything?"

"She saw as much as the others, but had nothing new to add. I thought it was best to let Falk handle it."

Arlene Chase made a sweeping gesture which forced Falk to duck to avoid getting hit.

Lawrence whistled. "She *is* chatty."

Sohm remained facing forward. "Like I said, I thought it

best to let Falk handle it. He's been wanting another promotion anyway."

Lawrence grunted in agreement. That settled, there was no further reason to put off what he'd been unconsciously avoiding.

Harry Gagnon was sitting motionless and alone in a chair in the middle of the auditorium. He looked wooden, as though he were beyond both pain and grief. He had to be questioned, of course, but Lawrence dreaded it. Talking to the family was always the worst part of the job and no amount of experience made it easier.

Lawrence sighed, rubbed his face again, then started forward.

***

Harry Gagnon barely noticed when Arlene left him, though he was glad for the peace that followed her departure. He did not hear Samantha's outburst and he heard nothing of the ensuing conversation. He simply sat, staring at his hands, trying to think, trying to feel, trying to grasp something that made sense.

Emma was gone. It was unbelievable but it was true.

He ought feel something. Pain, probably, sorrow definitely, but no emotion seemed to touch him. Everything felt as if it stood at a distance, as if he were simply an observer of a terrible event that had occurred to someone else, on television perhaps. He was numb. It was normal, he knew, it had been the same before, when he had seen combat. The terror, the anguish, the pain, it had all remained hidden away in his psyche, buried so deeply that he had not known it had existed. Fool that he had been then, he'd actually thought that he could get away with killing the enemy and their children without feeling regret.

He had soon learned differently. It took decades to get over the events that he had experienced, the things that he had witnessed, and he was in no way healed. He never would be.

"It's like an invisible scar, Harry," his therapist had told him. "The memories will always be a part of you, but they don't have to control you."

"I'm here, Harry. I'm always here for you."

How many times had Emma said that? Harry had often taken comfort in the fact that he was older than Emma. It had never occurred to him that he might outlive her.

Oh God...

The fallout would come soon enough. Harry knew it. The wrenching pain and the aching loss would emerge once the initial shock had worn off, when he was weak and defenseless. Then it would all become real and he would fall apart. Until then, he could function. He *had* to function. The others did not believe him. They thought that Emma had died from something natural just because she was older than they. Harry knew better. There was something wrong with her death. The arching back, the gasping for breath, the distortion of her features...

He stopped himself and leaned forward, groaning, willing away the image. Not yet. He could not indulge himself yet. Not until he was *sure* that they understood that this was not normal or natural. Her death was not right. Someone had to pay for it.

Someone slipped into the seat beside him. It was not Arlene. The scent was cologne and coffee, a vast contrast to her usual flowery, girlish perfume. He was glad it was someone else. It did not occur to him to look to see who it was. He remained leaning forward, his hands limp and useless on his lap. They looked, he thought, like *he* must look to them all; limp and useless.

Emma...

From what seemed a long distance away, Harry heard someone speak. He didn't feel capable of a response. He could not remove his eyes from his hands. The voice spoke again. His name was Lawrence, the man said, and he was the officer in charge of the investigation. He wanted to let Harry know how terribly sorry he was. He sounded competent, kind, and, though he must have spoken similar sentiments dozens of times in the course of his profession, he seemed sincere. Trustworthy even.

The man stopped talking. Harry knew he was waiting for a response, but he simply didn't have the energy to comply. When Emma collapsed, he had been paralyzed only for a moment, then he had gone frantic, rubbing her arms and back, calling for the paramedics, pleading with Emma to stay with him, insisting that Chase and Harris were wrong. He had been angry when they told him to wait and his resentment made him sit as far away from the pair as possible. Now, he was weak, nearly voiceless. But he had to speak up before it was too late, before Lawrence made up his mind, before he stopped looking for the truth.

When Harry finally spoke, his voice sounded robotic. "She had no allergies. There was nothing wrong with her. She was healthy, she was so… all *right* this morning. It can't have been an allergy – it *can't* have."

He sounded pathetic, even to his own ears, but there was no judgement in the detective's voice when he spoke.

"We'll find out, sir. I promise you that."

One could almost believe him.

Harry turned to face the detective and was pleased to see that he was not just a boy, like the other two detectives, the disheveled man and the prim one. This was a man of experience, one who had seen the world a bit and knew what it was really made of. He was someone that you could talk to. Someone who would hear what you had to say.

Lawrence was waiting for him to speak and Harry found the words in a sudden burst of renewed energy. "I saw a girl, running away."

"Do you know who she was?"

"One of Emma's students, she must have been talking to her…she just ran out on her, left her there to…" He choked up and looked away.

"What is the girl's name?"

Harry waved his hand in frustration. He had been beating his brains trying to remember, but nothing came. "She was just a girl in Emma's class. She met with Emma regularly. Flute I think, but I never know their names. A tallish girl, slim, brown hair. Typical."

There was something else too but he could not remember what it was. Harry Gagnon had never felt so old and helpless in all of his life. Weariness returned and he fell back into the seat.

The lack of information did not seem to concern Lawrence. "We'll ask around. Maybe she has some information."

Harry nodded and closed his eyes.

Emma...

"Is there some family member we can contact for you?"

His own voice sounded distant. "A son..."

"Oh?"

Harry shook his head. "Haven't seen him in years. We don't get on well."

"I see. What about your ward? Should I contact her?"

Harry shook his head again. He did not want her. He did not want anyone other than Emma. There was no point in saying that, no point in saying anything really.

Suddenly Harry did not want to be there anymore.

"Detective, I want to go home."

Lawrence was watching him intently, a thoughtful expression on his face.

He understands, Harry thought.

The younger detective had returned. His eyes were fixated on his phone as he waited by his superior officer. Behind both of them, Peter Chase was waiting, too, watching Harry anxiously.

Lawrence said, "All right, sir. We'll be in touch if we find anything."

He stood and Peter stepped forward, anxious to help. "Harry, I'll drive you."

Harry Gagnon nodded. He was exhausted. He did not care how he got home, so long as he got there, out of the sight of this dreadful place.

I hope he leaves Arlene here.

Harry walked towards the door with Peter at his side. As he shuffled slowly on trembling legs, he heard Lawrence speaking in resonant tones. "This isn't a murder, Sohm. It's a tragedy."

Harry Gagnon, leaving the scene of his wife's death, knew quite certainly that it was both.

14

Lawrence was working at his desk when his cell phone rang. It was late and the offices were nearly empty. The silence was peaceful after the long, busy day. He was finishing up his report on the Flynn case – the Gagnon death was still open – and ignoring a flare-up of carpal tunnel as he typed. He did not mind the pain so much as he minded the cure. Being hobbled by braces would have irritated him beyond measure.

He stopped to look at the phone, rubbing his wrists as he did so. With three open cases on his docket, four if you included the Gagnon case, he could not afford to ignore any call… or so he thought.

Janine.

He had been expecting this all day. He knew she would call as soon as she spotted the flowers on Lizzy's nightstand. She would tell him how beautiful they were and how Lizzy always loved carnations and how she was sorry that she missed his visit. She would try to sound pleasant and innocent, but behind every comment would be a question that she was too afraid to ask outright and that he had no real answer to anyhow.

He let the call go to voice-mail. For all she knew, he was in the middle of an interrogation or stuck in a meeting with the chief. She did not have to know that he was ignoring her, but she certainly did. They had been playing this game for weeks now, a game of silence and avoidance, and she knew why. She might even be grateful. If they ever did start talking, the damage might be too much to overcome. He could not afford that.

Stop calling me, Jeanie. You know it won't help...

The phone went silent.

Lawrence sat back in his chair and ran his hands through his hair as he sought to clear his mind. Harry Gagnon's destroyed expression came back to him,

At least he has some clarity. Death has one redeeming feature: it is, above all else, final.

Sohm's voice cut through his morbid reflection.

"Need me any more tonight?"

Lawrence dropped his hands. His partner was leaning up against the doorsill with his hands shoved into his pockets. He looked as though he had nothing on his mind or his conscience, an enviable position.

"I'm good," Lawrence said, keeping his tone light. "Did you run those background checks on the Gagnon case yet?"

"Sure did." Sohm pulled out his phone, "Nothing particularly interesting. You want the run down?"

Lawrence looked at his watch. It was six-thirty, way past the workday's end. Unless Sohm had a class or a meet-up, he would stay until Lawrence dismissed him. Sohm was not the motherly sort, but in the past few weeks, he had grown attentive. As Lawrence's marital problems pulled more and more at his mind, Sohm had stepped up into the breech, making the jokes that Lawrence would have made, volunteering for extra duties, and generally trying to be helpful. It was kind, but it was irritating. A man needed to work things out for himself and tonight was one of those nights.

"It's late." Lawrence said. "I don't think there's any rush. You can give it to me tomorrow." He gestured towards Sohm's phone. "Any interesting moves today?"

"Just put my king in danger, but I can handle it," Sohm said. If he noticed the subtle rejection of his veiled offer of support, he did not act as though he did. "Purple-Butterfly is an interesting player."

"Pity he has such a lame name."

Sohm paused in the doorway, raising an eyebrow. "*She* I would think, sir. Definitely a 'she'. But, still, it is a pity. Good night."

Sohm left and Lawrence turned back to his computer. He had several hours of work ahead of him and he allowed nothing, not his growing hunger, aching wrists, or the intermittent calls from his wife, distract him.

Thursday

15

Lawrence was stirring the second packet of sugar into his coffee and wishing that he had taken the time to actually eat breakfast, when his phone rang. He snatched it up and snapped without thinking: "Lawrence, here." He winced at the sharpness in his tone. *Definitely should have had breakfast...*

If Klugman picked up on his mood, he showed no sign of it.

"I've got the preliminary report," Klugman said, much too cheerfully for Lawrence's mood. "You're not going to like it, Mikey."

He was right. Lawrence did not like it at all.

He jotted down a few notes, asked a few questions, and hung up just as Sohm entered the office. Sohm was carrying several files and looked pensive. He stopped at Lawrence's desk expectantly.

Lawrence leaned back in his chair. "Just got the preliminary report, Sohm."

"Murder?"

"Or a massive overdose. Until we get the toxicology confirmation, we're considering it suspicious."

Sohm did not appear surprised. Unlike Lawrence, he

seemed to think that murder was as likely an explanation for this death as anything else, an open-mindedness that was not like him. Then again, he was a much younger man.

"Then this might be important." Sohm held up a file. "Emma Gagnon's office was broken into last night."

Lawrence sat up sharply. "*What?*"

"It was discovered this morning, reported by the administrative assistant, a man named Cumberbatch."

"That's quite a handle," Lawrence said absently.

Sohm grinned and went on. "Someone thoroughly ransacked her office, but it doesn't look like anything was taken. Since she is our victim, the robbery boys thought we'd be interested."

They were right. First a death, then a robbery. None of it made sense. Emma Gagnon was a model citizen, so proper and diligent that Lawrence doubted she had even run a stoplight in her life. Noble College, for all its rank and privilege, was not an especially wealthy school and Emma didn't seem the type to own anything worth stealing. But that, as he reminded himself, was pure guesswork. Until he had more facts to work from, he should not assume anything.

Lawrence looked at his watch. According to what Harry had said yesterday, he would not be home until somewhere around ten this morning. That bought Lawrence some time, not that it would help much. Telling a man that his wife had been murdered was never an easy task.

"I'm going to need to see everything you dug up with those background checks," he said to Sohm as he pulled himself out of his chair. "We've got some time before we need to go over to the Gagnons. Let's go check this robbery out, shall we?"

***

Finn Cumberbatch reminded Nick Sohm of every over-privileged college prat that he had ever met in his long, memorable stint in the hallowed halls of upper learning. He was solidly built with the correct blue sweater vest over a correspondingly blue shirt and he even, God help him, wore a bowtie.

If Central Casting were looking for a Harvard snob, Sohm thought, as he and Lawrence trailed the talkative egghead down the halls towards Emma's office, *they need look no further.*

Sohm had been an avid student in prep school and college, though perhaps a little too active and restless to be considered truly academic. His ability to memorize even the most trivial data made some mistake him for a prodigy. Others recognized his true talent, an ability to synthesize information and draw logical conclusions from it. There had been a time when he might have *been* Cumberbatch; working long hours over old books and looking forward to a lifetime spent behind the desk and in the library. Such a life might have killed him, but it would have suited his parents' ambitions far more than the career that he had chosen.

Sorry, Mom, he thought now. *If I hadn't have walked away, there would have come a day they'd have thrown me out. I know that much about myself anyway.*

"...I discovered it this morning," Cumberbatch was saying to Lawrence. He managed to appear as though he were looking down his nose at the man, despite the fact that Lawrence towered head and shoulders above him.

"*You* did?" Lawrence asked calmly. He looked worn today, but seemed so even before he met the young college upstart.

"Well... Janice did. She's student teaching, you know, and always gets to the office before Emma."

"I would have thought she'd know to stay away from Emma's office until the proper authorities cleared it out."

Cumberbatch rolled his eyes. "You don't know Janice." He stopped at a doorway and said, as he threw open the door, "Here we are. As you can see, they did a thorough job."

They followed him into a small office. There was a wall of glass behind the black desk that let in light but obscured detail. The room had a worn look, as though many years had passed since there had been a fresh coat of paint or a new rug. The walls were covered with framed pictures, musical charts, concert posters, and memorabilia from a long life. Their presence warmed the otherwise stark white and black color scheme of the place.

But it was not the walls or the framed archives of Emma Gagnon's life that first drew their attention. It was the sea of destruction that lay spread out on the floor and desk. The reports of ransacking had not been exaggerated. Someone had torn through the office, scattering books and sheet music, knocking over trophies and souvenirs, upending music stands and pulling out desk drawers. They had emptied the battered wardrobe of all of its uniforms and clothing and had even taken the few instrument cases - a violin, ukulele, and guitar - and emptied them of their contents before tossing the cases against the wall. There was even an impression left on the wall where a case had struck it.

Someone didn't just search the place, Sohm thought. *They had a bone to pick with Emma.*

A picture of Harry and Emma standing in front of a foreign temple lay with its glass shattered on the floor. Sohm, remembering the devastated man in the auditorium yesterday, resisted the urge to pick it up. Anger flared at the back of his mind, but he quashed it. This was just an investigation, like any other. He was not personally involved and should not be for that matter.

"Almost as though someone had it in for her." Cumberbatch's self-satisfied tone broke through Sohm's thoughts.

Sohm's dislike for the man went up a notch. "Is that likely?" he asked.

The college boy scoffed. "You obviously don't – didn't know Emma. She was everyone's friend, everyone's mother. If we had a difficult student, Professor Stewart would assign them to Emma. She was more effective than any of our student counselors."

Finn Cumberbatch sounded as though he did not like Emma one bit.

He's jealous – Emma was more influential than he is. Hardly surprising. I've been with him all of five minutes and already I'm dismissing everything he's saying.

Sohm began to snap photos with his phone, more for something to do than for any evidential purposes. Robbery would be in soon enough with their own cameras and professionals.

"So she was the motherly sort?" Lawrence asked.

If the doctorate student annoyed him, he showed no signs of it. One of the things Sohm admired about his partner was his stoic disposition. One rarely knew what Lawrence thought of anything, unless he chose to verbalize it.

Cumberbatch nodded. "Yes, very. She always had several troubled souls in her care."

"How about the alumni? Any trouble there?"

"She wasn't an academic star, so no professional jealousy, and she wasn't the type to run around on her husband. Any number of people might have been in love with her, but there was no drama. She wasn't the sort."

Lawrence nodded thoughtfully. "So, what is missing here?"

Cumberbatch shrugged. "I'm afraid I couldn't tell you. No instruments or computers, so far as I can tell and they are the only thing of value. We'll have to take inventory to be sure, and even then, I can't account for her personal items. I can't make heads or tails of this myself."

Sohm could not resist replying, "Well, now, that's what you called us in for."

Cumberbatch gave him a measuring glance. Annoyance glittered in his blue eyes.

"We'll be sending over a few lab boys to see what they can find." Lawrence said.

Cumberbatch sniffed. "They will be overwhelmed. This is a high-traffic office. What I don't understand is why they sent two homicide detectives to look into a break-in?"

Lawrence said smoothly, "Mrs. Gagnon's death has been

labeled suspicious. Until we determine the cause, anything to do with her is of interest to us. You understand."

Cumberbatch stared blankly at him. "Suspicious? That's ridiculous. She hadn't an enemy in the world!"

"Be that as it may, we have to cover all angles. Now, I'd like to talk with Professor Stewart, if he has a few minutes."

"He hasn't."

Despite their years of training, the two detectives stared. It was not often that they received an open refusal, especially from someone of Cumberbatch's caliber. It only took Cumberbatch a second to offer an excuse. Obviously even he was not secure enough to openly defy a police request.

"He's in New Haven today, at his vacation house. Besides," he shrugged, "he would know nothing about any of this."

Sohm caught Lawrence's glance and he knew that he was thinking the same thing: *That seems awfully convenient.*

Lawrence calmly nodded and handed Cumberbatch his card. "When he gets back, have him give me a call."

Cumberbatch took the card with two fingers, as though afraid that he would catch something. "And what should I give him for a reason?"

"Oh," Sohm said cheerfully. "Just tell him, he's a person of interest."

The look of horrified dismay on Cumberbatch's face made Sohm choke back a chuckle. His good mood followed him outside to the parking lot where Lawrence, with a pensive look in his eyes, turned to him.

"So, if no one wanted to kill the saintly Mrs. Gagnon, does that mean we're looking at a suicide?"

The question caught Sohm off guard. He had not once considered suicide and now, thinking it over, the answer was simple. "I think that's very unlikely."

"Why? Because she was Catholic?"

Sohm ignored this half-hearted dig, as he did whenever someone tried to rile him by use of his faith. He was used to hearing it from the other men at the office, but Lawrence was different. His disdain for the church had only manifested itself after Lizzy's accident. It was a symptom, not an argument.

In any case, being Catholic would not necessarily have stopped Emma Gagnon from taking her own life, but Sohm didn't think that a caring, motherly woman would have done it in front of her ward, or in such a public place. And it seemed a stretch to believe that the destruction of her office the night of her death was just a coincidence. The killing and the robbery were intimately connected. Sohm would have bet his badge on it.

But beyond these, there was yet another, more compelling reason to dismiss a suicide theory.

He looked at Lawrence and said simply, "No. Because she still had at least two troubled souls still in her care."

16

L arry Gagnon wasn't surprised when Lawrence and Sohm appeared on his doorstep. He invited them inside and ushered them through the comfortable, airy home. Bridget was there, moodily making herself coffee in the kitchen, her jacket and purse close at hand. Neither seemed particularly moved when Lawrence told them about the coroner's report. Harry had been expecting it, of course – it confirmed what he'd already thought – but Bridget was surprisingly stoic.

"It's ridiculous," she said. "But I guess you have to thorough, right?"

Lawrence and Sohm exchanged glances. They'd already decided that it would be more efficient to talk to Bridget and Harry separately so, according to their prearranged plan, Sohm asked Bridget to show him Emma's rooms.

"Why?" she asked, her dark eyes flashing with impatience.

"We'd like to get a feel for the kind of person she was," he said patiently. "It helps in these investigations, you know."

"Show him the play room, Bridget," Harry ordered.

His ward pouted, but obediently stalked off, Sohm following.

Harry took Lawrence into the living room. It was a bright, airy space, with bay windows looking out over the river. Emma's touch was everywhere. Pictures of her, Harry, and Bridget decorated the walls along with plaques of common inspirational quotes. Small angels sat on the window sills, arms raised in the sunlight. There were music books and paraphernalia scattered about on the tables, among them brochures for Friday's concert, and a small black and white poster announcing S. J. Harris' book signing at a local shop.

Harry did not offer Lawrence a drink. He lowered himself onto one of the matching couches and looked at Lawrence expectantly. His clothes were neat, a good brand, but he wore them carelessly and he looked as though he had not slept well. Lawrence sat on the window seat and told him about the break-in.

Harry was shocked.

"I don't know why anyone would want to ransack her office." He seemed to take the break-in as a personal assault. "There... there isn't anything in there anyone would want. Well, no one except for me and Bridget of course."

"She kept nothing of a personal nature in there?" Lawrence asked.

"I suppose she must have. She worked there for over twenty years. I used to tease her that she felt more at home at work than she did at home."

"Did anyone have a grudge against her? Any difficult students?"

"I can think of one."

Harry reached over to the coffee table and pulled out a picture of a college-aged girl in a gray hoodie, posing in front of the Washington Monument. She was slim and pretty with long, straight, brown hair and glasses.

Harry jabbed a finger at her image. "That's the girl I saw running away. I knew I'd seen her before. She was one of the girls that went on the DC trip with Emma last year."

Lawrence looked at the image more closely. College girls were not typically the type to use strychnine to off their rivals, let alone milquetoast college professors.

There's always a first time.

Lawrence flipped the photo over, but there was nothing written on the back. "What's her name?"

"Sarah Hopper. I remember because she caused some trouble on that trip."

"Do you know what the trouble was?"

"No. The police were involved, but Emma said it was nothing." He said this dismissively, as though Emma would have shrugged off Watergate. "But that girl is no good, always in trouble somehow. Emma said she came from a broken home, but what difference does your background make? Breaking the law is breaking the law, whatever reason you have for it!"

"Have she and Emma been having difficulties?"

"I don't know," Gagnon said bitterly. "I do know that Emma's been getting a lot of strange phone calls lately and she was worried. She wouldn't tell me about it. She didn't want me to worry. She..." his voice broke. "She was like that."

There was silence for a moment. Then he looked at Lawrence. "What happened to her?"

He voice was small, like that of a child.

"We're still in the process of figuring that out," Lawrence said. He switched to an easier topic. "Bridget's related to you, is she?"

Harry looked confused. "Bridget? No. No, she was one of Em's causes." He paused, then said softly, "She has - had a lot of causes…"

***

Bridget snapped on the overhead light and looked at the young detective apologetically. "It's kind of a mess."

The detective…*what kind of a name was Sohm?* …stepped past her, peering around. Emma's music room was as she had left it; old mixing equipment in the corner, fenced in by microphone stands, a few beaten instruments, some older than Bridget herself, and the two desks, piled high computer equipment, books, and hand-scribbled sheet music. Chord charts hung on the wall over the electric piano. Some of the students who came here knew little about their chosen instrument other than that their favorite pop stars played it. Emma never made them feel bad, though. She hung the charts so that they were easily visible and the less capable would not need to ask her for as much help.

"This is Emma's office?" Sohm was poking around Emma's CD collection. Emma was not exactly eclectic, but clearly some of her choices were surprising the young man.

An innocuous question – probably he was trying to get

Bridget to relax, to confide in him. It would not work but she could play along.

"She called it her play room." Bridget walked around him to one of the desks. "She used it for her own projects. Sometimes she helped students cut demos here."

"How long have you known Emma?"

"All my life. My mom started working for her after Dad died. I would sometimes go into the office with her."

She could not help but smile at the memory of her mother with her short dark hair and pretty smile. Bridget would sit in the corner of the office, listening to music on her mother's earphones, sucking on lollipops and daydreaming…

"When did your father pass away?"

She shook off her reflective thoughts. "Before I was born. It was a car accident, a hit and run, and he left my mother without anything. He worked for the college too, so Emma gave my mother a job. Then when Mom died" – did she sound as though she had a catch in her throat? - "she took me in and helped me get that scholarship."

"Sounds like she was a good friend."

"You should be grateful, Bridget! People aren't always so lucky to have friends like Emma."

How many times had she heard that? Yet, she could not live on gratitude or thrive on charity. She needed more. She had always needed more and could never find it.

She shrugged. "I guess. She was one of those people, you know? Never happy unless she had someone to help."

Emma couldn't have children of her own. She probably thought that Bridget could be her substitute daughter, but for all her warm smiles, offers of advice, plates of hot meals, she could never take the place of Bridget's mother. And Bridget, unable to grieve under the weight of charity, couldn't forgive Emma for trying to supplant her. No matter what Emma tried to do, Bridget never could forget that she was an orphan.

Now Emma was gone too, and it only added the weight of guilt to Bridget's burden of charity.

Emma was only trying her best. If only I could have believed her, believed that she really liked me, Bridget. If only I could believe that she wasn't just trying to be Saint Emma of Portsmouth…

Sohm was watching her, hazel eyes sober behind the ridiculous glasses.

Blinking back tears, Bridget said, harsher than she intended, "She was nice, you know? Really nice, but sometimes I'd think… well, that I was just another one of her charity cases."

Damn!

***

Harry Gagnon had slipped into melancholic reverie, shaken only when Lawrence brought up the name S. J. Harris. When Harry blinked at him, confused, Lawrence added helpfully, "Samantha Harris, the writer? She'd gone with Emma to hear Bridget."

He nodded then. "Oh, her, yes. Mrs. Harris was student of hers a long time ago. Emma hadn't heard from her in years."

"Just came back for a visit, did she?"

"No, she's here for some kind of lecture or something. Emma wanted her to hear Bridget's concert."

He waved at the pile of brochures and Lawrence reached for one. It was entitled *A Night of Music* with the name of some charitable foreign outreach program printed in smaller letters. Bridget's name was on the cover, along with two others. He flipped it over and saw Emma's name on the list of sponsors.

Peter Chase did say she was involved with everything...

"It's some kind of fundraiser," Gagnon was saying, as though Lawrence was unable to read that. "Another one of Em's causes, but they both treated it like Bridget's Broadway debut. Emma has...had been over at the venue almost every day, getting things ready for it." He turned wistful. "She was so excited..."

Lawrence watched him, alarmed. He was slipping again.

"Bridget says she's going through with it, as a tribute to Emma, that that's what she would have wanted it that way. I..." Harry shook his head and looked at his hands, "I just can't believe that she's gone..."

Lawrence gave him a moment, then asked, "She and Bridget got along well?"

Gagnon chuckled. "They were constantly at odds. Bridget is a difficult child, thinks the world owes her, but it was never anything serious, you understand. Just the normal parent-child thing. I always wanted to interfere, but Emma wouldn't let me. Said the child was delicate."

There was sarcastic emphasis on *delicate*, but Lawrence

let it pass. He was no stranger to the ways of a quarrelsome teenager and her mother.

"What did they quarrel about?" he asked.

Harry shrugged. "Money, studies, her future."

No boyfriends?

Gagnon was saying, "Emma wanted Bridget to finish her schooling here, then go on to Europe, but Bridget is determined to go to New York. One idea was as ridiculous as the other." He sighed. "But Emma loved her so. Despite everything, Emma loved Bridget. She loved me, she loved… she loved everyone, detective. She just loved."

***

Bridget Madden is a study in deflection, Sohm mused.

They had moved outside to the front of the house, Bridget having been unwilling to linger in Emma's old study, which was understandable. She tried to act as though Sohm's questions were not bothering her, but she was far too quick and too callous with the answers. Emma's death had affected her – only time would tell how deeply.

They walked through the garage and crossed the street to the sidewalk which ran along the inlet. Looking across the water, you could see the Memorial Bridge and the coast of Maine, bright and glittering in the mid-day sunlight. The Gagnon's had a dock here and a small boat. Harry was an angler, an interest that Bridget had shared with him until recently. Sohm let her lead the way, listening as she told him about her tempestuous relationship with her guardians, her voice always as controlled as her face. She told him about Emma's grand ambitions for her future and her own.

"She and Harry would argue about it sometimes," she said in a matter-of-fact tone.

The sun was strong, glinting off of her dark sunglasses. She stood a few feet from Sohm, her posture rigid. At Sohm's interested glance, she went on, "Harry was in the army, you know, so he's convinced that every place outside of America is some kind of terrorist stronghold or something. For once, he and I were on the same side. I'm not going to Europe. I'm going on Broadway. It's my life and I'm going to live it my way."

She said this as though she needed to convince herself as well as Sohm.

"You told Emma this?" he asked.

Bridget shrugged. "I tried, but doing it my way would have meant giving up the scholarship and Emma had just kept harping about that. *'People gave you that money so you could succeed, Bridget. You shouldn't just throw it away.'*

She turned to look over the bay. Small, colorful boats wound their way up and down the channel. When summer came, it would be crowded, even in the middle of the week as today was.

"She drove me mental," Bridget said after a moment. "But honestly, who would want to kill her? It would be like drowning a kitten or something."

Sohm did not question her assessment. "How was she with her students? Any problems there?"

The sound of a car horn cut through the air, two short

blasts. Bridget jumped and looked over her shoulder. Sohm followed her gaze. A non-descript, black, car, maybe ten years old, had pulled up in front of the Gagnon's house across the street from them. A heavy-set young man with straight, dark hair was looking at the house. He obviously had not noticed that his travel companion was standing on the dock with another man.

Bridget turned back to Sohm. "I'm sorry. I have to go. Did you have any more questions for me?"

"Not right now. You're going to be in the area for the next few days?"

"Yes." She seemed surprised by the question. "Why?"

"I may come up with a few more questions, to help clear up what happened, that's all."

"Oh. Well, anything I can do to help, you have my number."

The offer surprised Sohm with its sincerity. She turned to leave as her driver let go with another impatient blast. He had spotted Bridget on the dock and even from this distance Sohm could tell that he was not pleased.

Bridget took a step forward, stopped, then turned to face Sohm.

"My friend," she explained. She seemed embarrassed. "He's got an in with some people in Boston and New York and he's been introducing me around, getting me auditions. I, uh, couldn't tell Emma about it. She'd have flipped."

"I see." He looked at her more kindly. "Good luck, then."

"Thanks." She hesitated, clasping and unclasping her hands nervously. "It's going to be weird, you know? Not having her here. You grow to expect..."

She trailed off, looking helpless and suddenly very young and alone. Sohm found himself smiling at her in an almost fatherly fashion.

"I know," he said.

The horn sounded again, this time angrily. Bridget turned and raced across the road. Sohm watched her go, following her until she had hopped into the car. There was hesitation. The man in the car was gesturing, clearly upset. He was bigger than Bridget, possibly older. Was he just a friend, or was it something more? Were the gestures confined to the air or were they directed at her? Bridget had clearly been uncomfortable. Perhaps her discomfort was less about her guardian and more about her not wanting to get into the car with this man who had promised her a New York connection.

Uneasy, Sohm ambled over until he was on the sidewalk directly across from them, making certain that he was standing within Bridget's line of sight. She never looked at Sohm. She was arguing with the man, but though she appeared upset, she did not look as though she were frightened.

Finally, the man turned back towards the steering wheel, ready to drive off. He caught sight of Sohm, squared off with a granite expression, and for a moment, their eyes met and held. Then the man threw the car into drive and peeled off, taking the budding singer with him.

***

Harry Gagnon was hunched over, his head nearly touching his knees as he wiped his watery eyes with a ragged tissue.

The tears had come fast, but he managed to keep himself from making a sound. Lawrence said nothing. He sat there, a sturdy block of a man, impassively waiting. His very silence seemed to Harry to be a condemnation.

He probably thinks you a very silly old man.

Well, perhaps he was, but this detective had not known Emma and could not possibly comprehend the scope of his loss.

It was a struggle, but Harry regained control and straightened up. He thrust the tissue away with some embarrassment and glanced at Lawrence. The detective's piercing blue eyes were thoughtful, but distant. Yesterday, he had seemed understanding. Today, he listened politely enough, but he was here on business and there was no detectable sympathy in his face. There was a break-in and possibly a murder and the man had a job to do.

Emma's just another body, just another piece of paperwork, Harry thought. *He's grown accustomed to these things. He doesn't understand. He couldn't understand.*

"I'm sorry. I just..." Harry's hands moved in a gesture of helplessness, "I just don't know what I'll do without her."

His throat caught and he dropped his gaze again. *Damn!*

There was another moment of silence while he struggled. Then, gently, in an unexpectedly human way, Lawrence's voice broke the silence.

"I know," he said. "I've been there."

***

Thinking back on that afternoon, Lawrence never quite understood why he told Harry Gagnon about Lizzy. Perhaps it was because the man was suffering as he had suffered, or maybe it was because Harry was a stranger and it had been so long since Lawrence had talked to anyone about her. It was not something that could be shared with many people. It was a private, family matter, to begin with, and Lawrence was not the type to confide in others anyhow. Perhaps it was because after the investigation wrapped, he would never see Harry again. Maybe a remote part of him thought that, if he told Harry the story, Harry would be more inclined to see him as a confidante and tell him more.

Whatever the reason was, the story came out haltingly, slowly, regretfully.

"It was during that last big storm in January. Black ice, white out…I warned her not to go out, but… they didn't listen to me. The game was more important; the team was on their way to the semi-finals…"

He could still hear Lizzy's excited voice as he had heard it the night before as he spoke to her over the phone. He and Sohm had been wrapped up in a particularly tricky case and he had not been able to come home for two nights in a row. Lizzy understood, as she always did. She always called him at night when he was not home to give him the news and wish him goodnight.

"Too bad you can't come to watch, Dad. It'll be a good game – they are almost as good as we are…"

The other team was good. It was a tight game, but Portsmouth High had won, just as Lizzy predicted.

Lawrence forced himself to finish the sentence, "They hit

a patch of ice on the way home on 95 and spun out into on-coming traffic."

"Was she…?"

Lawrence shook his head. "She was in the passenger seat and was trapped in the car. The…driver was hardly touched and the people in the other car were fine. They'd hit the passenger side, pinning her. The paramedics thought she was…"

His throat caught. He shook his head, shook it off. Men did not cry. This was not about him. It was about letting Gagnon know that he was not alone…that someone understood. Because God knew that Lawrence could have used that himself a few months ago.

"Spinal injuries," he said. His tone sounded harsh with effort. "Cranial damage. If she ever wakes up from the coma, it's very likely she'll never move again."

Gagnon was silent for a moment.

"I'm sorry," he finally said. He sounded sincere.

Lawrence shrugged. "They say where there's life, there's hope. I'm afraid I don't always see it that way."

There was more silence and it became apparent that Harry had said all that he could today. It was time to leave and Lawrence was glad. He had been in that room, that house, Emma's house, for far too long. He rose to his feet and instinctively buttoned his jacket.

Gagnon watched his movements with a hollow-eyed gaze. He was alone in this. Despite anything Lawrence could tell him, the true fact of the matter was, Harry Gagnon and Harry Gagnon alone was going to have to deal with the loss of his wife.

There was still one thing that Lawrence could promise him.

"We'll find the person responsible for this," he declared. "Justice will be done."

Gagnon stared at him for a moment. Then he began to laugh. It was a hearty, bitter laugh, so cold that it sent shivers down Lawrence's spine.

It was not the reaction that he was expecting and his face must have shown his surprise because Harry reined it in and wiped his eyes. "I'm sorry, I'm afraid I lost my faith in the justice system a long time ago, detective."

It was so final that Lawrence could not think of anything to say in response. Naturally, Harry would feel helpless and naturally he had be upset, but this was a level of cynicism that Lawrence could not touch.

There seemed to be nothing more to do or say. Feeling curiously helpless, Lawrence turned to leave. He had already taken a few steps when Harry's voice brought him up short.

"Have you ever wondered what you'd do if you had that culprit, that driver alone for just five minutes, detective?"

Harry was leaning forward eagerly, his hand extended as though to grab hold of something. The expression in his eyes alarmed Lawrence. They were glittering with the kind of ice that he had seen in a few others – and most of those he had dealt with professionally.

Harry continued, almost dreamily, "Just five minutes... for *real* justice to be served. If only I could..."

Lawrence interrupted. "You leave that to us, Mr. Gagnon. Justice can turn into vengeance without our noticing."

Gagnon glared at him defiantly. "You can't blame a man for wanting…"

Then defiance turned into defense and he leaned out farther. "Don't you wish you could do the same? You can't tell me that you don't wish to do the same to that driver who ruined your daughter's life."

Lawrence's mouth went dry, but his voice came out steady. "I'm afraid it's a little more difficult in my case."

"Difficult?"

"The driver? The driver was Lizzy's mother – my wife."

****

Sohm was waiting for him in the car, so focused on his phone that he did not even look up when Lawrence got into the driver's seat. Lawrence was glad – he felt weary to the bone, as though he had aged a decade since getting out of that car an hour ago. He fell back against the seat with a sigh that he could not restrain and rubbed his face with his hand.

"Tough one?" Sohm asked.

"You've no idea," Lawrence muttered. He glanced over and caught a glimpse of the familiar chessboard on Sohm's phone. "Another one of those Sicilian moves?"

"Oh, no." Sohm showed him the board. The pieces were arrayed in what seemed to Lawrence to be a discordant mess. He was playing against Purplebutterfly87 again and it was obvious even to him that they were pretty far into the game.

"I started with a different gambit, but she caught on really fast," Sohm said happily. "As you can see I've moved queen's bishop to king's knight 3. That ought to keep her busy for a bit."

"I would think so." Lawrence replied, thought the move meant nothing to him. "Find out anything interesting from the ward?"

"Yes. Bridget Madden has a boyfriend. And I think I've seen him somewhere before..."

17

Matthew Harris knew his mother well enough to know how she was feeling from the way she spoke. For instance, yesterday she had been upset, frightened, and shaken. Nothing Matt did and nothing she drank could bring her around. Only when after she finally reached Jonathan on the phone and spoke to him for a half hour, did she regain her equilibrium. She hung up the phone, wiped her tears, and beamed at Matt.

"We are so lucky to have Jonathan in our lives," she proclaimed.

Matt was too relieved at seeing her improved condition to disagree as he normally would have.

The next morning dawned and her good mood held. She was busy working on her edits when Matt woke up. She spent the morning taking calls and getting her things settled into their house.

The house *was* nice, Matt had to admit. It was large and airy. He did not know the woman who had prepared it for them but he imagined that she was elderly, because the furniture was old fashioned and there was not a single game station anywhere. Good thing he had thought to bring his own. From the looks of things, the old lady's death aside, Portsmouth was going to be about as placid as you could get.

Even Jonathan had worried about that.

"Make sure you bring your games," he had advised Matt two nights before they left California. Jonathan had been leaning against the doorframe of Matt's room, watching him pack even though Matt had made it clear earlier that he wanted neither advice nor company. "And your outdoor gear. New Hampshire is supposed to be great for hiking and camping."

"Swell," Matt muttered.

The truth was that Matt loved nothing more than being outdoors and the idea of climbing Mount Washington had been the deciding factor which made him agree to go in the first place. Later, reality had set in hard; what good was going to a cool place to hike and camp if you didn't have anyone to go with? Mom didn't camp and wasn't likely to allow him to go alone. His best bet was that he'd meet someone who be willing to go with him. And *that* didn't seem very likely.

New Hampshire was going to be a drag. Matt had already resigned himself to that fact.

Jonathan was still lingering so Matt muttered something about being busy doing his summer curriculum. That usually worked on adults. They tended to get off his back if they could be made to think that he was serious about his academic work.

It did not work this time.

"It's going to be a long summer for you there without your friends," Jonathan remarked, folding his arms.

"Obviously," Matt said before he could stop himself. Then he quickly added, "It'll be fine. Mom'll be there."

"Well, sure, that'll be nice," Jonathan agreed.

There had been a pause in the conversation then. Matt had kept his focus on trying to shove his gym gear into his already over-stuffed duffel bag.

After a few moments, Jonathan spoke again. "Look, Matt... I've got a few slow weeks coming up in July and I could use some time away from the office. What would you say to me flying out there to tackle some of those White Mountains with you?"

The offer froze Matt in his tracks.

He wanted to explore more than anything else... but not with Jonathan. That would risk getting too close and Matt had lived through too many of his mother's relationships to want to do that. The men his mother chose were generally decent and usually tried to bond with Matt, acknowledging him as part of the package. But they always disappeared when the relationship ended. Matt had lived through many good beginnings and had been left with loads of empty promises. True enough, on paper Jonathan looked like the most sure bet, but Matt was not a child. He knew better.

Don't get close. That's how you get hurt.

Jonathan and Samantha were actually married now... but she had married Gary before him and that had lasted, what, two years? Then again, Matt really did want to climb Mount Washington...

Jonathan waited for his answer. Matt wrestled with himself for a moment, then shrugged.

"If you want, sure," he said, taking great pains to keep his tone neutral. "Whatever."

Jonathan had responded in kind, with so little inflection in his tone that Matt wondered if he would just drop the matter and not come. It was probably better if he did. Nevertheless, Matt had packed his hiking boots. It had taken everything he could not to ask his mother last night if Jonathan had said anything about flying out later that month.

He was thinking about this when he came downstairs that afternoon. Despite the lovely, late spring day, Matt spent the morning in his room, playing on his game station and trying to lose himself in world building. He had almost forgotten about Emma Gagnon's death, but recalled it instantly when he heard the almost frantic tone in his mother's voice, echoing in the nearly bare kitchen.

"Broke into her office? But... why would anyone do that?"

Matt immediately slowed down to listen. A burglary was interesting, provided it did not happen to him and his things. He came to the doorway of the kitchen. His mother was sitting at the counter, her lap-top open, a pile of manuscript pages next to it. She was hunched forward, a physical signal that she was totally engrossed in what she was hearing on the other side of the line and that she was worried by it.

Was she talking to Jonathan?

As he sidled into the kitchen towards the fridge, she began speaking again.

"They think she was *what...*? Oh my God..."

She was not talking to Jonathan, that Matt was fairly certain of, and she still had not noticed Matt's entrance. Her hands were moving now, she was trying to make sense of something. He reached up slowly for the door handle.

"But how was she…?"

The fridge handle clicked. Samantha broke off and turned sharply, spotting Matt for the first time. Her mouth opened into a little O and she looked horrified. Matt dropped his gaze, grabbed a bottle, and shut the door. If he slipped out quickly enough, maybe she would continue the conversation. He could listen in from the den…

No such luck. He was not even out of the room when she spoke quickly into the phone, "Look, can we talk? I can be there in a few minutes?"

Definitely not Jonathan, then. But if not him, who?

He did not get a chance to find out. Samantha ended the call in a hurry, packed her things and sprinted out of the house without another word. Matt stood at the den window. He watched his mother pull out of the driveway with aggravated haste and wondered what it was that could have upset her so much.

Suddenly, the house seemed much too big and hollow.

18

"So it wasn't natural causes?"

Chief Beverly DiFranco was a petite woman with a pleasant smile who did not like to waste time. She sat on the other side of her remarkably modest desk, listening to Lawrence's preliminary report with her head cocked to one side while beating time on the desk with her pencil. Being called into her office, as Lawrence had, usually meant that she had heard something that worried her. The doubtful expression in her eyes confirmed this assumption.

Lawrence shook his head. "We're still waiting on the lab, but strychnine seems the mostly likely cause of death."

"And you're thinking murder, not suicide?"

"She doesn't fit the role of a suicide victim: active in her community, regular church-goer, in a stable relationship, no history of depression or recent tragedy."

DiFranco frowned and tapped her pencil harder. "She also doesn't fit the profile of a murder victim. She's a music teacher. Why would anyone want her dead?"

Lawrence shrugged. He'd had the same conversation with Sohm only a short time ago and neither of them could come up with an explanation. "There must be something someone isn't telling us."

She raised an eyebrow. "Oh, you think?"

Lawrence grinned.

She sighed and got up from her desk to stand in front of the window. Her office was a large room with old-fashioned wood paneling left over from the prior chief. Her predecessor was a sportsman who loved 70s movies and decorated to taste. To DiFranco's credit, she did not immediately order a redecoration, though rumor had it one was in the works. Lawrence could not blame her. The dark walls made for a depressing space.

"Do you have any leads?" she asked.

"At present, Samantha Harris is our best suspect."

She turned to him, shocked. "Samantha Harris – the *writer?*"

"She got coffee with the victim and from all the witness reports, she was the only one who had the opportunity to slip something into it."

"But what's the motive?" DiFranco sounded annoyed. "Why would S. J. Harris fly all the way out from California just to murder her old music professor, twenty years *after* she left her class?"

So that's what's got you worried, Lawrence thought. *The celebrity.*

"I can't imagine," he answered easily.

"It's ridiculous."

"Maybe, but it's what we have right now."

DiFranco looked at him, her gray eyes sizing him up and

weighing his statements. Lawrence thought, again, how mis-leading appearances could be. DiFranco was five foot five, if that, with curly blonde hair and an easy laugh. She had a picture of her grandchildren and turquoise china owls that were too pretty for a police chief's office on the shelf behind her. Yet behind her softness, there was a granite wall that everyone in her department had run into at one time or another. She was a helpful, pretty woman who did not suffer fools easily.

Lawrence prepared himself for the lecture and it came.

"Look." She left the window and went back behind her desk. "You know I like to give my officers free rein on their investigations. If I didn't trust you, I wouldn't have you head-ing up my investigation here."

"Thank you, ma'am," he said automatically, and her eyes narrowed.

"But the people in this case..." She hesitated. "Noble Col-lege has connections, Lawrence. Within this town, the state, the country even. If you go in there like a bull in a china shop, we could have the roof brought down on us. You understand, right?"

He looked at her levelly. "You're asking me to proceed with caution."

"Proceed with diplomacy," she clarified. "Just keep in mind that every ripple has its effect. That's all I'm asking." She straightened up. "Besides, I like the runaway student as a suspect better."

DiFranco may allow her officers free rein in their in-vestigations, but that did not mean that she wouldn't give directions from time to time.

Lawrence repressed a frustrated sigh and stood. "I'll keep that in mind."

"And keep me in the loop on this one, right?"

"Always."

As he turned to go, she called out to him. "Lawrence – how's Janine?"

He froze. Something squeezed hard in his chest and he thought, *At least I feel something.*

"Fine, ma'am," he replied, without turning around. "We're all fine."

***

Sohm was at his computer studying reports when Lawrence came back into the office. Lawrence looked put out, but Sohm had been expecting that much. DiFranco only called in the lead of an investigation when she was preparing herself for some kind of political fallout. While Lawrence was knowledgeable and naturally gregarious - when he was not dealing with a personal crisis, that is– he had even less patience for dealing with political and PR problems than Sohm did. And that was saying something.

"You're back," he said as Lawrence took his chair.

Lawrence grunted. "Have you started those background checks yet?"

"Working on that now. Emma Gagnon got a parking ticket once."

"Figures."

Sohm turned in his seat to face Lawrence and put his

hands behind his head as he leaned back in the chair. "I've been talking with Peter Chase."

Lawrence was searching through his drawers and desktop. He stopped when he found a weathered, league-edition baseball. Grunting again, this time in satisfaction, he leaned back and began to toss the ball gently into the air. Sohm recognized the habit as a sign that Lawrence was puzzling over something particularly tricky. The rhythmic motion of the toss soothed him.

I hope it works, Sohm thought. *You've been wrapped up way too tight for too long.*

"What did Chase have to say?" Lawrence asked, keeping his eye on the ball.

"He told us pretty much what we already know. Emma was a regular volunteer at the hall but Harry and Bridget weren't. According to him, Emma was on every volunteer arts committee that would have her."

"Trying to avoid home?"

Sohm shrugged. "Maybe, but here doesn't seem to be any trouble there. As for Harry Gagnon, the grieving widower, he served in Vietnam, was medically discharged, and spent some time in various VA hospitals. He has a few things on his record." Sohm turned back to his computer to look over the list. "A couple of episodes of road rage, DUIs, drunken disorderlies, probably linked to PTSD. Nothing since he married Emma, though. Bridget's clean."

Lawrence nodded and tossed the ball, which Sohm neatly caught. "What about Sarah Hopper? Any record for her?"

"Oh yeah." Sohm tossed it back. "A few DUIs, couple of

citations for rowdiness. She's been pulled in for questioning a few times by the drug squad, but so far they haven't been able to prove that she's involved."

Lawrence got up abruptly and went over to the board where they had posted the pictures of all the suspects and witnesses. They had added the picture of Sarah Hopper that he had got from Harry Gagnon.

"Why was she with the victim at the time of her death? And why did she run away?"Lawrence wondered.

Sohm shrugged. "Scared, probably. But she can't be involved with her death. Emma would have had to have ingested that poison at least twenty minutes before."

"If it was strychnine," Lawrence replied. He wandered back to his desk. "Emma Gagnon never left New England. She taught music, which is hardly inflammatory. She was a housewife, a church-goer who never swore, never lost her temper. There's not one reason why anyone would want her dead." He dropped down into his chair and turned to Sohm."What about our celebrity, S. J. Harris?"

"I found a biography of hers online but its incomplete. She comes from money and she studied here for three years before moving back to California. She has not been back since. Her current husband is Jonathan St. Jean, a businessman who has offices in London and Paris as well as New York and Chicago and she has one son. She was invited here by Professor Stewart, who, coincidentally, is one of the ones working on the concert for Bridget."

"Any criminal record?"

"Nothing worth mentioning."

Lawrence sighed, "Well, we're going to have to talk to

everyone, I suppose, but let's start with Sarah Hopper. Have you got an address for her?"

"Home address and work address."

"You have been busy."

"Keeps me off the streets. Anyway, according to her online profile, she works part time at Atkinson's Books."

"Atkinson's Books?"

The question was sharp and unexpected. Sohm nodded, taking it in his stride. "Owned by Thomas Atkinson, longtime resident and Noble College alumnus. The shop is one of those trendy places, used books, offbeat music in the background, vintage albums sold in the back. You know it?"

Lawrence was searching his desk again. "No, but Atkinson is helping to put on Bridget's concert Saturday night." He held up a brochure triumphantly.

Sohm took it and flipped to the back. Atkinson's Books headed the list of sponsors. "Coincidence?"

"We'd better find out." Lawrence said briskly. He got up, suddenly looking brighter. Having something to do was always better than sitting around stewing about conversations with superiors. "But of primary importance is locating Sarah. You go to her place. I'll go to the shop. If she isn't there, see if you can poke around, get a feel for what kind of girl she is. If not, keep on with those background searches."

"Right." Sohm grabbed his coat. It was good to be on the move again.

19

Atkinson's Books was typical of many of the small trendy shops in Portsmouth. It was tucked into an alley, out of the way of the main street with only a folding sign with a hand-drawn arrow to point out its location. The building itself was tall and narrow, sandwiched between two similar buildings, all looking slightly apologetic for taking up space. There was room for Lawrence to park in front, but only just barely. The shop's front door was wide open, spilling AC into the bright street.

It took a moment for Lawrence's eyes to adjust to stepping into the dark interior. While he was blinded, he noted two things; that the shop smelled of old books and chili, and that Sohm had been correct about the type of music being played in the background.

The entry was cramped. Directly in front of him was a narrow staircase running up to a door adorned with a sign that read '*private*'. To the left was the doorway to the shop proper. The building was, Lawrence realized, a converted tenement-style apartment building built before code. The shop was one apartment while the stairs lead to the second.

When he stepped into the shop, he saw at once that he was right. Walls had been modified, doors and appliances removed, but the place bore all the signs of conversion, from the bowed front room to the tiny windows on the back wall which were blocked by the AC unit.

It was difficult to make out even these details, though, because the room was densely packed, both with shelves and with people. Hipsters with faded jeans and deliberately neglected hair mused over titles like *My Antonia* and *The 1994 Guide to Sci-Fi*. Two tourists were poring over tattered copies of Portsmouth History, and a few teenaged boys were engaged in an excited discussion over a faded copy of Queen's *Night at the Opera*.

Lawrence could not help but grin when he saw that. He had been the first in his class to get a copy of that album. For a brief time, he was the hero of his grade.

My dad was right —everything old becomes new again, if you wait long enough...

"Can I help you?"

A stuffy voice broke through his reverie. Lawrence started and found himself looking at a tall, lanky young man with thick black hair and a severe cold. He looked no different than any of the other Portsmouth natives in the room except that he was standing behind the counter, making him a man of importance.

"Is Sarah working here today?" Lawrence asked.

The young man looked at him suspiciously, so he reached into his jacket and brought out his badge. The young man's eyes went wide and Lawrence gestured for quiet. "I just need to talk to her."

"She's not here now," the young man whispered. "I don't know what her schedule is, sorry."

"Is your boss here?"

"Oh, yeah, he's in the office." He indicated the door that Lawrence had just walked through. "Up the stairs."

The staircase was old and the steps sloped in the middle. Lawrence had to pick his way carefully and when he reached the top he found the door open a crack. He pushed it wide and found that he was in another entryway about as small as a coat closet. The walls were yellowing and there were books piled around the edges, adding to the claustrophobic feeling. There was a light in the next room and he was about to call out when he heard a voice.

"I'm telling you, there's nothing for you to worry about, all right?" It was a man's voice, low and gentle, as though he were comforting a child. "I'm here. You know you can rely on me."

"I know, I know," A woman sniffled. "It's just… you know, after… I haven't been here since Bobby…"

The man cut her off. "Nothing is going to happen…"

Lawrence rapped on the doorframe just before he stepped into the room. He found himself in the middle of a kitchen, surprisingly open and airy, with beaten appliances and a computer station in the back. The walls needed paint, the floor re-tiling. The counters and few shelves overflowed with books, papers, and forgotten soda bottles, a bachelor's pad if ever Lawrence saw one. He did not spare much thought for the room; he was far more interested in its occupants.

A man and a woman sat at a table a few feet away from him. The woman was leaning on the table, her tearstained face in the man's hands until Lawrence's surprise entrance made her tear away in embarrassment. The man remained where he was, letting his hands fall to his sides. Lawrence did not know him, but he knew the woman who now had her back to him. It was Samantha Harris.

Lawrence was still staring at her when the man said sharply, "This isn't open to the public."

Thomas Atkinson hopped up from his seat and glowered at the newcomer. He was tall with a solid build and clenched hands. His hair was thick and long and he wore glasses that did not suit him. He looked like the shop itself – beaten, run-down, defeated, but defiant.

Lawrence held out his badge. "My name is Detective Lawrence. I'm looking to speak to one of your employees, Mr. Atkinson."

Samantha Harris turned her tearstained face to look at him with bewilderment. Even there, with her makeup marred and in those dismal surroundings, she had a glow about her.

What is a beautiful woman like you doing here with him? Lawrence wondered.

"Would you get away from the staircase then, detective?" Atkinson asked pointedly, "I don't want to advertise that one of my employees is wanted by the police."

Lawrence did as he was asked and Atkinson shut the door firmly. Lawrence looked at Harris.

Harris abruptly stood. "I'd better be going…" She gathered

her purse from the table and turned to go. She hesitated when her gaze met Lawrence's.

"Did I interrupt something?" he asked mildly.

Samantha Harris swallowed hard.

"Nothing." Atkinson's tone was harsh.

When Lawrence looked sharply at him, Harris intervened. "I have a book-signing in a few days," she explained and tried to smile. "We were just going over a few details."

It was a lie and a poor one at that.

Lawrence raised an eyebrow. "You always do that before a book signing, do you?"

Atkinson stepped forward. "We're old friends – went to college together here years ago. We were just..." He shrugged. "Catching up."

"Yes." Harris looked as though she had just been thrown a life-preserver. "Yes. Well, it's been nice, Tommy, but I'd better be going. Matt will be waiting for me."

She moved towards the door and Atkinson followed as if in lock-step.

"This has been nice," he said.

Harris looked up at him, startled. "Yes."

Lawrence took a step towards the window at the far end of the room, as much to give them space as to encourage them to talk.

"Maybe we can have... dinner while you're here?"

."Yes." Harris sounded cautious. "Yes, that'd be nice. Until tomorrow, then."

The door closed. Lawrence turned to see Atkinson standing alone, rubbing his chin in thought. After a moment, he turned to face Lawrence. He wore an expression of extreme politeness, but he had positioned himself between the police-man and the door through which his visitor had just left. Defensiveness radiated off the man.

"I'm sorry, detective," he said. "What did you say you wanted?"

"I'm looking for Sarah Hopper," Lawrence replied. "I understand she works here."

"She does. Is she in trouble?"

He was not concerned. Or perhaps, it was that he was not surprised.

"Not that I know of. We just want to talk to her. Is she working today?"

"No. She has a class."

"I see."

Another pause. Lawrence looked around the apartment, taking in the untidy sink, the desk covered in papers and books and the poster of Samantha Harris's book signing, taped up conveniently where someone sitting at the table eating might easily view it.

I guess some men never quite got over you, Lawrence thought.

Atkinson did not have a wedding ring. That meant little in some circles, but Samantha Harris wore not only a wedding ring but an expensive engagement ring as well.

And yet she was here, confiding in you. How does that make you feel, Mr. Atkinson?

The silence was making Atkinson nervous. He attempted to cover by stepping forward and taking a handful of files from the table. Lawrence watched him impassively.

"Well," Atkinson began, "if you don't need anything else..."

"How well did you know Emma Gagnon?"

Atkinson blinked. "Emma? I've known her for years. She taught back when I was at Noble. We've worked together on some community projects. And before you ask, I was here, in the bookshop, setting up for the day the morning she was killed."

Lawrence folded his arms. "Then you know that we consider her death suspicious?"

"Word gets around fast, but it's absolutely insane. No one in their right mind would want to kill her. It'd be like killing Mother Theresa."

"Then she didn't have any enemies or rivals?"

"Of course not. The woman never hurt a fly."

Lawrence was beginning to wish someone would say something different.

"Someone broke into her office this morning – trashed the place looking for something. Can you think of any reason why someone would do that?"

"No," Atkinson said firmly. "Is that what you wanted to see Sarah about?"

"Was she working yesterday?"

"Yes, as usual."

"What time did she get in?"

"A little after ten, maybe later. But surely you can't think that Sarah…"

"How well do you know Mrs. Harris?"

Atkinson turned white. "I told you. We're just good friends."

"And you all were just good friends with the late Mrs. Gagnon."

"Yes." Now he was turning red. "We were all good friends."

Lawrence paused for a moment. He had shaken the man, which was good, but he was shooting blind. There was something here. He knew it but he could not grasp it. Even if he was right, there was every reason to suppose that it was merely two consenting adults grappling with guilt over a proposed indiscretion. It could have nothing to do with Emma Gagnon at all.

DiFranco's warning came to mind: "Be diplomatic."

So much for that.

Atkinson was watching him, looking like a cornered dog who had already seen a few scraps. What Samantha Harris saw in him was anyone's guess, but it was none of Lawrence's business. Still, there was no reason to let Atkinson think that.

Lawrence smiled and drew out his card. "When you see Sarah, would you tell her that I'd like a word? It's Lawrence with a W."

Atkinson took the card without looking at it. "With a W," he repeated. "Anything else?"

"Not at the moment. Thank you for your help, Mr. Atkinson. I'll see myself out."

Lawrence left the room feeling rather like he had been walking through the fog and missed every sign that he had been looking for.

20

Sarah Hopper lived in the poorer section of Portsmouth, which meant only that the buildings were slightly older and still beyond the means of most young students who were not being supported by two jobs, a roommate, probably two, and the monthly support check from their parents.

Sarah Hopper is not alone in this world, Sohm thought, as he made his way up the steep, narrow staircase to the second floor.

The apartment was a on a quiet street where the buildings in front crowded out the sight of the North Church steeple. Not that one really lived in Portsmouth for the view. They came for the atmosphere, a lively feeling of being in a small, culturally aware community without the usual drawbacks of the larger cities like Boston. Sohm understood the appeal. He had not chosen the Portsmouth Police Department solely because it was on the East Coast.

Someone in the apartment was playing loud pop music so loudly that he could clearly make out the lyrics from halfway down the stairs. He had to knock several times before the music stopped and the door was wrenched open with an impatient jerk.

"Yes?"

The question was also impatient.

The woman facing him was pretty and young, but not what Sohm had been expecting. She had jet-black hair tied up in a severe ponytail, and her face carefully done up with makeup despite the fact that she was quite obviously in the middle of cleaning. She wore a faded pair of jeans and a worn sweater, and she held a duster in her hand. She was just as surprised by him as he was by her.

"I'm looking for Sarah Hopper," he said.

From the doubtful once-over that she gave him, he suspected that it was not often that Sarah received visitors in a jacket and tie.

"That makes two of us," she replied. "I'm Tina O'Reilly, her roommate. Who are you?"

He pulled his badge from his inside coat pocket. She sagged against the door with a weary sigh.

"Oh God," she said. "What has she done now?"

***

Tina O'Reilly was the only occupant of the apartment that afternoon, though she informed Sohm that there were three of them during the school year. Jenny, the third roommate was on a road trip and had been since the beginning of the month. As for Sarah, Tina had not seen her since yesterday morning.

Sohm sat at one end of the over-sized couch that cramped

the narrow, high ceilinged living room while Tina tried to call Sarah. The couch was several years out of date and, though otherwise clean, was coated in a fine coat of caramel-colored cat hairs. The walls were covered in pictures and old, tin signs – one of the roommates was a fan of kitsch. One corner of the room was devoted to a computer and a surprisingly high-quality printer. Stacks of photos in various sizes littered the small desk and the coffee table directly in front of Sohm was covered with photo albums, scrapbooks, scissors, magazines, more pictures, and shards of paper. Someone was apparently in the middle of a project.

Tina paced in the center of the room. She held herself well, though the presence of homicide detective at her door would have been enough to throw anyone off their game. Only the pacing and the way her fingers played with her straight hair betrayed any sense of nerves at all. She gave a huff of impatience as the voicemail came on.

"Sarah, give me a call as soon as you can." She turned to Sohm, raising her shoulders in a shrug. "I haven't seen her for days. I think she slept here last night because some stuff was moved around, but she was gone before I got up. I don't know when she'll be back."

She lowered herself on the opposite end of the couch and Sohm mentally noted the graceful movement.

"Is that unusual behavior for her?

Tina snorted. "Very. Usually I have to drag her out of bed to get her to work or class on time."

"Do you attend the same college?"

She laughed. "Thanks for that, but, no, I graduated awhile back. I work and sub-let the room to students."

"Very economical."

"You have to be to be able to afford rent in this town."

"How is Sarah to have as roommate?"

"We seldom see each other," she said delicately. "It works out best that way."

Weariness, but, again, no bitterness. Sohm was wondering what it would take to shake or annoy this woman.

"Did Sarah have any steady boyfriends?"

"Several."

"Anyone special?"

"The longest running one I know of…" she looked around the room, then got up and went to the desk, "…was this fellow here." She plucked a picture from the pile and handed it to Sohm. "Colin Rideout. But I think she's more interested in him than he is in her."

Sohm studied the picture. Sarah was smiling, her hair pulled back in the same loose ponytail that he had seen in Gagnon's picture. She had her arms around a stocky young man with dark hair and a pained expression. Despite the fact that he had a pretty young girl leaning into him, Rideout's arms were resolutely at his side.

A picture is worth a thousand words, Sohm thought. *Colin, Colin…does Sarah know about Bridget?*

"Do you know how I can contact him?"

Tina shrugged. "I don't have his number, but I do know that he lives on Essex Street and works at one of the restaurants downtown."

"Which one?"

She thought for a moment. "The Rusty Ale. He works the

bar, keeps odd hours. I think that's where Sarah met him." She grew serious then and leaned forward. "Look, is Sarah involved in anything serious?"

He met her gaze, unblinking. "We think she might be able to aid us in an investigation, that's all."

Tina sighed and leaned back. "That's a relief."

"You were expecting worse?"

"It wouldn't have surprised me."

There was sadness in her tone. For all Tina O'Reilly's cynicism, she really did not want to see Sarah in any trouble.

Almost as soon as Sohm noted this, Tina straightened and said, "But look, I keep my nose clean. I try not to get involved in her life. She does her thing. I do mine and we try not to annoy each other in the kitchen." Having spoken her piece, she sighed again. "But, no. It wouldn't have surprised me to learn she was involved with something."

Sohm waited a moment, but Tina offered nothing further, so he nodded. "I see." He pulled out a card and handed it to her. "We are really anxious to talk to her. If she returns, would you give me a call?"

She took it readily, studying the simple raised print. "Sure. Anything else you need to know?"

He decided to try a long shot. "You didn't know Emma Gagnon by any chance?"

"No. I mean, I heard she died, but that's it." She leaned forward. "Is that what you need to see Sarah about?"

Sohm replied lightly, his eyes wandering over the paper-strewn coffee table again, "We think she might be helpful, is all." A particular photo caught his eye and he leaned over to study it. "What exactly do you do, Miss O'Reilly?"

"I'm a nurse."

He plucked the picture from the table and held it up in askance. It was a photo of Tina dressed in corsets and lace and little else. She was on a stage with another girl, making eyes at the camera. In the image, Tina had a knowing smirk that was, frankly, intriguing.

The same knowing smirk crossed her face now.

"Oh," she said. "That's just something I do for fun."

Sohm could not help but return the smile.

21

DiFranco was not happy when she heard that Sarah Hopper was still missing. She came by Lawrence's office after the working day was through, casually, as though she had not a care in the world. Lawrence knew better. She wanted to make sure the investigation stayed on target, that he was not annoying the important principals. Sohm was too observant to be unaware of the undercurrents but he acted as though DiFranco's visit was nothing out of the ordinary. He recounted his interview with Tina O'Reilly for both Lawrence and DiFranco. He had a very favorable impression of Sarah's roommate, and Lawrence wondered idly if she was single.

DiFranco had a few questions about Hopper, but Sohm was only able to confirm what they already knew: Sarah was unreliable and skirted the fringes of the law. She was fast becoming the person of most interest, even in Lawrence's estimation.

"We've put out her description," Sohm said. "She'll turn up soon enough."

DiFranco grunted. She was leaning on the doorsill, her

arms folded. She had had once been a top-notch detective and sometimes Lawrence wondered if she ever missed the work.

"Who else do we have in the front running for possible suspect?" she asked. "Her husband?"

Lawrence snorted. "Harry Gagnon? Certainly not."

DiFranco looked at him sharply.

"He knew Emma's schedule and habits," Sohm pointed out. "He had access to her food and medications. He could have poisoned her toothpaste for all we know and then made sure he was in the presence of witnesses when the poison was likely to take effect."

"If he'd put strychnine in her toothpaste, she would never have made it as far as the hall," Lawrence retorted. "Anyway, what was his motive?"

"Insurance?" DiFranco offered. "He's putting his ward through college, isn't he? Maybe he'd run out of savings and needed the money."

"Kill his wife to put his ward through college? That's stretching it a bit, don't you think? Anyway, he's been wanting to retire *with* her."

"So he says," Sohm said mildly.

Lawrence glared at him. "Since we're pulling people out of the hat, what about your Peter Chase?"

His answer was prompt, "Absolutely no motive there and no opportunity."

"How about the ward, Bridget?" DiFranco asked.

"They had the usual family squabbles, nothing serious."

Lawrence sighed heavily. "That's the trouble with this whole thing, everyone liked Emma Gagnon. She offended no one, wasn't in a position to threaten anyone, and didn't have enough money to tempt anyone. There's no reason whatsoever for anyone to want to kill her."

"What about Thomas Atkinson?" Sohm asked.

"He's Sarah's boss?" DiFranco queried.

Lawrence nodded. "And he was working with Emma on Bridget Madden's charity concert *and* he knows Sam Harris – they went to school together."

"Any possible motive there?"

"Not that I can see."

"Just a tightly knit group of professionals," Sohm said.

"I got the impression that Atkinson wanted to be more than professional with Sam Harris," Lawrence said.

"That still isn't a motive to kill Emma Gagnon," DiFranco sighed. "The only lead we have right now is the fact that minutes before her death, Emma Gagnon was involved in an argument with a young student who has since gone missing. Unlikely a suspect as she may be, Sarah Hopper is still our best lead."

Lawrence grimaced. She was right. Strictly as the evidence went, there was no one else but Sarah. The *why* still hung heavily in the air, as well as his own gut feeling that there was more to this than met the eye. And he still couldn't shake the question of why Samantha Harris always looked so guilty.

DiFranco straightened up. "Well, keep at it. Something is bound to turn up."

"If we're lucky," he replied.

She gave him a sympathetic look that surprised him. "Goodnight, boys."

She left and Lawrence glanced at the clock. It was past six and he was tired. He went through the shutdown procedures for the night, told the night shift that he was to be notified the minute someone found Sarah Hopper, and spent a good ten minutes deleting emails before shutting off his screen for good. He grabbed his coat from the back of his chair and then wandered over to the board to examine the pictures.

Samantha Harris' carefully staged photo contrasted sharply with the casual poses in the other photos. He stared at her for a moment. Janine came to mind and he wondered at his own motivation. Was he truly interested in Sam as a suspect? Or was he being swayed by her physicality? No doubt about it, she was a pretty woman...

He remembered the expression on her face that afternoon when he surprised her at the bookshop and shook his head. No. It was not physicality that was making her stay on his mind. She was a piece that did not fit into the overall puzzle. When Lawrence turned from the board, he saw that Sohm was sitting quietly behind his desk, scowling at his phone.

"Your mother again?" he asked.

Calls from Sohm's mother happened every few weeks or so and though Sohm tried to brush them off, they always upset him. Lawrence did not know what the issue was but there was something there.

Sohm, however, shook his head at the question.

"You aren't going to believe this." His tone suggested that he still did not himself. "But Purple butterfly just moved queen's bishop to king's four."

"No!" Lawrence deadpanned and Sohm nodded vigorously.

"That scuttles my gambit." He held out the phone for Lawrence to see. "I'm going to have to reconsider my position."

Lawrence examined the little board on the screen. "You could move your king to the left."

Sohm arched an eyebrow. "That would hardly do," he said in mock reproof. "I might as well concede the game. One could never do that."

"Go down fighting, Sohm."

"Always, sir," he said cheerfully, pocketing his phone. "Always."

22

Janine Lawrence awoke with a gasp. The TV was on, cycling through an episode of a show that she had forgotten that she had been watching. She had fallen asleep on the recliner again. She had fallen asleep *alone* again. The remote was lodged between the cushions and she had to dig to pull it out. She snapped the television off and fell back against the recliner, letting the sudden silence and darkness drench her like a warm bath.

Silence without stillness, quiet without peace.

Janine had forgotten how noisy an empty house could be. In the past few weeks especially, she found herself growing reacquainted with creaks and groans and mechanical sounds that came with the shift of seasons in New England.

In contrast, she had never realized how truly quiet the neighborhood was. At any given time there was hardly more than the occasional sounds of lawnmowers or children riding bicycles. Sometimes on the weekends she would hear the neighbors next door, arguing about who was taking which child to which practice. They were so loud at times that she'd wonder whether they were on the brink of a divorce. She hoped not. In an odd way she envied that couple. Arguments were a sign of communication - poor communication, but communication nonetheless - and noise was a sign of life. As long as they could argue and resolve, they could survive. Where there was noise, there was life. Where there was life, there was hope. It was silence that killed.

Janine knew about silence. She had lived with it these past few months, a constant pressing weight on her chest like a relentless, driving, master of conscience. She could escape it during the day when she was at work or even in the hospice where Lizzy's monitors and unsteady, weak breath kept the monster at bay. Where there was noise, there was life.

But at night, when she was alone, the silence was unbearable. It was amazing to think that she had once complained to Michael that Lizzy's friends were too loud. "What I wouldn't give for a little peace and quiet," she had said.

The price had been way too high.

Restless, Janine threw off the blanket and went into the kitchen. She saw the time on the clock and felt a rush of despair. It was 11:30 p.m. There was still so much night ahead of her and no hope of sleep.

She filled the kettle and set it on the stove to boil. Her sister had recommended herbal tea to help her sleep. It didn't work but the act of preparing it was soothing. Earlier that evening, her sister had called to fuss: "You shouldn't be alone. Why don't you come and stay with us for a few days? We've got the guest bedroom already made up."

Janine was tempted but ultimately turned the offer down. She was a grown woman. An empty house should not intimidate her. Besides, there was always the remote chance that Michael might need her.

Michael.

The kettle began to grumble. She found a clean mug, the honey bear, and the box of tea. She wondered, idly, where Michael was, then squashed the thought brutally.

He'll come in his own time.

The absence was a condemnation all of its own, a cruel sentence she disputed at times and accepted at others. She had, after all, been at fault. She had driven the car. She had made the call to head home. She could have stayed put. She *should* have stayed put. But the sky had looked clear and she had wanted to go home. *"I'll outrun it,"* she'd told herself.

She had miscalculated. It was winter and with New Hampshire's own brand of unpredictability, the storm had come on fast. It was her fault, but it *was* an accident.

Accidents happen, she had been told. *It was no one's fault. You're not to blame.*

They had all said that to her– family, friends, doctors, therapists, priests. They had said the same thing to Michael too, for all the good that it did. In the beginning she believed that he had forgiven her. In the first few weeks after the accident, when Lizzy's life was in the balance and Janine was so hopped up on pain medications for her whiplash and broken arm that she could not think straight, Michael had been present. He'd watched Lizzy, consulted with the doctors, fended off the various well-wishers that had come to the door, and soothed Janine when she woke in the middle of the night, sobbing from the nightmare that replayed over and over again: "It'll pass, Janine. It'll pass."

He was right. The nightmares faded and she only got them every once in a while now. She healed and Lizzy stabilized. For a while things seemed as if they were going in the right direction. That was when the distancing started.

Michael never accused her directly. Only once, a month into their long ordeal, had he even come close to making a charge. He had drank a little too much with their friends and came home to subside sullenly on the couch.

"Why did you go out that night, Janine? Why didn't you stay put?" he'd asked.

That was all. That was enough.

Wracked with ever-present guilt, she tried to explain, but what could she say other than it did not seem that bad out and she had wanted to go home, to be in her own bed? It was a poor explanation– it seemed a worse now. Michael didn't ask her again. He never accused her of negligence or foolishness. He never said anything and eventually he stopped talking altogether. As winter turned to spring, he began to avoid the house, often staying away all night. Where he slept, she did not know. The one time she had asked, he had brusquely answered, "Jim's place."

Jim was his brother.

"I wish you'd have let me know," she had said and he had replied with a simple, "I forgot," and disappeared into the bedroom to change. It was apparently not open for discussion.

Janine never knew when he would be home. Sometimes she would return to discover that he had stopped by, leaving new clothes in the hamper and taking food from the fridge.

He was not eating well, she was certain, and he probably was not sleeping either. His frigid expression, on the increasingly rare occasions when she saw it, implied that this was none of her business.

No, he never verbally accused her of negligence. He did not need to say it out loud. Her brother-in-law told her that men react differently to pain.

"Give him time," he said. "He'll come back."

Jim was often right, but what really frightened Janine was the realization that on nights like this, she did not want Michael to come back at all.

The kettle whistle jerked her out of her reverie. Water fountained over the top, the whistle gurgling as though it were drowning. She had put too much water into the kettle and the sputtering overflow burnt her hand when she reached to pull it off the burner. She swore and slammed on the cold water in the sink, shoving her reddened hand beneath the cascade of cool water.

Anger came swiftly now, too. She was angry that she had only been able to have one child when she had wanted a houseful and that one child was slipping away. She was angry that Lizzy was in the hospital, the only one so badly injured in that stupid accident and the only one who could claim true innocence in its cause. It was wrong for Michael to abandon her, to make Janine grieve alone, knowing that they both needed each other to stay strong. It was not right that she should have to bear everything alone, including the great big shell of a house which had become nothing more than a haunting reminder of better times.

There wasn't an item in the room that didn't remind

her of them, of Lizzy, laughing, running, playing, beautiful, and Lizzy's father, grounded, solid, handsome, and full of fun. There were pictures on the walls of their vacations and Lizzy's trophies lined the shelf that Michael built. Lizzy's schedule on the fridge, her skates on the mat, Michael's coat slung on the kitchen chair, his Disneyworld mug on counter by her hand. Reminders of good times – of her life as it had been, as it *should be* now.

Her hand was almost numb now. Janine slapped the water off and tucked her hand under the other arm, pressing it to herself, fighting off the sudden tears that stung behind her eyes.

She was sad. She was frightened. She was angry. She was lonely. She was overwhelmed. She was lost.

Then the tide crested and something broke free in her. She would not stay here tonight. She would not torture herself with the silence and the memories. She would go where she was needed. She would leave now before she changed her mind. Janine Lawrence grabbed her purse and her keys with such haste that she nearly forgot to turn on the alarm when she left the empty house.

***

Like every proper hospital and medical facility, the hospice had strict rules about visiting hours and stricter policies on overnight stays. Meadowbrook, where Lizzy had come after all her surgeries had been completed, learned swiftly that neither Michael nor Janine would abide by those rules which had resulted, finally, in an exception being made for them.

Nevertheless, the night nurse Candace Miller looked startled when Janine pushed through the double doors at five minutes to midnight, wearing sweat pants and a tired tee-shirt and looking like hell.

"Mrs. Lawrence!" she said, with her signature wide smile instantly in place, belying the exhaustion in her eyes. She glanced at the clock. "It's a little late for you, isn't it?"

Janine nodded, feeling her defenses slide down and bone-weariness settle in. The hospice decor tried to be warm and welcoming but it could not mask the fact that the building was still an institution, with the same sanitary smells and impersonal furniture as any other. The staff, at least, were genuine and human.

"I couldn't sleep," she confessed, adjusting the heavy purse strap as she leaned up against the counter. "Can I see her?"

To her surprise, Nurse Candace hesitated, biting her lip as she glanced in the direction of Lizzy's room. "Well, uh..."

Janine was suddenly alert. "Is something wrong?"

Nurse Candace's professional training settled over her again. "Everything's fine," she said, soothingly, putting out a hand that came within six inches of touching Janine's shoulder. "It's just that..."

Again, she stopped, this time looking embarrassed.

"What?" Janine demanded. "Tell me."

There was another moment of hesitation, then the nurse beckoned for the mother to follow her. She led her down the now familiar hallway to the wide bedroom door marked E.

Lawrence. Then, with her finger pressed to her lips, Candace pushed the door open.

A shaft of muted light from the hallway fell across the darkened room. Comforting sounds of breathing mixed with the regular noises of the monitors wafted over Janine. The familiarity brought an odd-sense of peace. Lizzy should not be here, perhaps, but she was still here, and that was enough for now.

Lizzy lay propped up on the slanted bed, her beautiful face as still as death, her silky hair limp on the pillow, the last vestiges of her highlights almost grown out now. Michael's flowers were a bright spot in the darkness, perky and pretty in the borrowed vase. Lizzy's teddy bear, the last holdout from her childhood belongings lay by her side where the nurses, in their kindnesses, always left it.

But this evidence of the compassionate care given to Lizzy was not what made Janine's heart catch in her throat and her eyes grow hot with sudden tears.

Lizzy was not alone in the room. Michael was sprawled in the chair beside her, his head thrown back, and his legs akimbo. He was still wearing his work clothes, a worn jacket and rumpled white shirt with a tie loosened around his neck. They had bought it for him two Father's Days ago. His left hand dangled over the armrest, the wedding ring glinting dully in the new light. His other hand was closed around Lizzy's.

Anger, frustration, fear- it all fled ahead of the tidal wave of grief, sorrow, and intense loneliness. Janine pressed her hand to her mouth, a gesture of restraint. Tears flowed down her cheeks, but she would not sob. She would not wake them. Candace was watching her, a kindly, respectful guardian.

Of course, Janine thought. *She's been watching us. She would have noticed that we don't come together anyone, not even for Lizzy's birthday. Doesn't take much of a detective to realize that we are falling apart.*

She took her hand away from her mouth and said, steadily, "I won't disturb them."

Candace merely nodded. It was not her place to judge and Janine was grateful. She took one last, lingering, look at her family before the door swung shut again.

23

It was late when Colin Rideout finally called it a night. When he was not actively driving Bridget to her appointments, he had spent the entirety of his day on the phone, trying to smooth ruffled feathers and keep everything he was juggling in the air. As he inserted his key into the outside door of his apartment, he had to admit that he had no clue as to how successful he would be. On the bright side, he had not been killed today. Working in the lines that Colin did, survival was not a given, even when everything was going well. As it was, he had been barely able to smooth-talk his way back into their good graces.

"Of course, everything is going well? Trouble? What trouble? There aren't any delays, just a hiccup or two, nothing I can't handle. Tony's just nervy because his girl is out of town. Everything is going great, Mr. H, don't you worry."

Whether or not Mr. H believed him was immaterial. What mattered was he had bought a stay of execution, at least in the short term. Hopefully it would be enough.

That stupid, stupid girl, he thought, ripping the key out savagely. *She better pray I find her before they do.*

He took a deep breath and hoisted up his backpack once more. *Easy, Colin. You start acting scared and you'll start acting dumb.*

There was no room for that.

He snapped on the stair lights and checked the door before he opened it. The little piece of clear plastic that he had stuck in the jamb was still where he had left it. The door had not been opened since he had left that morning. Colin relaxed some and unlocked his apartment door. It swung silently on its hinges and he stepped in.

It was a large, somewhat shabby studio with irregular hot water and a constant odor of Chinese food, curtsey of the restaurant downstairs, but it was his own place and weary as he was, he wanted for no better.

It was not until he dumped his backpack on the floor and shut the door that he realized he was not alone. He froze in the small entryway, listening. The apartment was shrouded in darkness. He could not tell exactly what he heard; a breath, a sigh, the shuffling of cloth as someone moved. It was enough to set the hairs on the back of his neck on end and cause his heart to start pounding in his chest.

For a brief moment, Colin Rideout was terrified. So he did something foolish: he called out, "Who is it?" just like the first victim in a horror movie would.

He heard the sound again, the rustle of cloth on a body. The lamp by the couch snapped on. The room was not exactly flooded with light. It was an old lamp and the bulb was weak, but it was enough to make Colin blink and step back.

In his momentary blindness he did not recognize the figure that rose from the couch.

"Colin...?"

Sarah Hopper emerged from the shadows. She looked pale and drawn and more terrified even than Colin. Her hoodie was grubby, as though she had rolled on the ground and her hands dry washed each other in anxiety.

"Colin," she whispered again. "I need your help..."

Embarrassed by his show of fear, Colin's surprise quickly turned to anger. He drew himself up and stepped towards her, his hands tensing. "Have you got it?"

Sarah flinched as though he had hit her. She made the smallest of head moves, *No.*

Colin swore and turned away from her, swinging his fists. Sarah stepped as though to follow him, stopping short when he turned on her again.

"You *stupid* girl!" he hissed. He could not risk shouting it, but he might as well have for the reaction he got. "Do you realize what you've done?"

"Colin-"

"The police are all over now!"

Her eyes were huge, pathetic. "I know, I know, I'm so scared - Colin, if you knew-"

He stepped forward and she stepped back. "I don't give a crap," he snarled. "Tell me you at least *found* it, Sarah. Tell me that."

She hesitated... then shook her head.

In the blinding cascade of fear and frustration, Colin barely heard her attempt at an explanation. He did not even try to listen. All he really heard was her gasp the first time he hit her.

Friday

24

It was only four days into her new regime and already Karen Thompson was regretting it. She'd dragged herself out of bed at 5:30 a.m., leaving Jake to slumber under the comfortable covers while she splashed cold water on her face and laced up her now-hated sneakers. The gray skies outside were a mixed blessing, promising cooler weather than yesterday while threatening rain. If there was one thing Karen hated more than early mornings, it was rainy mornings.

Just get going. You'll feel better once you start.

She grabbed her iPod and cell phone and headed out the door resolutely.

Four days in, she thought. *Only four months to Monica's wedding. That green dress is going to fit.*

Her mood improved once she got outside. Portsmouth was a beautiful town at any time of the year, barring only slushy March and April, but May and June were transition months that really brought out the best in her; new leaves, fresh grass, blue waters, and brisk breezes, the cheerful knowledge that summer was on its way. It may have been a few decades since she was a student but Karen had never lost her excitement for summer fun.

And I'll be ready for it this year, Karen thought, putting her earbuds in. *For once.*

She followed her usual route, down her street, across another, and headed for the harbor. Few were out this early and the idea that she was ahead of everyone lent vigor to her workout. She found herself sailing along down the streets, singing under her breath to her favorite tunes, through Prescott Park and over the bridge to Four Tree Island.

It was nearing six when she crossed the bridge for Pierce Island. One or two pickup trucks satin the departing gloom of the tree-lined parking lot, their drivers loading fishing tackle after their early morning attempts. In the background, cranes looming at the naval yard sat silently across the harbor waiting for the day to start. Four Tree Island was connected to Pierce Island by a land bridge several yards long and covered in gravel, just wide enough for cars to comfortably pass. Karen lengthened her stride as she worked her way down the bridge towards the picnic areas.

Despite the overcast, it was a perfect day for a run, and she was beginning to get her second wind. She followed the curve of the drive, passing the circular building in the center of the island, and keeping the Naval Yard on her right.

I'll jog to the point, she thought. *Then it's selfie time.*

After all, what was the point of getting up early and doing all this work if no one knew about it?

As she approached the tip of the island, she slowed her pace so that she could check her progress on her phone.

Overhead, seagulls were beginning to circle and call to one another. Traffic between Maine and New Hampshire was picking up on the two bridges. A small powerboat whined past, headed out to sea, perhaps to fish or on its way to one of the many small, rocky islands of the Isles of Shoals that dotted the coast.

Jake and I should take a trip out there some time, Karen was thinking. *I've only lived here all my life and I still haven't been...*

Something caught her eye, cutting off the thought. The island was high above the tide and slick rocks lined the steep drop of the shore. This was, after all, the mouth of the Pascataqua River, not the ocean proper. There was something jutting up from the rocks, something that did not belong, that she could only just make out...

Karen took a step forward, then another, squinting as she tried to focus. Some sixth sense buzzed in the back of her head, warning her to be cautious. She stepped forward once more, pulling her earbuds out.

"Oh my God..."

25

When Lawrence arrived, Four Tree Island was already a hub of activity. Sohm, or maybe Falk, had already seen to sealing off the front gate. It was only by flashing his badge that he was able to drive onto the island at all.

The park crawled with activity. The crime scene was bound in yellow tape with Officer Burns standing watch in front. A few yards away, Officer Whatley spoke quietly to a pale woman in jogging clothes who sat under a covered picnic area. The poor woman looked frightened and it was no wonder. Discovering a body while out for her morning jog had to be something out of the ordinary for her.

Lawrence stepped out of the car, welcoming the warm, salty air that greeted him. His back was sore from the night spent on a hospice chair and he was exhausted from the dreams that had assailed him all night, not that he could re-member any of them. Their memory had fled when he woke, although he was sure that Janine was in one...

Sohm came striding up to meet him, dressed with his usual care in a gray suit and vest. "Morning, sir," he said as he lifted the caution tape.

Lawrence stepped under it, nodding to Burns as he passed. "What have we got here, Sohm?"

"Looks like we've found Sarah Hopper."

They approached the rocky edge. Klugman, dressed in crinkling white plastic, was making his awkward way back up the rocks, holding his clipboard in one hand as he climbed. When he reached the top, he nodded to Lawrence by way of a greeting, then gestured below to where Sanders was hovering with his camera over a prone figure.

"As you can see," Klugman said, "she was not universally loved."

Looking down in the indicated direction, Lawrence had to fight back a sudden feeling of dizziness. The loose, brown hair, matted with blood and dampened with dew and spray, fell across young shoulders clad in a hoodie. Jean-encased legs sprawled unnaturally. It was a sight that was much too familiar to him.

The dizziness only lasted a minute but his stomach moved uneasily as he studied the blood spattered remains. Even from where he was standing he could see where the back of the head had been beaten in.

Not universally loved, indeed.

"Bludgeoned to death?" Sohm asked unnecessarily.

"Sure looks that way," Klugman agreed. His tone was different this morning. He had a daughter, too.

Lawrence turned away, forcing himself to focus, a task that would have been easier had the body not been in his immediate sight. *Head in the case, man, head in the case. Who, what, where, when, why...*

"Time of death?" he asked.

"I'd said sometime late last night," Klugman said. "I'll have a better idea once we get her back to the office."

Lawrence nodded as he scanned the park. The coroner did not need to tell him that this girl had not died here on the rocks. She had been dumped there after the fact. Now the question was, was she killed in the park, or somewhere else? A head wound like that would have left a lot of blood.

"What was she doing out here?" Lawrence said, more to himself than to anyone else.

Klugman answered quickly, trying to cover his own unease with another attempt at humor. "That's out of my area of expertise. I do the how and the when. I leave the whos, the whys, and the whats to you and Sohm here. Need anything else from me?"

"Just that report."

"As soon as I can."

Klugman turned back to his clipboard and subject. Sohm followed Lawrence as he walked back to where the witness sat chatting with Whately. His eyes unconsciously scanned the grassy expanse looking for signs of a struggle - blood, tire tracks, anything - but the ground was undisturbed, the grass tight and new, showing little.

"How was she identified?" he asked Sohm.

"Student ID in her back pocket," was the prompt reply. If Sohm had been moved by the girl's plight he would not show it. It was a matter of pride for him.

"Anything else? Purse? Backpack? Cell phone?"

"No purse, no backpack, no cell phone. And there's no sign of a weapon yet."

"There wouldn't be, but search anyway."

"Right." Sohm swung about to face him, sunlight glinting off his oversized glasses. "Do you think this is related to Emma Gagnon's death?"

"I don't know." They had reached the yellow tape that marked off the crime scene and Lawrence stopped. He nodded to the woman at the picnic table. "She found the body?"

"Her name is Karen Thompson. She was out for an early morning run when she came across it and called us. Want to talk to her?"

"I guess I'd better..."

Falk appeared at Sohm's side, looking rumpled as always. He waited until Lawrence looked at him before plucking at Sohm's sleeve. "Excuse me, sir, just one quick thing."

Lawrence nodded and Sohm ducked under the tape to follow Falk across the way and down another rocky edging.

"Hold it just a second, sir..."

Burns's voice was authoritative, warning. Lawrence turned and saw that he was holding off a well-dressed man with aristocratic bearing who held two small paper cups. He was politely trying to argue with Burns and was clearly growing impatient. He had good cause, but Burns, who was part-time and new in the area to boot, would not know that.

Lawrence strode over to interfere. "It's all right, Burns. He's all right."

Burns reluctantly stepped aside and Lawrence extended his hand to the newcomer. "Good morning, John. I didn't know we'd called the Staties in."

To his relief, Lt. John Gordon of the NH State Police shook his head, "You haven't, as far as I know." He gestured over his shoulder. "I live just up the street, heard about this on the scanner, thought you could use this."

Lawrence accepted the offered cup gratefully and took a sip. Coffee, black and bitter, just the way that he had preferred when at the academy. Naturally John Gordon would remember that. John was a detail-oriented company man, a good man, but definitely a company man. Where Lawrence focused on the case at hand, John was a team player and an excellent politician in his own way. As a result, John was comfortably situated in the upper echelons of the State Police and Lawrence had been passed over twice for promotion.

Not that it mattered much. Lawrence preferred casework to deskwork and DiFranco knew it.

John leaned in confidentially, keeping his eyes on Burns. "Though from the way things are going, you'll be calling us in pretty soon. Two bodies in two days? What have you got here, a serial killing?"

It was a good question. Unfortunately, there was no clear answer to it. The short summary would be no, based on the MO, but the fact that Sarah Hopper was a student of Emma Gagnon kept the possibility in play.

"I don't think so. It *is* connected but..." Lawrence looked back at the crime scene where Klugman and Sanders were bent over the hidden form. "I've got a feeling about this one, John."

John studied him and Lawrence had a flashback to study periods, when he had got the same look during flash card sessions.

John was kinder this time.

"Well," he said, "from what I recall, your instincts have never been off."

Lawrence blinked in surprise. Something caught John's attention and he checked over his shoulder. A short distance away, a man in a jacket and tie was striding along the path, microphone in hand and cameraman at his side. The press had arrived.

It begins, Lawrence thought and wished John had thought to bring a larger cup of coffee.

John said, "Well, looks like the press is here. I'd better get going before they recognize me and blow this into something bigger. You know where to find us if you need us."

He strode off hastily, somehow managing to escape the reporter's sharp eye.

Lawrence turned back to the witness. She was still talking to Whately, but her attention had wandered towards the new arrivals. Her color had much approved. No doubt the idea of possibly of being interviewed on TV was helping to revive her flagging spirits.

Better talk to her before she starts rehearsing what she's going to say on TV, he thought. *Thompson, Karen Thompson...*

Karen Thompson was pretty and excitable and unable to add anything more to her statement, though she was grateful for the attention. Sohm and Falk came back up onto the grassy area and Sohm gave Lawrence a nod. Lawrence excused himself and met them half way.

"Find anything?"

"Looks like Falk found her purse. It was tossed on that shore a little way down from here. And this," Sohm held up a pink-encased phone in a clear evidence bag, "was inside." He hand edit to Lawrence.

"Sharp eyes, Falk," Lawrence said.

Falk, flushed with success, handed over another evidence bag, this one containing a small, brown, cloth purse.

The phone was unresponsive, the bag wet and sandy. Lawrence gave them both to Falk. "Take these back to the lab for analysis, will you?"

"Yes, sir." Falk hurried off.

Lawrence turned. In the distance, the bridge was raising on the Piscataqua River, a large barge waiting on the other side. The sun glistened on the statue of 'My Mother the Wind' that stood at the end of the point. On the river, small boats zipped along the edges of the coast, heading out to sea, their captains looking at Four Tree Island with curiosity. On the Maine side of the river, trees rustled quietly. On the New Hampshire side, Portsmouth was starting to wake up, with sounds of cars and voices drifting over on the fresh breeze. For all the business of the harbor, Four Tree Island was a restful place.

Usually, Lawrence thought and then Sohm spoke.

"It's a different MO, sir. We might be looking at two different killers."

Lawrence shook his head and began to list on his finger. "She argued with Emma Gagnon, went to school with her ward, works for Thomas Atkinson, and she just happens to die after we've issued an APB. There are way too many co-incidences for me to believe it's not related. The question is, how?"

Sohm was silent.

Lawrence looked back over to where Sarah Hopper lay. The ambulance had arrived and the EMTs were readying the gurney, laughing with Burns as they worked. The morning was bright and under normal circumstances, the park would be filling with retirees and moms with young kids. In a few weeks, the higher summer traffic would start and they would have had a much harder time keeping the curious away.

Thank God for small favors, he thought, then said, "Where are her parents?"

"Out of state," Sohm said.

"Then we'll have to find someone to ID the body."

At least they won't have to do that. They'll get the call and they'll know from the first ring that something isn't right. Then some disembodied voice will tell them and they won't believe it at first, but they'll know, deep down. They'll know...Mind on the game, Lawrence.

He sighed heavily and turned to his partner. "What on earth is going on here, Sohm?"

Sohm had no answers for him.

26

"We do know that the victim was a student at Noble College and that the police are treating her death as suspicious. Only two days ago, popular music teacher, Emma Gagnon, also of Noble College, died of poisoning in Noble Concert Hall...."

The statement yanked Sam out of her zone and back into the real world. She was sitting cross-legged on the white leather couch, boxes of her books at her feet and her editor's latest notes on her lap. Unlike yesterday, she was finding it easy to concentrate. Delving into the escapist world of dashing Martin Cromwell worked not only on readers, but on the author as well.

She had left the TV on since breakfast and it played softly in the background as she worked. Matthew was upstairs somewhere, quiet and sullen as always. The TV helped to mask any lingering anxieties that Martin Cromwell could not dispatch. She had learned to tune out the drone but Emma's name cut had through her concentration.

Sam looked up. The local station was on and most of the reports revolved around one of Portsmouth's parks, but she had not been paying attention. The banner below spelt out the news that a student's body had been discovered this morning.

The handsome reporter was finishing his statement, "When pressed for details earlier this morning, the police would not confirm that the deaths were related."

The scene switched and to Sam's astonishment, the reporter was interviewing none other than Detective Lawrence, looking as haunted as ever.

Bastard, Sam thought.

"Is this death connected with Emma Gagnon's?" the reporter asked.

Lawrence faced the camera and said, almost mechanically, "We can neither confirm nor deny that possibility here. Right now we are viewing both deaths as suspicious and will be searching for the truth in both cases."

Sam's heart caught in her throat.

They are related. They must be. He would think so too, otherwise he'd have dismissed it right away.

"Should students and faculty be on the alert, after two killings in three days?"

The detective answered quickly and firmly, "There is no reason for anyone to be alarmed. All the appropriate steps have been taken."

His expression indicated that this was all he would say and they cut to an interview with a student.

Sam turned away from the TV.

There must be a connection – the police would deny it

immediately if there weren't, otherwise they'd be facing what they're facing now; rumors of a random serial killing.

She thought back to the day of Emma's death, the dreadful sounds, that girl's panicked face. *I'll bet it's that girl. It has to be that girl. Whatever they were arguing about lead to her death.*

I was wrong.

Lightness overcame her. She felt an upsurge of relief and something which bordered on joy. Frantically, she pulled out her phone, found Tom's number, and began to text: *Guess I had it wrong! Nothing to worry about after all.*

She smiled as she pressed send.

Good old Tommy, she thought. *He'll be a bit disappointed that he can't ride to my rescue after all...*

The sound of footfalls aroused her. Matt was walking through the living room, his phone in his hand as always. For once his melancholy disposition could not touch her triumphant one.

"Hey, Matt!" she said brightly. "Feel like lunch?"

His head jerked upward and he blinked in surprise.

"Um… sure…" As she got up, he ventured to ask, "So… you're feeling better?"

She laughed and the sound reverberated through the room.

"Oh," she said, "you have no idea."

27

Tina O'Reilly awoke with a start. For a moment, she lay in a bewildered fog, half asleep and half alert. She was on the couch. The TV was on, the newspaper reporter reporting on some incident on Four Tree Island, but that was not what had awakened her. She had heard something. But what?

The sun was coming in strong through the windows, its position telling her it was noon even before she focused on the clock. Tina had worked the 7-7 shift last night, coming home at about eight in the morning to find the apartment empty and the note she had left for Sarah still pinched between the freezer and the refrigerator doors. Sarah would not notice if the apartment were engulfed in fire, but she seldom walked through the apartment without grabbing something from fridge. That the note was untouched told Tina that her roommate had spent the night elsewhere – a not infrequent occurrence. Once again, Sarah had ducked the all-important conversation about rent. If this kept up, Tina was going to have to go over her head and talk to her parents. That would only make the situation worse.

Now, rubbing sleep out of her eyes, she called out, "Sarah?" No answer.

She groaned and rolled over. Four hours of sleep was not nearly enough. Why on earth was she awake? She heard it then, a suspicious, muffled sound, like someone opening drawers very, very carefully. There was someone in Sarah's room. Suddenly, all her sleepiness was gone and Tina was wide awake.

It *could* be Sarah – but it was not. Sarah would never be so considerate and quiet. She was never intentionally mean, but was often thoughtless and forgot that Tina worked nights.

Jenny, her other roommate, was in New Mexico. No one else had a key.

There was a shuffling sound and then more noise. The person was moving quickly about Sarah's room now, shifting things around. They had not answered her call. Tina got up quietly, slipping through the living room into the dining room. Sarah's room was just beyond that. The door was ajar and slowly, creakingly opening wider. Tina saw movement.

Someone was in Sarah's room. Someone who was not Sarah.

There was a small, orange chest of drawers to the right of where she stood and Tina dove for it, pulling it open with a trembling hand. A pistol lay nestled among the cloth napkins. She snatched at it, tapping the magazine and racking the slide like her father had shown her so many times. Her dad had given it to her when she moved out. He had trained in the Marine Corps and took her out Saturday after Saturday until she was as comfortable using it as he was.

"A girl needs to know how to protect herself," he had said. "But I hope you'll never have to use it."

She hoped so, too.

Tina moved down the hall.

The sound of searching continued, growing more frantic. She did not allow herself to hesitate before stepping into the room. Someone in a black tee-shirt hunkered down on the other side of Sarah's oversized bed. He had not noticed her yet. He was too busy pawing at Sarah's things.

Tina held the gun in both hands, her heart pounding. "Hey!" she called.

The intruder lifted his head.

Relief washed over her. She lowered the gun, "Colin! Did you forget some-"

She never got a chance to finish the sentence.

28

Sohm dropped the phone back into its cradle.

"The school is sending us Sarah's file," he announced and stood, stretching his back as he did. He prided himself on keeping in good shape, but his back was a constant source of worry. *Too many falls from horses and motorcycles,* he thought wryly.

Chief DiFranco was in the office studying the cork board with Lawrence. Her mouth was tightly drawn and she leaned forward with her hands on her hips, looking at the array of photos. Her unusual interest in the case and her presence in their office told them that she was not at all pleased with how things were going.

Lawrence turned to Sohm, his hand under his chin. "Any word from the roommate?"

"Not yet." Sohm joined them at the board. "I've contacted the hospital where she works. Her supervisor said that she worked the seven-to-seven shift last night and never left her post."

Lawrence grunted. "Good enough alibi, not that she was ever really a suspect."

DiFranco made an impatient movement with her hands. She had not wanted to hear that. It only brought home the fact that for all their suspects they had no real leads.

"I've had the Dean and the college on the phone all morning," she said. "You're *sure* they don't have to worry about this becoming an epidemic?"

It was a good question, one that Sohm had already put to Lawrence. But his answer was the same as it had been earlier. "I don't think this is a serial crime."

"We're going to have to give them a better reason than 'I don't think so,' Lawrence. People are jumpy and they'll seize any opportunity they can to panic. Frankly, I don't blame them." She paced and then turned back to him. "You don't think this is a serial crime, but you *do* think these two murders are related?"

"Yes." Lawrence leaned back, crossing his arms in front of him. He was a big man and managed, even in the middle of complete uncertainty, like now, to convey calm and assurance, something that Sohm envied. "We're working on the how right now." He turned to Sohm. "Have you got anything on Sarah Hopper yet?"

Sohm nodded. "I spoke with her student counselor and pulled up her police records. We've got more on her than Emma and she's a third the age."

"A criminal record?" DiFranco asked sharply.

"Minor. Some trespasses, one count of underage drinking." He pulled out the file and flipped it open. "Background is she has parents and two sisters in Virginia. I guess she has some talent with the camera. She's won two contests and has had pictures published in the newspapers a couple of times."

"Have the parents been contacted yet?"

Lawrence shifted uncomfortably. "Not yet. We were waiting for the roommate to ID the body, but we still haven't found her."

She shook her head. "It may be too late by the time you do. Get the student counselor in hereto make the formal ID and quickly, before this turns into a PR nightmare. *I'll* make the call to the parents." She paused. "Do you have *anything* I can tell them?"

Lawrence's voice was level in reply. "Tell them that we're following up every lead and hope to have answers for them soon."

It was a textbook stall, the type of answer that would satisfy no-one. But there was no other answer to give and they all knew it. DiFranco made a wry face as she walked towards the door.

"Terrific," she complained. "On top of that, I've got to pull something together to calm the press down." She stopped in the doorway. "You find anything else, you let me know immediately, right?"

"Of course," Lawrence replied. It was only when she was gone that his shoulders sagged. "This is a mess."

Sohm looked at their latest picture of Sarah Hopper. She stood among a group of friends, wearing that same hoodie with a Red Sox cap. She could have been anyone's daughter, sister, or friend. There was no indication that she was any different than anyone else in the image, except, perhaps, for the fact that of all the other girls in the picture she was the only one not looking at the camera. She was facing it, true, but her eyes were directed at something else almost as though she could not bear to look straight at anything.

He shook himself and went back around to his computer. "By the way, I also pulled the record on Colin Rideout, Sarah's on-again/off-again boyfriend. According to Tina O'Reilly, she was currently seeing him."

Lawrence looked interested. "And?"

Sohm pulled up the file as he spoke. "DUI, possession, battery, and the drug boys think he's a player in the local ring. A real nice guy."

"Think he's involved somehow?"

"When last I saw him he was picking up Bridget Madden at her house." He paused before delivering the final blow. "The first time I saw him was at Joshua Flynn's hearing."

There was a pause while Lawrence digested this. Then he nodded and got up purposefully. "Alright, you go and talk to him. I'll wait here for the counselor to ID Sarah."

"Right." Sohm shut off the screen and reached for his jacket.

"And swing by Sarah's apartment. See if the roommate's home."

Sohm did not mind that in the least.

29

The dean was on the campus by noon. He had called Finn Cumberbatch even before the police did and informed him that he was cutting his vacation short so that he could help deal with the situation. When his assistant feebly protested that the auxiliary dean was volunteering to cope, Stewart came down hard.

"One of our students has *died*, Cumberbatch," he said. "A member of our college family. This is not something that is to be left to underlings."

He hung up, leaving Cumberbatch in such a state that it never occurred to him to ask why the dean would insist on returning for this death and not for Emma Gagnon's.

When Stewart arrived, he looked rumpled from the long drive, but otherwise alert and ready. He strode through the office, indicating that Cumberbatch should follow him, which of course he did, answering his questions as they walked: No, he did not know the cause of death, only that the police had confirmed it suspicious. No, no one else was involved, that he knew of. No, the police spoke of no connections to Emma Gagnon's death.

"They'd be foolish if they didn't think there was a connection," Stewart remarked.

He was correct of course. Already the newspapers and media were calling for comments and conclusions and they were only just starting to get phone calls from concerned families and friends. The phones were ringing off the hook and both men knew that this was only the beginning of the deluge.

"As you would expect," Stewart sighed. When they reached the security of his small office, he went right around to the desk. "That poor, poor girl. Have the police been in touch?"

"Yes, even before this." Cumberbatch gave him a quick run-down about the break-in and the homicide detectives that had answered the call. He finished by handing him Lawrence's card. "Detective Lawrence wanted to talk to you about Emma."

"Lawrence?" The dean took the card and looked at it. "He was the detective they interviewed this morning."

Cumberbatch shrugged. "I guess it makes sense that they'd assign him to both cases, seeing as there is the connection to the college." When Stewart looked at him sharply, he explained, "I mean, they both have connections to this school."

Stewart nodded and looked at the card again.

Cumberbatch felt a swift pang of sympathy. After two years of planning, the project to rejuvenate Noble College and raise attendance had only just begun. Already they had reinvigorated the front hall, painted all the dorms, updated their software, and started on the new gardens in front of the administration buildings. The celebrity lecture series with Samantha Harris would begin in a week and the waiting list of applicants was still growing. This year was supposed to be the dawn of a new era for Noble, a prosperous time of growth and popularity. Now they had not one, but two deaths, one of them verging on sensational. This kind of notoriety was exactly the kind of thing that would kill any chance they had at revitalizing the school and saving it from the closure that was sure to happen if attendance was not improved in the next two years.

It was a devastating set-back. Yet when Professor Stewart looked up, Cumberbatch did not see despair or even disappointment in the professor's eyes, however. All he saw was quiet determination.

"Well, then," Stewart said. "I suppose I'd better give the detective a call."

Cumberbatch was overwhelmed with admiration. He should have known that the dean would not be thrown by this. He was too big a man, too big an intellect, too kindly and wise to be disturbed by anything. Cumberbatch had worked under him for more than four years now and only once had he seen the dean come close to losing his composure. That was two years ago and there had not been a crack in the exterior since. Cumberbatch could only hope to be half the man the professor was.

He left the room, grateful that Professor Stewart had decided not to leave this terrible situation in the graceless hands of his auxiliary.

30

"That's Follansbee's car." Falk said.

He was driving while Sohm sat in the passenger seat, checking through his messages while giving directions to Tina's apartment. Sohm had been about to go to Rideout's by himself and only when he practically collided with Falk in the hallway on his way out did he reconsider. Even if Rideout had nothing to do with the two homicides, he had been at Flynn's hearing and he did run with a dangerous crowd. Going alone was probably not the wisest of plans. Fortunately, Falk had been happy for an excuse to get out of the building and volunteered his car.

Sohm looked up as Falk eased the car to a halt in front of the time-scarred building. A patrol car sat in front of the building, lights flashing. It was empty.

Something clenched tight in Sohm's chest.

"Come on," he said and wrenched the door open.

Falk followed without a word. Sohm forced himself to trot up the narrow entry stairs at a decent pace, not running, not panicking, no reason to worry. Even his knock sounded restrained and when Follansbee opened the door, Sohm continued to maintain his composure.

"That was fast," Follansbee said, stepping aside to let them enter.

Sohm's gaze swept the room as he entered. It was as cluttered and colorful as it had been the other day, with no signs of a fight or struggle or even of the owner.

Then his gaze fell on the tiny metal dining table and his heart stopped. There was a gun, magazine out, racked back and secured.

"What's going on here?" Sohm demanded.

"Breaking and entering and assault and battery." Follansbee sounded like he was reading a report. He added, "The woman who lives here was attacked."

"Is she okay?" Falk asked.

"She's bruised but okay. Heck of a woman. Chased the perp off with a gun. I've already called the ambulance."

As he spoke, Tina came out of the kitchen. She was holding a pack of ice against the back of her head with one hand and carried a glass of water with the other. She looked white and unsteady, but otherwise okay. She lowered herself into a chair and slid the glass over towards Follansbee, wincing with the effort.

Sohm went over to her, crouching so that he could look up into her face. There was a scratch on her neck and he felt his jaw tensing.

"Are you alright?" he asked gently.

"Shaken, but not stirred." She attempted to smile but the curve of her mouth trembled. "He went for me, then my gun went off and he ran away."

"Did you recognize him?"

"Oh yes. It was Colin Rideout."

Sohm nodded slowly, fighting against the tidal-wave of guilt and recriminations. *We should have known. We should have foreseen this.*

But how could they have known? It was not uncommon for boyfriends to lash out at their girlfriends, but the violence usually ended there. Unless, of course, there was more to Sarah's death than a simple case of domestic violence.

Tina was still looking at him, her large brown eyes surprisingly free from tears. Sohm could think of nothing to say. He patted her arm reassuringly and got to his feet. Falk and Follansbee were by the front door talking in undertones. They stopped when Sohm strode up.

Follansbee began, "Nick..." but Sohm interrupted, "Stay here with her until the ambulance arrives. Then you stay behind and secure this apartment until you're relieved. Falk, you come with me."

Falk jumped for the door and Follansbee called after them, "But where are you going?"

Sohm turned back to him, his face grim. "We're making a house call."

31

Colin Rideout was sweating bullets and it had nothing to do with the fact that his cramped, crappy apartment had no air conditioning. His hand was throbbing almost as badly as his head –a souvenir he had picked up in Sarah's apartment when her roommate surprised him in the middle of his search. He had hoped to subdue her, to buy himself a little more time to look, but her gun going off had frightened him and so he ran. Now he was in real trouble. Tina O'Reilly knew him by name and even if she did not call the police, one of the neighbors was sure to do so after hearing a gun shot. They would be coming for him, but the police were the least of Colin's concerns.

Getting caught by Tina was only one of two stupid mistakes that Colin had made. The second mistake was parking his car across the street from the front of her house. When he took off like a scared rabbit, he had run a half a mile towards his apartment before remembering where he had parked. By then, it was too late to go back. He ran the remaining distance to his place in what must have been record time for him, not that he knew or cared. All that mattered was that he got his stuff and cleared out.

He burst into the apartment at full speed and, grabbing his backpack, threw things in it with reckless abandon. There wasn't much; Colin had long ago become accustomed to away of life that necessitated quick retreats. There was some cash hidden in spots, a change of clothes, and a few small pieces of equipment that were too valuable to be left behind.

As he rushed about, he wrestled with himself. He could try to stay, try to explain, avoid the police and talk to the boys. They would understand. Every organization had weak players. Colin was not one but Sarah had been. Colin was smart, valuable, they had understood that he was too important to...

But that was the purest of folly.

Within five minutes of his arrival, Colin was ready to go. With a final sweep of the room, he ran to the door and yanked it open.

He froze.

Two men stood there, a man with heavy shoulders holding his badge out and another man in glasses and a gray suit that he recognized, but only vaguely.

"Ah, Mr. Rideout," said the man in glasses. He had, Colin noticed, as though from a great distance, a nasty little smirk. "Going somewhere?"

Colin did not stop to think. The heavy backpack slammed into the chest of the man with the badge, making him stumble backwards. Colin whipped the door shut, the automatic lock clicking into place, and fled for the back entrance. He hit the backstairs fast and slipped on the mossy surface, nearly losing his balance. He grabbed at the railing and hurtled forward, his heart in his mouth.

There was a crashing sound from the apartment above him – they had broken through the door.

Run, run!

The stitch in his side re-opened, but he paid it no mind. He was nearly at the bottom of the stairs when he heard a shout. The big cop had spotted him. The staircase rattled under his weight. Colin jumped the last few steps to the ground and the uneven pavement threw him off balance. He fell and rolled, popping up to his feet and sparing a second to look around. The cop was already half-way down the stairs, shouting for him to stop. The alleyway reverberated with the sound of his voice.

Rideout ran. If he could get to the street before the cop got him, he could duck into Tony's shop just around the corner. Tony owed him a favor and he was discreet; Colin would not even have to explain.

Colin was almost at the end of the alley, the shaft of sunlight already hitting him full in the face. Just round the corner and slip into Tony's back room and he'd be...

The fist came swinging out of nowhere and Colin ran face first into it. The world exploded and his feet lost contact with the ground. When the fireworks stopped, he was on the ground, pain and dampness seeping into his back as the cop with the glasses stepped over him, shaking his right hand out, the hand that had so nearly broken Colin's nose.

"That wasn't too smart, Mr. Rideout," he remarked calmly.

Colin rolled over, groaning.

The other cop came pounding up behind him. Hands hauled Colin to his feet, thrusting him up against the wall. Colin's cheek pressed hard against the grain of the bricks and he regained his breath as the handcuffs snapped around his wrists. He was caught.

The man with the glasses was saying, "Now you're coming with us for a little field trip."

He had enough breath to protest, "You can't touch me! I didn't do anything!"

A hand turned him around. The big cop was still breathing heavily, but the man with the glasses, who must have run faster than the pair of them down two flights of apartment stairs and around the corner to meet Colin in the alley, looked as pristine as if he had just stepped out of his car. His nasty smirk was firmly in place.

"Well, now, that's all in the interpretation," he said and looked at the other cop. "Didn't that look like assaulting a police officer to you, Falk?"

The big man nodded in all seriousness, rubbing his chest where the backpack had hit its mark. "It sure felt like it."

"That's what I thought, too," the man in glasses said cheerfully.

Falk grabbed Colin's arm and pulled him away from the wall. "Come along Mr. Rideout. Time for you to take a ride in the nice, shiny police car."

"And if you're a very good boy," the man with glasses said as he followed after them, "we'll even sound the siren for you."

32

They were still waiting for the student counselor to arrive when the call from Professor Stewart came through. DiFranco spoke the necessary soothing words, then paged Lawrence the moment she got off the phone.

"Did you demand an interview with the dean of Noble College?" she asked.

"I requested an appointment." Lawrence replied, "That was yesterday, in connection to the break in. He's out of state."

"Well, he's back and nervous as hell."

"He hasn't any reason to be, so far as I know."

She grunted. "Right, well, I think he needs someone to go down there and tell him that. I'll assign someone else to the identification. You get out to his office asap and make it look like we're on top of this thing, will you?"

Lawrence was more than happy to comply.

The drive out to the college offices was pleasant. It was a warm day and the traffic was not bad, though downtown was busy. He had to park in the parking garage and drove all the way to the top on a whim. From his vantage point he could seethe steeple of North Church and the Memorial Bridge suspended over the Piscataqua. There were some advantages to living in Portsmouth and the view was definitely one of them.

Cumberbatch had lost none of his officious air in the interim. He ushered Lawrence into the Dean's office and told him that the professor was on his way, having been called to reassure a nervous group of sophomores.

"These events have everyone on edge, naturally," Cumberbatch said.

Lawrence, looking around the surprisingly small office, nodded. "That's understandable."

Evidently, this was not the answer that the assistant was looking for. He hesitated.

He's going to try to probe me. Good luck, son, Lawrence thought.

They were both spared by the ringing of telephone in Cumberbatch's outer office. He excused himself to answer it, leaving Lawrence to wait in merciful peace in the office. He used the time to study the room.

Professor Stewart's office was smaller than he expected, though with enough space for a desk, bookshelves, and several chairs for visitors. It was a comfortable office, pleasantly populated with items but not overstuffed. There was a teapot in the corner, with a supply of tea and honey on hand. Asian prints lined the walls while Dickens, Thackeray, Austen, and Pope filled the bookcases. While the case was predominantly English literature, Lawrence did spot some textbooks, French novels, historical treaties, and an entire shelf devoted to Agatha Christie, Margery Allingham, and Raymond Chandler.

Stewart didn't have many personal items on display. Citations, diplomas, and awards were arranged almost carelessly and there were no pictures of either the professor nor anyone else. In one corner of the room there was a pile of cards and gifts, presumably from grateful students. One of the gifts was a rather garish poster with a guillotine and the words, "It was the best of times, it was the worst of times – Charles Dickens –*A Tale of Two Cities.*"

Lawrence was still studying this when the door swung open behind him and a man that he recognized as Professor Stewart came striding in. Stewart moved quickly and paused in front of the poster, looking at it with a critical eye.

"A gift from my honors class," he explained. "I appreciate the gesture, but I'm afraid it really doesn't fit with my décor."

Without any more introduction, Stewart went around to the chair behind his desk. "This has been simply dreadful! Two deaths in three days!"

He gestured towards a chair and took his own, still talking, oblivious to the fact that he had not introduced himself. Not that Lawrence needed the introduction. They had actually met once before at a fundraiser several years ago, something that Janine had dragged him to. It was a brief introduction and it was unlikely that the dean would remember.

"I didn't know this Sarah Hopper, poor girl," the professor was saying. "But Emma Gagnon was a simply wonderful human being, just wonderful. Warm, motherly – I'm still in shock."

He did seem genuinely upset. His babbling attested to the state of his nerves.

Lawrence nodded, lowering himself into the seat. "Did you know Emma long?"

"Oh, yes. We started out teaching together 25 years ago. She was a mother hen even then. She was always looking out for the underpowered kids, always taking time out to help others with their studies." He was relaxing, smiling as he fell into the comfortable pattern of gossip, "She wasn't a brilliant musician, truth be told, but she was a born, gifted teacher. It was a real shame that she couldn't have any children of her own."

"I thought she had a son."

Stewart's smile turned knowing. "That's Harry's son from a previous… arrangement."

"I see."

"I don't know that I'll be much help to you, detective. I've been in New Haven the past three days, at my summer residence."

At this point, Lawrence did not know either. *Stewart doesn't need to be reassured,* he thought. *He wants an audience.*

"Getting ready for summer break?" he asked.

"No, preparing to sell," The professor smiled indulgently and Lawrence suddenly felt as though he was being spoken to from a great height. "I've reached a plateau in my life, detective. Time for something new. Anyway, I'm afraid I really know very little about what's been happening here."

One minute in and you already want to leave. Lawrence was amused. He reclined comfortably in his chair, letting his hands rest in his lap, the picture of ease. "I'm just looking for some background information. I know that she and Samantha Harris are friends."

Stewart cocked his head. "Emma taught a few classes that Samantha attended here when she was a student. I don't know that they were any closer than that."

"Mrs. Harris was with Mrs. Gagnon at the time of her death. They'd gone together to hear Bridget Madden sing."

"Really? I had no idea."

"How does Samantha Harris happen to be here?"

"I met her and her husband at an event in California two years ago and invited her out here to do a guest lecture series." He leaned forward, speaking low, confidentially. "You see, the college isn't doing as well as I'd like. I thought having a celebrity as a guest teacher would help boost our visibility, as the young people like to say."

The detective thought it unlikely that an author who specialized in thrillers marketed to the middle-aged and senior crowds would be a massive draw for the young, but he refrained from mentioning it. "And she's doing this pro-bono?"

"There have been some… generous donors that made her appearance possible. You don't think *she's* involved, do you?"

Stewart looked concerned and Lawrence really could not blame him. On the face of it, it seemed a ridiculous idea. The woman had only just returned to the college after a long absence and within a day Emma Gagnon dropped dead. There seemed to be no connection at all. Yet he could not shake the memory of that expression, the hostility and fear that crossed Samantha Harris' lovely face when he had questioned her. Not to mention Thomas Atkinson's defensive posturing when he was questioned.

"I'm just trying to be thorough," Lawrence replied.

He was searching for his next question when his phone buzzed. He pulled it out instinctively and glanced at the face. It was a text from Sohm: *Have Rideout in custody – assault and battery. Waiting for you.*

That was all.

Assault and battery? Lawrence thought about Rideout, the drug connection, and Sarah Hopper's mangled body. *It's very likely I'm barking up the wrong tree concerning Samantha Harris.*

He pocketed the phone and asked the first question that came to mind, "Would one of those donors have been Thomas Atkinson?"

Again, Stewart's answer was delivered with just the slightest hint of condescension. "Our donors have asked for anonymity. But I *can* tell you that Thomas and Samantha were students here together and were considered a couple at one point."

There was some satisfaction in the delivery. It was a juicy morsel of gossip, but Lawrence had already figured that much out.

"They seem an unlikely pairing, don't they?"

Stewart nodded thoughtfully. "I'd have thought so, too, but girls of that age are more prone towards, shall we say experimentation?" He smiled again. He smiled often and easily, Lawrence noticed. "In any case, it didn't last long."

Lawrence nodded. "Sarah Hopper – how well did you know her?"

"Not at all. You'd be better off talking to her student counselors. I'm still in shock about her death."

"And Colin Rideout?" He tossed the name out casually.

The professor blinked. "I'm sorry – is he a student here?"

Oh, well...

"No," Lawrence admitted. "I was just wondering if you knew him."

"Is *he* involved?"

"We suspect that he and Sarah Hopper were a couple and that drugs were involved. Now, I know she studied under Emma. Any chance that...?"

Professor Stewart almost recoiled at the suggestion. "Absolutely not." He sounded insulted. "Emma Gagnon was above such things."

"How about her ward, Bridget?"

That seemed to amuse him.

"Oh," he said, airily. "I wouldn't think so, no. I doubt she'd taken the time. Our Bridget is a driven woman – one can only hope that her talent equals her ambition."

While Lawrence was recovering from that surprising piece of criticism, Stewart's phone buzzed. The professor reached over and picked up the receiver, "Yes?... Oh, right, tell them I'll be a minute." He hung up and looked to Lawrence. "I have another appointment waiting for me. Was there anything else?"

Lawrence took a brief second to study the man. He was charming, well spoken, and steeped up to his hairline in college life and academia. In a way, he *was* Noble College. Being dean was the role he had been made to play and it was a role that he obviously loved, right down to the nitty-gritty of fundraising and parent soothing. Professor Charles Stewart, then, was probably the most content man Lawrence had ever met.

And yet...

Yet, there was still something.....Like Bridget Madden and Samantha Harris, Professor Stewart was role-playing and Lawrence had never liked masquerades.

Stewart was waiting for an answer, not that he expected anything but a quick and immediate exit. He had practically dismissed the detective from his office and it was his experience that people were so much in awe that they usually obeyed with alacrity. Lawrence felt no such compunction, but there was no reason to stay any longer.

He got to his feet, buttoning his coat. If the professor wanted to role-play, he could oblige.

"That'll do *for now.*" The slight emphasis on the last two words made the professor's eyebrows raise a hair. "You aren't planning any more overnight trips, are you?"

That amused the great man.

"Why, detective?" he purred. "Do you really expect me to skip town?"

Lawrence could not help but grin in reply.

33

If Lawrence were a betting man he would have laid money on the idea that Colin Rideout was not as upset about being taken into custody as he should have been. The young thug had been advised of his rights (a needless formality, as he could practically recite them himself), submitted to the usual check in procedures with indifference, and meekly asked for medical attention. He had no lawyer to call and when pressed, he admitted to running away, but defensively held that he had only done so because he was frightened by the attitude of the two cops who had come to call.

"It's not like the police in this country have a sterling reputation or anything," he said.

Lawrence could see the tension ripple through Sohm's face, but from Lawrence's perspective there was a compelling reason for Collin's docile manner.

Colin is relieved to be here, that's why he isn't playing too hard to get.

He wondered if Sohm saw the same thing.

The younger man was taking the lead on the questioning, playing up the part of interrogator so that Lawrence could field as the voice of reason. Sohm seemed to have taken the break in at Sarah Hopper's place personally and he was convinced that Colin had battered Sarah to death. All they had to do was get him to admit it.

Sohm thought it'd be easy, Lawrence not so much. For some reason, Rideout was content to be in jail, but he wasn't about to cop to a murder charge. And while Sohm might have made up his mind about Sarah's death, Lawrence hadn't.

Rideout was already starting to sweat. Sohm paced, jacketless with his empty holsters trapped over his waistcoat. He looked like a panther, ready to spring. Rideout's pallid face told Lawrence that he was thinking the same thing.

Sohm whipped around on his victim and grabbed a chair. Straddling it backwards, he leaned forward until he was within inches of Rideout's face.

"What were you doing in Ms. O'Reilly's apartment?" he demanded.

It was the fourth time that he had asked that question and the dogged answer was the same. "I was just there to get some of my stuff, you know? It's my girlfriend's place. I didn't steal anything."

"You broke a window, ransacked a room, and assaulted the occupant."

"She scared me, all right?" Rideout's voice went up in perfectly practiced pitch. "Coming around the corner like that-she tried to kill *me*! Why aren't you pressing charges against *her*?"

He winced and touched his face as though to remind them

who the victim was here. Sohm was not any more impressed by his theatrics than Lawrence was.

"She had a license for that gun, and the right to defend her life and property, whereas you had no right to be in that apartment." Sohm's voice lowered to a menacing tone. "What were you looking for, Colin?"

Rideout's hand dropped away from his injured face.

"I don't have to tell you," he sneered. "It was personal stuff. Sarah was going to give it back to me anyway, but now that she was dead – well, it was going to be more difficult."

"So you knew Sarah Hopper was dead?" Sohm asked. "How?"

There was a moment of ominous silence. Rideout realized that he had just walked into a trap and he was panicking.

Lawrence gave him a few seconds to flounder, then came in himself. "She was only formally identified this afternoon, around the time that you were fleeing the O'Reilly apartment. How did you know that Sarah Hopper had been killed before the rest of the world did, Mr. Rideout?"

The man stared at him wild-eyed. He licked his lips and shifted. "I... I..."

Sohm turned to Lawrence. "Could it be because he was the one who killed her?"

"No!" Rideout cried.

The two officers ignored him.

"Sarah's roommate did say that their relationship was on the rocks." Lawrence mused. "Perhaps he wasn't ready for her to move on."

"Could be." Sohm gave Rideout a studious once over. "He's already admitted that he has no real alibi for last night."

"Now, that is a shame," Lawrence gave the sweating suspect a disappointed look. "You should always have an alibi, Mr. Rideout. That's criminal training 101."

As Rideout gaped, trying desperately to come up with a response that would save him, Lawrence produced a case out from his pocket. He put it on the table in front of him, extracted a swab from it, and held the swab up under the terrified gaze of their suspect.

"You wouldn't mind giving us a DNA sample, would you, Mr. Rideout? A beating like Sarah got is bound to leave traces."

"I didn't kill her!" The protest was desperate, breathless, as though Rideout were struggling against drowning.

Lawrence smiled. "Then you have nothing to worry about, do you?"

"I-"

Sohm interrupted. "According to your neighbor's statement, you had a violent argument with someone in your apartment last night, an argument so loud that they were about to call us in. My guess would be that you were arguing with Sarah, and then you, Mr. Rideout, lost your temper and hit her."

"Yes!" Rideout turned on him in terrified fury. "Yes, all right, I did hit her, but I didn't kill her. She'd screwed up on... something and I lost my temper, I'll admit it. I slapped her around a bit, but she left on her own, *okay?*" He faced Lawrence again. "She left around ten and she was all right."

The memory of the girl, with hair so much like Lizzy's, swept over Lawrence. "Bruised, but all right."

"Yes, yes. I didn't kill anyone, I swear." He was close to pleading now, looking back and forth between the two of them. "I only knew it was Sarah because I was at the park this morning. I saw her arm – I recognized her sweater. I thought -"

He broke off and looked down at his hands.

Sohm waited a moment. Then he leaned back, folded his arms, and asked, "This argument that you were having – was it about the drugs she'd lost?"

If the suggestion was a shot in the dark, it was a good one.

"How did you-" Rideout gasped and Lawrence cut in with sharpness meant to deliberately rattle the young man, "Just answer the question, Mr. Rideout."

"It *wasn't* drugs," he protested lamely.

"Colin," Sohm pulled his glasses off to rub his nose. His voice was calm, a deathly sound. "We have men going over your apartment and Sarah's as we speak. Already they've found enough evidence of possession and dealing to put you away for a long time." He put his glasses back on and gazed through them at Rideout. "Now, it'll help if I can tell the DA that you were – forthcoming in this interview."

His tone suggested that there was not much that could be done, in any event.

Rideout waved a hand dismissively. "Forget it."

"What if we do?" Lawrence asked. "What if we let you back out on the streets, Mr. Rideout? Would that make you happier?"

Any color that had been left in Colin's face drained from it, leaving him a ghostly shade of white.

Sohm jumped on it. "I'm guessing it wouldn't. You've already lost so much time that you're afraid your suppliers are getting suspicious, maybe even worked out what happened. You're afraid that they're coming to you for... answers."

The word sounded like a death knell in the tiny room. Rideout fidgeted uncomfortably. His color was returning but his movements betrayed his agitation. They had hit the nail right on the head. Now, to drive it home...

Lawrence stood, an abrupt movement that made Rideout start.

"Still don't want to cooperate?" Lawrence shrugged. "Have it your way, Mr. Rideout. We have enough evidence here to ask the DA for murder one, so why don't we..."

"No, *wait!*"

Lawrence waited. Rideout wiped away the perspiration that trickled into his eyes. Sohm cleared his throat and Rideout glared at him.

"All right," he said in a steady voice. "You're right."

Lawrence sat back down and placed his hands on the table in front of him.

"Go on," Sohm ordered.

Rideout reluctantly did as he was told. "Sarah worked for me. She needed money and I needed a courier, so I used her to make deliveries around the area. I modified her backpack and made a secret pocket. It was brilliant – I mean, no one would suspect her, right? She was a bit of a flake but she knew all the places on campus that weren't covered by security cameras, and she was honest; nothing ever went missing. Then last week, I picked up a big order. She was supposed to make deliveries but something went wrong. She lost the backpack."

"Lost it?" Sohm asked.

"She got into an argument with one of her classmates and was pulled out of the classroom for discipline. By the time she got back, the backpack was gone."

"So what did you do when she told you?"

"I told her to find it, before we got into trouble." Rideout was starting to sound panicky, as though he were reliving the moment. "She knew the risks – we could both eat it if the backpack fell into the wrong hands." He drew a shaky breath. "Anyway, she told me that she knew who had it and that she could get it back."

"Who had it?"

"I don't know, man!" he whined. "I think maybe one of her teachers? If I knew, I never would have gone to her place today."

Sohm's gaze was measuring. "Go on."

"Sarah came to me last night to tell me that she broke into an office and everything to find it but she turned up nothing. She was terrified that the police would find it first. She was really falling apart. She asked me for help, but what could I do?"

"So you slapped her around," Lawrence said, as though that was the most reasonable thing in the world to do.

Rideout turned on him, defiant and defensive. "Her stupidity was going to get us both *killed*. I told her that she'd better come up with the goods, because I wasn't going to take the fall for her."

"And they say chivalry is dead," Sohm quipped. "What did she do then, Colin?"

He had the grace to appear uncomfortable. "She cried and all. She said she had one more place to look. She wouldn't tell me where – I think she was afraid I'd go with her and… well, do something. She was pretty afraid of me by then." He looked directly at Lawrence. "She left to go find that backpack, detective."

"What about Bridget?" Lawrence asked.

Out of the corner of his eye, he saw Sohm's surprised expression.

Rideout looked honestly confused. "What about Bridget?"

"Isn't she part of your little enterprise?"

"*Bridget?* She would have turned me in if I even suggested it."

"So you weren't training her as a replacement? For when Sarah finally flaked out and you found you had to… remove her from the scene?"

"*No!*" Now Rideout was horrified. "No, it wasn't like that at all. I slapped her around and she left. She left to go look for it. Look, I may be a lot of things," he said, his voice rising in pitch. "But I'm *not* a killer. Sarah Hopper was *alive* when she left me, and that's the truth!"

***

After that, Colin Rideout decided that he had had enough and he would wait for the court to assign him counsel before he would talk to them again. When pressed, he folded his arms and clenched his jaw. He was done. The interview was over.

Lawrence left the interview feeling as though they'd taken three steps forward and four steps back. Sohm was thoughtful.

"If he's telling the truth," Sohm mused as they walked back to their office, "that backpack might be the reason Sarah came to see Emma Gagnon the morning she died."

Lawrence nodded. "But if he is telling the truth, it doesn't explain either killing and it leaves us with even more questions."

"Where is that backpack?"

"And if Bridget isn't one of Rideout's dealers, just how *does* she fit into all of this?"

34

Matt was not happy. Samantha knew that without having to ask. He had been sulking up in his room all day, leaving it only when she insisted that he have dinner with her before she left for the concert. In the kitchen, he pushed the food around his plate and glowered until she could not take it anymore.

"Are you certain you don't want to come along?" she asked half-heartedly. "There'll probably be kids your age coming too and you could meet them."

He snorted. "Bunch of band geeks? No thanks." He waited until she turned to place her coffee cup in the sink before delivering his one-two punch. "Besides, I wouldn't want to be the third wheel."

Her face went up in flames and she whirled around to glower at him. "What do you mean, young man?"

"I mean," he said, without taking his eyes off his plate. "Tom Atkinson."

With a great effort, she forced herself to count to ten. She had already explained to Matt that Tom was a friend, how he'd had a pair of tickets, thanks to being a sponsor of the concert, how she had planned on going anyway, as a sort of tribute to Emma, how she had already told Jonathan about both the concert and her escort and Jonathan was perfectly all right about the whole thing.

"I'm only sorry I couldn't have met the woman myself," Jonathan had said. "Have a nice time."

She had laid it all out for Matt, so that he would know what the score was. She had always been honest with him. Well, as honest as she could be, given that circumstances could change and sometimes you never really knew where you would end up. She had done her best and he...he...

Counting to ten didn't help. She was angry, so lit up that her hands began to shake. She wanted to fire something back at him, say something that would take that malice out of his tone and make him feel like a perfect fool. But just as she was opening her mouth, she saw the slightest tremble about his lips and she realized: Matt wasn't trying to be a jerk. He was frightened.

She knew why, of course. He had lived through several of her relationships and though it was not her fault that these had fallen apart, he would not see it that way.

Neither did her mother, when it came down to it. Her mother had actually said, "Samantha, I don't want to tell you how to run your life, but if you can't hold a man, you've no one but yourself to blame."

No doubt Matt was afraid that this thing with Tom was about to become an affair. A few years ago, it might have happened. Tom was tall, good looking, single, and obviously in love with her. That would appeal to any woman, especially the old Sam, the Samantha before Jonathan. Jonathan had changed everything.

Nothing was going to happen tonight. Of that, she was certain. It was unfortunate that Tom was alone and still stuck on her but that was *not* her fault. She had not encouraged him, not really. She had made it clear that she was going to be faithful to Jonathan.

At least… she hoped that she had made that clear.

If I hadn't, he'll know by the end of the night. She sighed inwardly. *Oh, God, Jonathan, how I wish you were here instead of in California! Tom would be so much easier to put off if I knew I were coming home to my man.*

Sam found her voice. "It's just a concert with an old friend, Matt. That's all."

Doubt was clearly etched across his face, so she added, "But if you're really worried, why don't you come with us?"

To her surprise, Matt hesitated for a long moment. Then he shrugged.

"'S'all right," he said. "I want to watch TV tonight."

There was no more trouble after that. Matt went to his room and Sam went to her own to get ready, but the conversation had its affect: she selected her most chaste black dress for the night and paired it with simple pumps and pearls. It was an attractive look, fetching but not overly so. Tom would be impressed but hands-off was the message in an outfit like this.

Tom arrived right on time, smiling when she opened the door. He was dressed in a gray jacket that was a little too snug over a colored shirt with a tie that did not quite go with the outfit.

You need a woman to pick your clothes. She only just caught her tongue before saying it aloud.

"Ready to go?" he asked.

"Just one second," she said, and darted back to the entryway where she had left her clutch and program. Her pill box rested beside both and she slipped it into her clutch. Her temples were tightening ominously. She had promised to get a drink with Tom afterward, but if she had another one of her headaches...

Matt had not made an appearance so she called up the stairs. He came out of his room and leaned on the balcony rail, looking resigned rather than sullen. If Samantha had not been so flustered she might have noticed the loneliness that shrouded him like a heavy overcoat.

"I'll be back late," she said. "You'll be all right here alone?"

He shrugged. "Yeah, whatever."

She beamed up at him. "All right. Have a nice night, honey. Love you!"

He waved dismissively and she turned and smiled at her escort. "I'm ready now."

Tom gestured towards the driveway. "Your chariot awaits."

Samantha's heart fluttered with excitement as she stepped out into the early evening light.

35

"**A**nything I need to know?"

DiFranco's voice snapped Lawrence out of his usual, end-of-day lethargy. He had to shake his head clear. He had been staring at the computer screen for what seemed like hours, scouring reports and records and trying to make sense of the spreading mess.

When he did raise his head to look at DiFranco, it was to react in surprise at her appearance. She had shed her usual workday outfit in favor of a black and purple dress with golden highlights that accented her hair. Her hair was free and loose as usual but she was wearing heels and jewelry, a decidedly feminine look that became her. DiFranco seldom dolled up and a glance at Sohm showed that he, too, was surprised.

She was still waiting for his reply, so he cleared his throat. "We're researching a possible connection between Rideout, Sarah Hopper, and Bridget Madden and the other characters in this case, especially Thomas Atkinson. So far nothing. You look nice."

She accepted the complement gracefully. "Thanks. I'm

going to see one of your chief suspects in concert tonight." She held up the now-familiar pamphlet announcing Bridget's debut.

"Now, that surprises me." Sohm leaned back in his chair, folding his arms across his chest. "I had you pegged as a Madonna fan."

She inclined her head towards him with a grin. "I prefer to be a material girl, but Arthur loves this stuff."

It was clear from her tone that this outing was something of a marital compromise, a concept that Lawrence understood rather well. He once sat through an entire Josh Groban concert in exchange for a night at a Bruins game. Janine made out better on that deal. It turned out to be a miserable game with an embarrassing loss.

Still better than three hours of Groban, he thought and his gaze wandered across the desktop to where Janine's picture sat. He looked away at once.

DiFranco was speaking with mock seriousness in her tone, "If you need me tonight, don't hesitate to call."

She might as well have been saying, *Call me, rescue me.*

"We wouldn't dream of interrupting your cultural experience," Lawrence said, just managing to keep the grin off his face. "Besides, you deserve a night off."

"I heartily concur," Sohm agreed. "Go forth and enjoy."

She looked from one to the other with a sigh. "Some help *you* two are! Don't work too late, boys."

She left. Chuckling, Lawrence turned back to his computer and caught sight of Sohm bent over his phone again with the now-familiar puzzled expression.

"Purplebutterfly again?" he asked. "Or a new game?"

"New game, same player." Sohm shook his head. "I'm using the Calabrese counter-gambit, but her offensive is very weak tonight."

He sounded sincerely concerned.

Oh, dear, an emotional connection to a mysterious online woman. Watch yourself, Sohm, or you'll find yourself meeting some out of work, married, mother of three from a farm in Idaho...

"So you're going in for the kill, of course," Lawrence said.

Sohm arched an eyebrow at him. "To do otherwise," he said solemnly, "would be an insult."

36

Peter Chase was running about the backstage seeing to the myriad of last minute details that only he could handle, when he heard angry voices echoing out from Bridget's dressing room. Though he should have ignored it and moved on, he instead stopped to listen, anxiously twirling his pencil in his hand.

The hour before a performance is not *the time to have a personal discussion,* he thought annoyed. *Bridget should know better by now.*

If there was one thing that Peter Chase had learned in his long years of service at Noble College, it was that no prima donna ever thought the rules applied to her. Bridget, coddled and encouraged as she had been by Emma, was one of the worst offenders in his memory.

Emma was a lovely woman, but her indulgence was a disservice to this girl. She's going to learn the hard way that the world doesn't revolve around her.

Honestly the college would be served well by this opportunity to hire new blood in the music department. Emma Gagnon had ruled the roost a little too long and her ways were now entrenched. Had it been left up to Emma, Bridget would have sung almost exactly the same program that every other star pupil had debuted with. Fortunately for the loyal patrons of Noble College concerts, Bridget Madden was too stubborn to strictly adhere to her teacher's suggestions.

Now that Emma was gone, God rest her soul, the council would look more favorably on Peter's suggested replacement. Jameson Carter was brilliant at music theory and bored to death with his position on the West Coast. He was looking for a change of scenery and his prestige would add to Noble's. Peter tried for months to convince the council to offer Emma early retirement in order to take advantage of Carter's interest but they were reluctant.

"Emma embodies the spirit of Noble," they had said. "We can't really do without her."

Well, now we'll have to, and who knows, we might actually do all right.

The argument in the dressing room continued, growing in pitch. Peter sighed and looked at his watch. He would have to break it up, of course. Neither he nor anyone else would be served if Bridget wore her voice ragged before her big show.

Rose Chancellor, Bridget's accompanist, hurried past, dressed in her concert blacks and studying the sheet music that she carried. She looked startled he tapped her on the shoulder.

"Rose, do you know who is with Bridget?"

A knowing look crossed her pretty face. "Oh. That'd be Harry." She shook her head. "He brought flowers and everything. I thought he was going to be civil tonight."

Peter sent her on her way and waited until Rose was out of sight. Then he moved closer to the door so he could make out the words of their conversation.

Gagnon was saying, "It would be for *her*, Bridget!"

Bridget cut him off. "*This* is for her! God, do you have any idea what you're asking?"

"Don't you think you owe it to her?"

"It's too much. You're asking too much! She knew what I wanted and she would have understood, Harry."

"I've *told* you not to call me that-"

Harry stopped abruptly when Peter stepped into the room.

Bridget was standing by the wardrobe, dressed in a long, red dress that magnificently set off her black hair and olive skin. Harry, pale and shaking, stood across the room from her with his hands shoved into his pockets and his eyes hard. They both looked ready to chew stone. They turned to Peter in unison, their conversation entirely drying up in his presence.

Peter ignored the obvious tension. "Bridget, we need you for a last sound check before we let the audience in. Can you come now?"

She tossed her head and sent Harry Gagnon a withering look. "I'd be delighted."

Bridget swept past Peter and exited into the hallway. Peter looked at Gagnon but the older man was looking at the floor, his face blank.

Peter waited a moment and when the other man did not move, he said, "We've reserved a seat for you in the front row."

Harry blinked at him in momentary confusion. "Oh," he said at last. "Yes. yes, I saw. Thank you."

"Arlene will be right next to you tonight. She doesn't like to sit alone."

There was another moment of uncomfortable silence. Then Harry sighed and gave Peter a sad half-smile.

"Neither do I, Peter. Neither do I."

He shuffled out the door, leaving Peter alone in the dressing room, wishing he'd never entered it.

37

In hour later, Lawrence and Sohm had gotten no further. There was nothing to connect Atkinson to Rideout, save Sarah Hopper. If they were going to prove a drug connection, they would need to get it by sweating out a confession in the interrogation room. Sohm wanted to bring in Atkinson right away, but Lawrence deferred.

"He won't crack on this evidence," he said. "He's too smart for that and I'll bet my pension that he's stubborn. We won't get him to talk until either we have the evidence to back the accusation, which we don't, or I can make him think that we've got Samantha Harris on something."

"Samantha Harris?" Sohm sounded skeptical.

"I'd also lay money on this," Lawrence said. "Atkinson is the last of the true romantics."

Sohm was not convinced but he had not seen the man and the woman together.

It was too late to do anything more so they began to close up shop. It was while Sohm was out, returning some books to the front desk, that Klugman stopped by.

"Hey, Mikey," Klugman said, leaning against the doorframe. He was dressed in civilian clothes with a jacket draped over his muscular arms, obviously on his way out. "I just sent you the preliminary report on Sarah Hopper."

Lawrence glanced at his desktop monitor. Sure enough, there was an email sitting in his inbox. However, if Klugman was here at his office that meant that the coroner had noticed more than he could disclose in his report. Instincts were not, after all, facts.

"Want to give me the highlights?" Lawrence waved to the empty chair by his desk.

Klugman declined the chair but launched into the report with an eagerness that told Lawrence any qualms he might have had this morning had been lost in the renewed interest of his work.

"Looks like she was killed with a cylindrical object, like a bar." He held his hands about twelve inches apart to indicate the length. "Probably plastic or metal. Time of death was between midnight and two in the morning. Some of the bruising came from earlier in the day, maybe several hours earlier." He dropped his hands. "She fought back, though; some skin and blood under her fingernails. Looks like this girl had a rough night."

Lawrence thought of Rideout. "You can say that again. Any sign of drug use?"

"Oh, yeah, she was a user. Upper arm like a pincushion. We're running a tox on that too." His eyes brightened. "I have something new for you on the Emma Gagnon case."

"What did you find?"

"Looks like Agatha Christie did it after all. All the symptoms are consistent with strychnine, which we knew, but we've located the remains of a pill in her upper digestive tract and there are traces of a second pill. We'd missed them earlier. Quick dissolve, nothing unusual in appearance. We're sending them to the lab now." Klugman took in the way Lawrence was suddenly sitting forward with heightened interest and nodded in satisfaction. "Thought you'd like that."

Lawrence did like that. He liked that a lot. "You think the pills are the method of poisoning?"

"In the absence of other food or drink, and seeing as the coffee washed out, I'd say it was a reasonable guess. I've already sent the medication you found in her house to the lab, though that all looks normal to me. I'll let you know as soon as I do." He pulled out his vibrating cell phone, looked at the screen, and sighed. "I've got to go. Promised the old lady I'd take her to dinner tonight."

"Romantic."

"It would have been, only her birthday was actually last week, not tonight." He made a face as he stuffed the phone back into his pocket. "Women."

"I hear you. Good luck."

Klugman left and Lawrence leaned back in his chair, tapping his hands against his mouth as he thought. He was still sitting there when Sohm entered a few minutes later, rubbing the bridge of his nose in a tired way.

Lawrence's tone arrested him. "They've just discovered a pill in Emma Gagnon's digestive tract. Klugman's having it analyzed now."

Sohm folded his arms and leaned against his desk, his hazel-green eyes glittering. "Didn't Samantha Harris say she offered Emma headache pills that morning?"

"She did. She also said that Emma refused them."

"What if she changed her mind?"

Lawrence raised an eyebrow. "Are you suggesting that Mrs. S. J. Harris hasn't been completely open and honest with us?"

"Dare I?"

"What do you say to paying Samantha Harris a little call tonight?"

"I think," Sohm said solemnly, "that would be a most enjoyable way to spend the evening."

Lawrence felt almost eager. He jumped out of his chair and reached for his jacket. "We might just be able to wrap everything up tonight."

"Yes… I just don't see a motive here."

"Neither do I. Maybe the lady herself will provide it."

38

The first thing Beverly DiFranco thought when she entered the concert hall was, *Lawrence should be here. We'll have a full house tonight.*

The concert hall was a traditional New England building of white clapboard with black trim, sturdy construction and wood throughout as opposed to stone or brick. A broad staircase lead to the hall upstairs. DiFranco knew, from the crime scene photos, that Emma had been discovered on the second floor landing, just outside the meeting hall.

Arthur was an old-fashioned gentleman and offered her his arm as they walked up the stairs. The banisters were polished from decades of use and the stairs were wide and deep. The walls were lined with old photos of Portsmouth and the surrounding areas, part of a historical research project done by students several years earlier. The building echoed with the sound of polite laughter and enthusiastic chatter-subdued by most concert standards.

They were halfway up the stairs when Beverly stopped short, pulling Arthur with her. The landing was just in her view and if she had asked for a group photo of almost all of the suspects, she could hardly have arranged it better.

Professor Stewart, exuberant and fatherly, was talking genially with Samantha Harris and Thomas Atkinson. Samantha was laughing, her eyes sparkling, her dress modest yet shapely. She reached out to touch Stewart's arm as she spoke and there was an air of shared, delightful confidences in the exchange, though Beverly could not make out what the subject was. As for Thomas Atkinson, standing an awkward head and shoulders above the pretty authoress, he looked distinctly out of place, both in the conversation and in his own ill-fitting coat.

Samantha's laughter seemed to annoy Harry Gagnon, the grieving widowers, who stood afoot or so away with Peter and Arlene Chase. Gagnon's face was white and his hands were jammed deep into his pockets. He seemed impervious to the friendly overtures from Arlene, who was doing her best to draw the man out of himself. Arlene's black dress complimented her husband's suit and highlighted her red hair. Though she was taller than her husband by a head, they seemed well matched.

With the exception of Peter Chase and Professor Stewart, Beverly DiFranco knew each only by their photos and the conversations she'd had with her officers. She could not help wondering, as she stood there observing, how it was that Harry Gagnon could tolerate being on the alcove where his wife had collapsed only days before.

Maybe it was a good thing that Arthur dragged me to this affair. I'll have a chance to observe everyone without Lawrence's input.

"Honey?"

Her husband's voice cut through her ruminations and made her aware that she was openly staring. They ascended the stairs and passed through the knot of suspects without being addressed by any of them.

It was a peculiar quirk of Arthur's that whenever he went to a classical music concert heal ways chose the seats by sound amplification rather than by whether or not you could actually see the stage.

"What difference does it make what Pavarotti looks like?" he would ask whenever challenged. "I've come to hear him, not see him. Besides, the closer you are, the more expensive the seats."

Under normal circumstances Beverly found this annoying. If she could not enjoy the music she would at least like to see the staging. Tonight, though, she was grateful for Arthur's discrimination. The seats he had picked out were mid-way from and to the left of the stage proper, the perfect vantage point, as it turned out, to observe Harry Gagnon's head in the front row and Arlene Chase sitting next to him. A few moments before the start of the concert, Thomas Atkinson and Samantha Harris slipped into the aisle seats a few rows back from Gagnon, perfectly in Beverly's view.

Almost as if I'd arranged it, she mused. She surprised Arthur when she smiled at him and squeezed his arm affectionately. As much as Beverly DiFranco enjoyed her work and position in the department, there was a part of her that missed the actual investigation work. She had not realized quite how much until tonight.

As the house settled in for the performance, she observed Arlene leaning over to speak to the immobile Gagnon while Peter disappeared behind the curtained stage. Samantha bent over her phone while Atkinson, at once protective and respectful of her space, watched her fondly.

Lawrence thought there was something going on between those two, Beverly thought while Arthur studied his program. *But so what? The more interesting connection is the fact that Atkinson is, or was, Sarah Hopper's boss. I wonder if Lawrence will find anything besides Sarah that connects Atkinson with Rideout's operation...*

The house lights went down and the stage light revealed Peter Chase stepping from behind the stage curtain with his characteristic blend of showmanship and modesty.

"Good evening everyone and thank you for coming tonight. As you know, not only are we to enjoy one of Noble College's finest young talents but we are doing so in a good cause..."

He launched into an enthusiastic description of the charity, one that Beverly was unfamiliar with and could not care less about. She was watching Samantha Harris. The writer pulled herself away from her phone and tucked it into her purse, sparing a smile for her escort. It was not the secretive smile of a renewed amour. It was the carefully cultivated smile of a woman keeping her distance.

Lawrence is only half right about her involvement with Atkinson, Beverly thought.

Peter Chase invited Professor Stewart up onto the stage. Stewart, beaming like a benevolent Santa Claus in a blue and black suit, spoke a few words of praise for the young song-stress and her accompanist. Then his jovial manner sobered.

"As you all know," he said, in his resonant tone, "we have lost a beloved member of our musical staff this week. Our friend, Emma Gagnon, was a talented musician, a gifted teacher and a marvelous human being."

Beverly craned her neck to catch a glimpse of Harry Gagnon. Even shrouded in shadow, his rigid form spoke volumes about his distress. Arlene was out of view.

Professor Stewart was saying, "She devoted her life to her students, her family, and her charitable works. Emma Gagnon could see the best in everyone and knew how to help others shine. She was everyone's friend, everyone's confidant, everyone's 'Mother-Away-From-Home. She will be missed, not only by her students and her family but by the people who were fortunate enough to call her friend. I, myself, still do not know how we will manage without her espirit de corps."

Harry Gagnon slumped then, defeated and tired.

"I'd like to ask now," the professor went on, "for a moment of silence for my good friend, the keeper of confidences and the defender of all, Emma Gagnon."

Every head bowed as one. Every head, that is, except for two. Beverly made a motion as though to lower her head, but instead raised it. Professor Stewart had his hand clasped behind his back, his chin on his chest. Peter Chase was out of sight. Arlene rubbed Harry Gagnon's back while he dabbed at his eyes. Thomas Atkinson stared at his hands on his lap, a somber, mournful expression on his face.

His date, however, was sitting bolt upright with an ex-pression that might have been carved out of stone. Her gaze was not on the floor, but on the stage. Her expression was frozen, her color white, and if Beverly DiFranco had been the fanciful type, she might have thought that Samantha Harris was at that moment looking into the face of death itself.

39

Matthew Harris had his mother's eyes and hair, but someone else's height and his own sour expression. He stood in the doorway in the late afternoon sun, arms folded and legs spread to deny them entry.

If I had a nickel for every over-indulged rich kid I ran across in this job, I'd end up in a new tax bracket, Sohm thought wearily.

"Where is your mother, son?" Lawrence was asking.

Sohm knew the answer to that a breath before the boy decided to answer.

"She's at some sort of concert thingy," he said reluctantly. "She won't be back for hours maybe."

Bridget Madden's concert, Sohm thought. *Of course, if she'd gone to the rehearsal, she'd probably go to the concert, too, if only for Emma's sake.*

"Did she go alone?" he asked.

The boy's resentful blue eyes shifted towards him. "What do *you* care?"

The question caused Sohm to blink, but Lawrence interjected smoothly, "It's all right. We'll come back tomorrow. Thank you."

The boy shrugged and stepped back into the house. Plainly distrustful, he did not shut the door fully until the two policemen were halfway down the walk.

"Suspicious little cuss," Lawrence remarked in an undertone. His voice did not hold a trace of the frustration that Sohm felt.

Sohm shoved his hands into his pockets, wishing he could shed his jacked and loosened his tie. Technically he probably could. It was nearly seven in the evening and Lawrence had the look of a man who was done for the night. Sohm, though, could not bring himself to look even slightly disheveled. The coat and tie would remain in place until he could change. In the meantime, rather than wrapping up a tricky case, as he had hoped that they would be doing by this point, they had run into yet another obstacle. Emma Gagnon might have been nearly a saint in life, but in death she was a real burden.

"So," Sohm said, with a sigh, "do we go to the concert?"

Lawrence shook his head. He reached into his pocket for his cell phone. "No, let's not cause a stink. She's obviously not going anywhere."

Not to mention DiFranco would have something to say if they dragged Portsmouth's only celebrity out of a concert in front of everyone on the flimsy evidence they had. That meant this interview would not take place until tomorrow at the earliest. It was another disappointment that Sohm had to swallow. He was ready for this affair to be concluded.

Still, there was nothing to be gained from pouting.

"All right, then," he said. "Dinner?"

Lawrence had stopped short. His face was white as he put

the phone up to his mouth. "Yes, Lawrence here," he snapped into the receiver.

He listened for a moment and though it seemed impossible his face turned a shade lighter. "*What?* When?... I'm on my way."

Then he was running for the car, his panic radiating outward with every step. Sohm was only a pace behind.

"What's wrong?" Sohm called.

Lawrence yanked the car door open. "Just come on!"

Sohm barely got into his seat before the car shot backwards down the drive.

"Is it Mrs. Harris?" Sohm asked as he fumbled with his seatbelt.

Lawrence, his eyes riveted on the approaching road, his mouth tight and his face hard, shook his head.

"It's Lizzy," he said. "They've messed up her medications or something. She's going into shock."

***

They broke several traffic codes and took the turn into the hospice parking lot so fast that Sohm was convinced that they would overturn the car. Thankfully, the parking lot was not even half-full and there were no pedestrians to get in their way. Lawrence barely threw the truck into park before he was out the door and bolting for the entryway. Sohm took a moment to lock the doors before following him. He had to sprint to catch up.

Meadowbrook Hospice hummed with low-level activity.

Sohm had only visited once before and vaguely recognized the waiting rooms, hallways, and staircases they raced down. Patients and visitors gasped, nurses and aides shouted for them to stop. Lawrence was blind and deaf to their warnings. He tore through the stairwell door and bolted up the stairs, Sohm hot on his heels. They rushed through the entryway and brushed past Janine Lawrence, who stood at the nurse's desk speaking with the on call nurse.

"Michael?" Janine called.

"Wait!" the nurse called. "Sir, you can't-"

Lawrence either did not hear her or did not care. He burst into the hallway beyond and ran towards the door marked 'E Lawrence'. It was here that Sohm slowed down, suddenly conscious of who and where he was.

Lizzy's room was bustling with activity and Lawrence barely took a step inside before he was politely but firmly shoved out again.

"What is it?" he was demanding. "What's going on?"

Sohm had never heard his superior officer so close to breaking down as he did then. He felt a sudden moment of panic strike his chest and squelched the sensation immediately.

"She's all right, sir, she's just had a reaction to one of her medications..." The nurse spoke gently but firmly.

"One of her medications?"

She gave him one last shove. "She'll be all right. We're stabilizing her now. We'll call you when there's any change."

With that, the door swung shut.

Michael Lawrence stood before the closed door, shoulders slumped, his chest still heaving from his recent effort. He ran both his hands over his face and stopped, his frame still and silent. For the first time since Sohm had known the man, Lawrence looked completely helpless and lost.

****

There was nothing to do but wait. Lawrence brushed off Sohm's murmured comforts and his own wife's offer of a hand. He paced madly out in the entryway, frustrated and withdrawn. Janine sat in the waiting room, as still as Lawrence was fidgety.

Sohm sat next to her with his hands folded and his gaze studiously ahead. He was keenly aware of the awkwardness of his presence. He was Lawrence's partner, but not his friend, and he had just inserted himself in the middle of a family crisis. Multiple family crises, if he read the situation correctly, and judging from the curious way the nurse behind the desk watched both of the Lawrences, he had. Not only was Elizabeth in trouble, but so were her parents. This emergency was only making the problem more obvious.

This was no place for him. If Sohm had brought his own car, he would have left, but somehow calling a cab seemed too insensitive. He was stranded with Lawrence as his ride. So he sat, staring straight ahead and trying not to draw attention to himself.

Mrs. Lawrence shifted, reaching into first one pocket, then another, then her purse. Only when the nurse offered a box of tissues did Sohm realize that the woman was silently crying.

Poor woman, he thought, then, *Not your affair, Nick. Leave it alone.*

So he sat still and pretended that he could not hear Janine sniffling in the chair next to him.

An eternity passed before the doctor came out into the waiting room. He was a stocky man with curly hair, a harassed attitude, and a clipboard, which he tossed on the counter in weariness. The other nurse was close behind him, holding a laptop. Sohm and Janine got to their feet.

"Mrs. Lawrence?" the doctor said, as he took the laptop from the nurse.

"Is she all right?"

Sohm had not realized that Lawrence was in the room until he materialized beside him.

The doctor nodded in response to Lawrence's question, his eyes on the computer screen. "She's fine. You can see her now." He held up a finger to the nurse. "Only one at a time, mind. I've got to go. Anything happens, buzz me."

He left, brushing past Lawrence.

Lawrence took an eager step forward, then halted and looked at his wife. Sohm, standing awkwardly in the middle, took a step back and almost fell into his chair.

Janine Lawrence looked at the nurse, then her husband. "It's all right. You go first, Michael." Her voice was faint and somehow sounded faraway.

He did not pause to thank her but strode off and disappeared down the hallway, leaving his wife standing alone, staring after him.

40

To Beverly's relief, there was an intermission during the concert. After a solid hour of incomprehensible arias, Italian ballads, and solo piano pieces that lost their distinction from one another, she was ready for a good stiff drink. Arthur, too, was ready to move around. His leg, which had never fully recovered from a ski incident several years ago, grew stiff after prolonged sitting. He got to his feet with a sigh of relief once the lights came up and beamed at Beverly.

"Isn't she marvelous, Bev?"

"She's the best I've heard." Beverly said. She did not mention that she could not tell one soprano's voice from another.

Atkinson and Harris had risen together but she lost sight of them when Arthur led her out of the hall. Gagnon, Stewart, and the Chases were last seen chatting by the stage. If she had come alone, Beverly might have found away to insert herself into the conversation, but Arthur always took it so hard when she mixed business with pleasure so she restrained herself.

It's not my investigation, she chided herself. *Put yourself in*

Lawrence's position. You wouldn't like your superior officer messing with your suspects on his off hours, would you?

The answer to that was obvious. She had not liked much of what her former chief used to do and had, consciously or not, patterned her own leadership in direct opposition to his methods. He would have interfered tonight if only because he liked rubbing elbows with Portsmouth's brightest and most influential. He made her job that much harder by doing so and she would not do the same to Lawrence and Sohm, no matter how much her curiosity itched.

The gathering space was crowded. Arthur slipped up to the bar and brought her back a glass of white wine. She kept to the periphery, watching and listening while Arthur swapped notes with some of his acquaintances. Atkinson came in once, looking distracted, and she could hear Arlene Chase's voice floating above the general milieu.

After about ten minutes the heat and the noise began to get on Beverly's nerves, so she put her glass down and touched Arthur's arm. "I'll meet you upstairs."

He nodded and she slipped up the staircase with the intention of sending a few emails from her seat before the concert began. When she reached the top of the staircase, she immediately revised that plan.

Harry Gagnon stood at the window, his chin on his chest, his shoulders slumped, and his hands crammed deep into his pockets. He was alone, staring out over Prescott Park and the river beyond it, the same river, Beverly knew, that Sarah Hopper had been pulled out of only this morning.

She hesitated but he looked so lost and lonely that she put aside her earlier concerns and approached. "Mr. Gagnon?"

He looked over at her, weariness etched deep into every line of his face. "Yes?"

She put out her hand. "Beverly DiFranco, Chief of Police."

The lines hardened. He ignored the extended hand.

Understandable, Beverly reminded herself and soldiered on. "I just wanted to say, on behalf of the whole department, just how sorry we are about your wife."

"Have you found her killer yet?"

His disdain was palpable, dripping off of every word.

She answered carefully. "We're making progress. I wish I could say that we had the person in custody but..."

Gagnon's eyes narrowed. She felt liked he was pinning her against a wall and to her own surprise the standard script fled from her memory. She groped about for words and finished lamely. "We're doing everything in our power to find her killer, sir. We'll get her justice."

It was a speech that would have been difficult to sell in a movie and Gagnon was no easy mark.

He grunted. "I'm sure. Excuse me."

He stalked back into the auditorium. Beverly watched him go, torn between sympathy and embarrassment. She should have handled that better. Her intentions had been good but she was never very talented in the art of mingling.

This is why the department has a PR person...

A penetrating voice cut through her musings.

"You'll have to excuse poor Harry, Chief." Arlene Chase, beaming with the nervous excitement of a fan about to meet a minor member of the band, came around to stand in front of Beverly. She nodded towards Gagnon's retreating back. "He's a broken man."

Beverly had been fixated on Harry and shook her head to clear it. "Yes, of course, and you are..."

She knew already, of course, from Lawrence's photos, but telling someone that you know them from their suspect profile was never a good way to start a conversation.

"Arlene Chase." Her hand fluttered to her chest – there was a ring with a large stone on her finger. "I'm Peter Chase's wife."

Beverly nodded and took in her new informant carefully. The woman was well dressed inexpensive clothes and her hair was done professionally. From her manner, she liked to move about exalted circles, but still felt as though she did not belong there herself. As such, she would be a useful source of information; people like Arlene loved to be helpful.

"You know Emma and Harry well, then?" she asked.

Arlene answered eagerly. "I know everybody here. We were all absolutely shocked by Emma's death. She was such a dear woman and poor Harry! He worshiped her, you know – would do anything for her. I don't know what he'll do now. He had a hard time of it, you know, after the war."

"War?"

Had Lawrence mentioned that Harry was a vet? Does it matter?

"Vietnam." She leaned forward confidentially, putting her hand on Beverly's arm. "He came back with all sorts of problems. Ruined his first marriage and almost killed him, but then he met Emma. He relied on her heavily. I used to think he was jealous of the pull her students and her ward had on her time. Doesn't speak much, you know, but he never looked happier than the day he was talking to me about her retirement."

"Was Emma happy about it? About retiring, I mean?"

Arlene shrugged. "I suppose so. She never talked about it to me. I think she was afraid that she'd miss her students."

Beverly nodded, tapping her program to her lips. There was not much more here than what Lawrence had but it painted in some of the blank spaces in Emma's portrait. Did it mean anything, though? And was it connected to that student's death?

People were starting to come back up, crossing the room behind them and buzzing with muted conversation. She was about to ask another question but Arlene cut her off by leaning forward again. Her eyes were gleaming with illicit pleasure, a sure indication of gossip. "Do you know, *I* heard that…"

She did not have the chance to finish. The lights in the gathering space blinked and when they came on again, Arthur was at Beverly's elbow. "We'd better find our seats, hon."

Beverly hesitated, but the moment was broken. She smiled at Arlene and thanked her, then followed her husband into the auditorium. They settled into their seats and Di-Franco found her phone in her hand, ready to send a text to Lawrence when she reconsidered. It was Friday night and the man already looked weary. Besides, she had learned nothing that was really new or necessarily of great importance. She, herself, had a better idea of the kind of people that Lawrence was dealing with, a discovery that would allow her latitude to guide him better. That did not warrant a text message on a weekend.

She slipped the phone back into her purse as the lights came down. The pianist began her solo piece. She glanced at Arthur and saw that his eyes were closed, a sure sign that he was reveling in the music.

Good, she thought, then movement caught the corner of her eye.

Atkinson was moving down the aisle towards his seat, his hunched manner suggesting that he wished he were not quite so conspicuous. He was alone and seemed surprised when he discovered that Samantha's chair was empty. He sat down quickly and looked towards the entryway. Beverly craned her neck in that direction, too, but the doors remained closed. The author was nowhere to be seen.

41

If the first wait had been long and awkward, it was nothing compared to the torment of the second. Sohm sat in his uncomfortable chair, feeling like an interloper while his boss's wife sat patiently next to him. Janine Lawrence was a cop's wife and used to stress and waiting periods. She no longer cried, but sat quietly, picking at her sweater and waiting for her husband to return.

After about ten minutes she began to talk. She told Sohm that she worked during the day, but visited Lizzy every morning or afternoon without fail. She told him about Lizzy's team and her prowess on the soccer field and her dreams of going to law school. She told him how kind the nurses were to her and Michael, how understanding they were when she or Michael came after visiting hours, which he often did. She did not have to say that he did not come with her. Sohm already knew that. He shifted in his seat and wished that Lawrence would return.

Janine was a nice woman, motherly and sharp as a whip, as good a counterpart for Lawrence as could be asked for. Sohm had met her a few times before at department events and the few times the Lawrences had hosted parties at their home. That had been before Lizzy's accident, of course, back when the Lawrences were on speaking terms. Why they were not now was a mystery not only to him, but to most of the department.

"This whole incident just hit him so hard," she was saying when Sohm tuned in again. "I know I've been..." She shook her head and rushed on. "We haven't spoken about this. Not really. For a little while, we pretended we could, that we were fine, but..."

Janine hesitated and Sohm shifted again, wishing she would stop.

You shouldn't be talking to me. You should be talking to your husband and straightening out whatever is wrong.

Once released, however, the confidence could not be bottled up again.

"He can't talk to me." Her voice cracked with the admission. "He can't even *look* at me anymore. I don't know what I can do. I don't know how to reach him, how to say I'm sorry. He's shut me out and..." She drew in a deep breath and looked ahead, steadying herself. "And I just don't know how to open that door."

Sohm knew Lawrence far better than he knew Janine, so it is perhaps understandable that he would assume that Janine was the cause of their marital problems, the silent one that could not be consoled. Now, looking at her tear-stained face, the way she still held herself erect and apart, not asking for anything more than a listening ear, he began to question those assumptions.

He did not have long to do so. Lawrence came striding back in, re-buttoning his jacket. He looked as though he had been to hell and back, but his professional expression was firmly fixed into place.

Lawrence barely glanced at the pair of them before looking down at the buttons he was fiddling with.

"Thank you," he said to Janine. "She's… she's fine, needs her mother." Then he gestured to Sohm. "Come on, Sohm, let's go."

With that, he was leaving through the entryway.

Sohm and Janine stood still for a moment, stunned.

That's it? Sohm thought incredulously. *Your daughter and wife… and you just leave?*

He barely had time to shoot Mrs. Lawrence an apologetic look before rushing after his partner. Lawrence was already reaching for the door to the stairs, his broad back to Sohm. Sohm had a sudden instinct to grab the man's arm and swing him around.

This is wrong…

"Michael Lawrence!"

The voice that rung throughout the little room was not Sohm's, but Janine's, strong and angry and hard enough to stop Sohm in his tracks. Lawrence froze, his hand on the doorknob. Sohm half turned, feeling dreadfully out of place.

Janine was standing with her hands on her hips, her eyes sparking in anger.

"We can't keep doing this, Michael," she said. It wasn't a plea. It was a statement of fact. "You can't keep running away from me. We *have* to talk. We have to do it now."

Slowly, Lawrence turned, a great boulder shaken loose from its place by seismic action. His expression had not changed, except perhaps to go even blanker than before, and his eyes were icy.

Sohm, watching, barely recognized the man he knew.

Janine stood her ground. "I know you don't want to talk to me because you're angry with me. You're angry because I drove the car, because I…" She broke suddenly, pain swiftly twisting her features. She rallied, but lost volume and force as she continued. "Because I caused what happened in there."

Sohm wanted to run away more than anything he had ever wanted in his life but something kept him rooted in place. Lawrence remained unmoved. His wife took a step forward and unconsciously extended her hand.

"You can't just keep running away from me, Michael. We *need* each other. Lizzy needs both of us." She took another step. "Please, Michael – just talk to me. Just talk. That's all. Please."

The moment stretched out for what seemed like a lifetime. Sohm saw the painfully raw loneliness in Janine's face, in her body, in her very pose. He saw months of silence and misunderstanding, all underlined with the dreadful uncertainty of their daughter's recovery. He saw the guilt and the self-loathing and the longing for relief, while feeling that the punishing exile from her husband was deserved.

When he looked at his partner, all he saw was a white face and a mouth drawn up in a rigid line.

Then Lawrence spoke.

"This isn't the time, Janine," he said, harshly and gestured towards the door behind her. "Lizzy's waiting for you. Sohm…"

Every word was like a lash. Lawrence did not stay long enough to hear her response. He turned on his heel and left the room.

Sohm felt as though a blow had knocked the air from his body. The door swung shut behind his boss and Sohm looked at Janine. Her face had crumbled, tears streaming down her cheeks. His anger flashed hot. Sohm tore open the door and charged after Lawrence. He caught up with him in the parking lot. Lawrence, showing his own temper, ripped his truck door open and slammed it shut behind him. Sohm pulled open his own door. One look at Lawrence's beet-red face was enough to moderate his tone, if only slightly.

"Sir…" he began.

Lawrence cut him off. "Get in or walk."

There was nothing else to do but concede.

42

The diner Lawrence chose was one that Sohm was familiar with but seldom selected when he had a choice. The tables and chairs were scuffed remnants from another era. Guitar-heavy rock played perpetually in the background. The food was served hot, fast, and fried, and when the place was full, it was noisy, close, and not at all what Sohm would consider relaxing. Even now, close to empty and quiet as one could expect on a main street, he could not relax. However, that may have been because of the argument that he had not yet had with his superior officer.

Lawrence had not said a word on the drive over. He clutched at the steering wheel like a drowning man would a life saver, pulled into the parking lot sharply, and left the cab without saying anything. Sohm followed, selecting the furthest table away from the counter where Lawrence went to place his order.

The dying, evening light flooded the table in a funeral mood. Sohm sat leaning on his hand, looking out the window at the traffic outside. Cars moved back and forth slowly, stopping every few yards to allow pedestrians to cross. Young women traveled in packs of three, four, and five, their costumes always similar, their laughter loud and uninhibited. Men in khakis and polos or shorts and printed t-shirts walked in pairs between the variety of pubs boasting local brews. Older couples and young parents moved with a swiftness that spoke of shows to catch or early bedtimes to make. Threaded throughout were the artistic and drifter types, each in shades of dishevelment, some smoking cigarettes, a few pipes.

It was a lively, typical evening for Portsmouth and Sohm took some comfort in its normalcy .In his line of work, one had the tendency to forget innocent pleasures and the truth that there is sanity and working relationships in the world. Until early this year, he had had a working example in his partner's marriage. Until earlier this evening, he had respected his partner's privacy, but after what happened in the hospice tonight, he could do so no longer. If he intended to call Lawrence friend, he could not let this go.

Lawrence came back over carrying a plate heaping with gravy and cheese. Only when he put it on the table did Sohm realize, with something approaching horror, that the thick, brownish gravy was slathered over French fries, crisp, brown, and freshly fried.

Gesturing that Sohm should help himself, Lawrence dropped into the opposite side of the booth and grabbed a handful of fries. A long string of yellow cheese pulled up with his handful. He artfully wrapped the cheese around the fries until the string snapped, then shoved the whole bunch into his mouth. Making little whooshing sounds -the plate was still steaming after all –he grabbed a napkin and swallowed hard while reaching for another helping.

After his second mouthful, Lawrence became aware that Sohm was not joining in and looked up with a defensive frown. "What?"

"What *is* that?" Sohm was incapable of suppressing his initial disgust.

"Poutine. It's a Canadian specialty." He defiantly shoved another gravy-drenched fry into his mouth. When Sohm continued to eye it doubtfully he shoved the plate towards him. "It's good. Try some."

Sohm shook his head. "Thanks, but I like my arteries as they are."

Lawrence shrugged and pulled the plate back.

There was a moment of silence while Sohm groped for an opening.

"How long has it been since Lizzy's accident?" he asked.

Lawrence threw drown his napkin in annoyance and glared at him. "Just can't leave it alone, can you, Sohm?"

"Janine's a good woman. She shouldn't be going through this alone and neither should you."

"And neither should Lizzy!"

Lawrence's voice echoed off the walls, catching him off guard. He stopped, sighed, and rubbed his face. Sohm recognized the movement; Lawrence was trying to buy time to come up with something to say.

Sohm leaned forward in sudden concern. "It *was* an accident, right?"

"Of *course* it was!" Lawrence snapped.

Sohm sat back, shaking his head. "Then… don't you think you should forgive her?"

"Forgive Janine?" Lawrence dropped his hand and glared. "For what, Sohm? For having an *accident?*"

Sohm felt like squirming but held still, forcing himself to hold Lawrence's gaze. The older man looked ready to explode but his voice when he first started speaking was low and terrifyingly monotone.

"It wasn't anyone's fault, except maybe God's, for making its now, or mine, for having to work that night instead of driving Lizzy myself, or the other driver's, for being on the road. Maybe I should blame the state for dereliction in snow removal, or the weather station for being caught off guard by the storm or the school for not cancelling the match, or the coach for not making the call herself." Lawrence leaned forward, his gaze darkening. "I could blame the school system, the team, the DMV, or WMUR, but you know what? I can't. I can't blame anyone. Because it was just an accident and accidents happen and no one is to blame. Lizzy's in the hospital, a 17-year-old vegetable and Janine can't sleep out of guilt, and I can't do a damn thing about anything because I'm just a father and a husband and a cop and there's no one to arrest today."

He brought his fist down on the table with a ferocious bang that made the dish of poutine do a nervous tap dance. His tone, steadily intensifying, was piercing in its thinly veiled anguish.

"She's just a kid, Sohm," he said, and for the first time his voice cracked. He looked away, out the window towards the groups of families strolling by and enjoying the warm evening. "Her life was ripped apart and destroyed. There's no way to fix it. No one to punish. No-" His voice hardened. "I've just got to sit on my hands and put on a good face and go in there and watch what used to be a bright, vibrant human being with her whole life in front of her suck up her dinner through a feeding tube. And there's not a damned thing I can do to make it better."

There was a beat. Sohm watched Lawrence and once again, he felt like the interloper, intruding on what should have been a private moment. He felt at once ashamed and embarrassed. He should have left it – but how could he have known?

I didn't know. I couldn't have known. Oh, God, will I ever get to a point where I understand?

Lawrence turned to him. He seemed to have recovered his equilibrium somewhat because, to Sohm's relief, his face was brick again. He pointed a finger at Sohm.

"So, no," he said. "I don't want to talk about it. I *never* want to talk about it. Get it?"

After a moment, Sohm nodded. "Got it."

"Good."

Lawrence grabbed a bunch of fries and began to eat again, moodily and disinterested, but determined. If there was un-usual moisture in the big man's eyes, Sohm did not feel compelled to draw attention to it. Instead, after a moment, Sohm offered, "If you ever do need to talk..."

"I won't." Lawrence said sharply.

The silence stretched uncomfortably.

Sohm drew in a breath and nodded. "Right. Well. Look, about your arteries..."

As he had hoped, Lawrence snorted and shoved the plate back at him. "Just shut up and take a damn fry, will you?"

Sohm was happy to oblige.

***

Lawrence got the call as they were walking out of the diner. The sun had dropped below the tree line, bathing the city in shades of blue. Sohm, feeling uncomfortably saturated with oil, gravy, and cheese, stopped at the top of the diner's stairs, buttoning his coat and listening to the one-sided conversation.

"Ma'am?" Lawrence said when he answered.

That meant the chief and that could not possibly be a good sign. The small hairs on the back of Sohm's neck rose.

"That can't be," Lawrence protested and listened, shaking his head. "Yes… Yes, Sohm's here. We're on our way."

He hung up and Sohm asked, "What's wrong?"

"There's been another murder," Lawrence said heavily. "At the concert."

Faces flashed through Sohm's mind: Bridget, Peter, Arlene, Harry… they would all be there. They all had connections, Bridget probably the strongest of all of them.

If only we'd caught on about Samantha and her pills sooner…

"Who?" he asked.

Lawrence gave him a side-long look. "Our number one suspect, Samantha Harris."

<h1 style="text-align:center">43</h1>

The body was not in the concert hall as Sohm had initially assumed, but in the adjoining Prescott Park, a short distance from the diner. They drove in a heavy silence. Sohm, noting the working of Lawrence's jaw, could guess what he was thinking.

If only we had acted sooner.

Sohm flashed back to his academy days and the speech given to his class by a former Boston policeman, who been present in the manhunt for the Patriot's Day terrorists. He spoke like a movie cop but his experience and commonsense approach elevated his speech: "There will be a day, for all of you, when you will find yourself thinking, 'If only.' Don't go there. It's a dead-end. You go to work, you do your best every day, and sometimes it won't work out. Sure, if you were clairvoyant you'd be able to stop all kinds of things before they happened. But you aren't. Do your best and that's all you can do."

It was easier said than done.

Prescott Park was crawling with life. A knot of well-dressed onlookers stood in the safe, yellow light of the concert hall, murmuring to each other while late-evening strollers slowed to stare curiously at the unexpected activity. Thick-chested patrolmen stood in front of the yellow tape barricade, arms folded and faces stern. This, after all, was not their first rodeo.

Whately was there – working a double shift again, apparently – and nodded to them as they stepped under the tape. "Busy day."

Lawrence's sharp glare silenced any further commentary.

Sohm's eyes swept over the inner circle. Straight ahead lay the harbor with the Navy Yard beyond. Boats slipped by on the still waters. A black shape lay crumbled and silent by one of the memorial benches that lined the waterfront walkway. A police photographer was already snapping pictures in the dimming light, her hair loose in the evening breeze.

Dr. Emily Evans, a pretty brunette who covered Klugman's off hours, was there, too, suiting up as she spoke with Falk. On another bench, as far from the body as he could get without leaving the circle, Thomas Atkinson sat with his head in his hands and his back towards the activity.

Sohm saw all of this in the moment before his attention was arrested by Beverly DiFranco, striding forward like a general in a purple cocktail dress.

"That was fast," she said, by way of a greeting. "She's over here."

As they walked, she explained in an undertone, "I was at the concert with Arthur and noticed that Atkinson came back from the intermission without Mrs. Harris. After a couple of songs, Atkinson slipped out and I followed him. I saw him find her here – it wasn't pretty."

She gestured to the body and Sohm had to agree with her assessment. Samantha's back was arched and her once pretty face was twisted into a gruesome grimace, teeth bared and glinting in the light of the photographer's flash.

"This shouldn't have happened." Lawrence's statement was stark and tortured.

Sohm looked at him and the big man turned away, rubbing his mouth as though he were fighting back nausea.

Sohm's training kicked in. He looked at the body, then his gaze swept over to the bench. A black clutch lay on top, open, the contents spread out over the seat. "Cause of death?" he asked.

Falk, who was hovering in the background, stepped in to answer. "Mr. Atkinson discovered her about ten minutes ago. She was dead when he found her. Looks like poison again, sir."

DiFranco shot him a look that was as cool as her tone. "Thank you, Falk. Now let's see what the *coroner* has to say."

Evans, jotting down notes on her pad, shook her head. "I can't give you a definite until we get her back to the lab but what I'm seeing here is consistent with strychnine poisoning. Looks like we've been having a run of that around here lately."

"I'm afraid so," Sohm said and he glanced at Lawrence. His senior officer was by the railing, looking out over the inlet.

He turned his attention to the contents of the purse which lay on the bench, mentally listing the items: lipstick, phone, compact, packet of tissues, lip balm. Did Samantha empty her purse, looking for something when the pangs started? Or had someone else?

He had the feeling something was missing from the little pile, but wearily thought, *How would I know what a woman keeps in her purse?*

He called to Evans, "Anything else you can tell us, doctor?"

"Looks like there was something of a struggle." Evans tapped her pencil to her teeth in concentration. The lamplight glinted off the rings in her ears and nose. "There's fresh bruising on her wrists, like someone was holding her down. No other signs of trauma that I can see right now, aside from what would have been caused by the spasms."

So there may well have been a third party here. Maybe that person emptied her purse. But why? His eyes dropped to the front of the stone and he read aloud the first part of the dedication: "Robert Grey."

DiFranco stepped closer and bent over for a better look. "Is he a relative?"

Sohm shrugged and Falk commented, "It looks like she was just walking along when she collapsed. Maybe she wanted to visit this stone."

It was a possibility, of course, but if Falk ever wanted to make detective, he was going to have to do better than state the obvious.

Sohm read the rest of the stone's dedication, "'*It is a far, far better rest I go to than I have ever known.*'"

Evans looked up. "Dickens, right? Tale of Two Cities?"

Sohm nodded and stood. "Yes. A story of a grand sacrifice for love. Probably has nothing to do with this case."

He felt weary and annoyed. None of this was making sense.

DiFranco sighed and then frowned as she caught sight of Lawrence by the railing, silent and still when he should have been leading the initial inquiry. She strode over to him and Sohm, sensing trouble, followed.

"Lawrence, what's wrong?" DiFranco demanded, planting herself in front of the big man. Her voice was low enough to keep Falk and Evans from hearing her, but dangerous enough to warn Lawrence to choose his words carefully.

Lawrence, his face tight and white, waved a hand over the scene. "This shouldn't have happened. We went over to her house tonight to question her. She was our main suspect."

If Sohm did not know better, he would have said that the man's tone indicated that he was about to breakdown.

DiFranco was even and cool. "And now she's your latest victim."

"We should have pursued it – she'd still be alive if I'd…"

Sohm hastily interrupted, "We have no way of knowing that, sir."

"Knowing *what?*" DiFranco sounded annoyed.

Sohm, feeling like he had stepped, yet again, in the middle of something that was none of his business, hesitated. However, DiFranco was the Chief of Police and not answering was not an option. He went ahead, feeling Lawrence's heavy gaze on him as he spoke, "We went over to her house to question her tonight. There's evidence to suggest that she gave Emma Gagnon pain killers laced with poison. When we learned she was here at the concert, we elected to wait until morning."

"If I hadn't been so damned concerned about appearances..." Lawrence rumbled dangerously, "she'd still be alive now."

DiFranco turned on him, snapping, "Unless you ordered the hit on her yourself, you are *not* to blame for this, Lawrence. For all we know she took the damn dose herself." She took a step closer. "Do I need to put someone else on this case, Michael?"

Lawrence drew in a breath and looked at his feet. Sohm, glad the dusk hid his reddened face, looked around at anything other than his two superiors.

Lawrence found his voice ."No. Thank you, ma'am."

His reply was cool, distant, and professional with just a hint of resentment. Sohm's gaze darted to DiFranco, but she was only nodding slowly.

"Very well," she said firmly. "Get on this and quickly. Three murders in four days is a very poor reflection on my department. Now, if you don't mind, I have a statement to make to Falk."

Resettling her shawl firmly around her shoulders, she turned on her heel and went to find the hapless Falk.

The verbal slap was not lost on either man. Sohm shoved his hands in his pockets and stared at his feet, waiting. Lawrence looked around the crime scene, running his hand through his hair. His gaze passed swiftly over Samantha's body – the sight of it disturbed him apparently.

Finally, Sohm broke the silence. "We can take Colin Rideout off the suspect list. He was in custody."

It was the wrong thing to say apparently. Lawrence

turned on him, his face black and his lips tight. His tone was taut with tension and sarcasm. "It was *poison*, Sohm. Rideout didn't necessarily have to *be* here to force-feed it to her."

Sohm suppressed a groan but allowed himself to wonder, *When is this day going to be over?*

He spotted movement across the lawn. Someone was talking with Whately, gesturing and arguing. He was too far away for Sohm to make out his face, but he thought he recognized the stature and movements as belonging to Peter Chase.

Lawrence had moved on. "What is going on here? Where's the connection between Emma Gagnon, Sarah Hopper, and Sam Harris? What are we missing, Sohm?"

His voice was pitching high and all at once Sohm was done with him and his shifting moods. He turned his own glare on his superior officer and growled, "I. Don't. Know."

With that, he left Lawrence to his own sour musings and strode to meet Peter.

Despite Peter's insistence, Whately was not about to let him pass through. Sohm was surprised that it was Peter and not Peter's wife who was trying to pass the roped off area to snoop around. When he glanced at Noble Hall, he could see Arlene, red hair glowing in the warm light, talking excitedly to Arthur DiFranco.

Poor guy, Sohm thought.

Both men turned to Sohm as he walked up.

"Peter," Sohm said. "I'm going to have to ask everyone to stay inside the hall until we've taken their statements."

Peter did not object but he did not immediately turn away either, "Yes, yes, of course, Nick." He gestured over Sohm's shoulder towards the stone bench and Samantha's lifeless body. "But I wanted to tell you something. That stone, the one they found Mrs. Harris laying in front of?"

"Yes," Sohm said slowly. "Robert Grey – did you know him?"

Peter nodded. "Yes, in a way." Then he said the last thing that Sohm expected him or anyone to say: "Robert Grey was the student that killed Bridget Madden's father in a hit-and-run accident twenty years ago."

Saturday

44

F riday night was a marathon session of statements, evidence gathering, and report work and it was well into the early hours of Saturday before Sohm went home. Even in the silence of his small, neat apartment, it was difficult to calm his mind enough to sleep. After a few fitful hours, he gave up, showered, dressed, and scrounged up a stale bagel from his close-to-empty kitchen. He toasted it, lathered it with cream cheese, and stood at the counter to eat, thinking about Samantha Harris and the pallor on Bridget's face when he spotted her behind stage at the concert hall, giving her statement to one of the officers.

By now, everyone, including DiFranco, had the girl at the top of the list of suspects and Sohm could not blame them. The connections there were easy to make. She was, after all, intimately connected with everyone: Emma, Sarah, Rideout, even Samantha Harris after a fashion.

Despite that, Sohm could not think of Bridget Madden as a killer. She was ambitious, but by the book in a lot of ways: college, then career, and Broadway after various small theatricals. She wouldn't risk her fledgling career for the quick, dangerous money that Rideout could have offered her. And murder by strychnine did not seem to suite her style. Theatrical a poison as it was, it was old fashioned and he doubted that she would have even heard of it before her guardian's death. Actually, the use of strychnine bothered him precisely because it was old-fashioned and theatrical, not to mention risky. If the dosage was too low the victims might survive and the murder plot exposed before the deed was finished.

Then again, what did he *really* know about Bridget? Only what she and others had said about her and what her peers said had not exactly been flattering. Also, she *was* friends with that low-life Rideout. Sohm might very well have sized her up all wrong.

The thought upset him. He tossed the rest of his breakfast into the trash, pulled on his jacket, and headed for the office. A few hours perusing files and studying up on the principals would make him feel better.

It was early when he pulled into the parking lot and the building was quiet as he made his thoughtful way to his and Lawrence's office. He had been expecting to have the place to himself and so was surprised when he came around the corner and found the office light on. He was even more surprised when Lawrence emerged, still dressed in yesterday's outfit, shirt rumpled, tie loose, and jacket held jauntily over his shoulder.

Mostly, it was the glow of accomplishment and the satisfied Cheshire-Cat grin on Lawrence's face that really threw Sohm.

As Sohm stood trying to make sense of this, Lawrence spoke.

"Sohm, you did it." He held up an old, beaten file.

Sohm shook his head. "Wait… did you stay here all night?"

He could hardly have gone back to Janine's after that incident in the hospice.

There was no guilt in Lawrence's movement or tone as he shoved the file into Sohm's hand and answered, "Yep. Now, hurry up and study that file. DiFranco will be here in about an hour. But you did it, Sohm! A-plus!"

He was past Sohm and half-way down the hall whistling before Sohm could call after him. "But…but what exactly did I do?"

"You found our missing connection!" Lawrence called out cheerfully over his shoulder. "Now read the file!"

Completely mystified, Sohm went into the office to do as he was told.

45

DiFranco, exhausted from the events of the night before, could barely summon the strength to crawl over to her phone when Lawrence called her that morning. She icily informed him that, given the circumstances, of course she would be at work that morning, even though it was Saturday. It was only when Lawrence had gone on to explain that he had had a break in the case that curiosity broke through her early-morning blues.

"A break?" she asked, her voice softening. "It was a long night, Lawrence, you wouldn't be pulling my leg here?"

"Come down and see. Sohm's already here."

She rushed through her usual morning routine and dressed hastily, pulling a relaxed jacket over a salmon blouse and jeans. Breakfast was a cup of coffee and a granola bar, which she finished in the car.

She found Sohm and Lawrence in their office, bent over documents spread across Lawrence's desk. When Lawrence looked up to greet her, she saw at once that he must have spent the night in the office, possibly sleeping at his desk. Despite this, he looked like a new man – calm and triumphant.

She was relieved to see the change. She had tossed and turned last night, worrying about his unusual funk the night before and wondering whether she had done right to leave him on the case.

Glad I didn't have to make that call. No one likes being pulled from a case.

Nevertheless, she was not about to let them relax. She plopped herself down on Lawrence's chair and crossed one knee over the other.

"Okay, boys," she declared. "Impress me."

Lawrence and Sohm grinned at each other, then Lawrence stepped over to the case-board and pointed a new picture on the board. The image was a mug shot of a man, not much younger than Sohm, with brown eyes and hair and a lop-sided, charming smile.

"Let me introduce you to the newest member of our cast," Lawrence said. "Robert Francis Grey, born January 18th, 1977, in Lawrence, Massachusetts to Nancy Grey, father unknown. In 1995, he started attending classes at Noble College on scholarship, despite a somewhat checkered past."

"I think we met last night," she said, remembering the name from the stone.

"By age eighteen, Grey had already spent some time at the juvenile prison." Sohm supplied. "His early record was sealed, of course – we're still trying to access it."

"Right, of course. But how exactly does a dead man figure into this?"

"Robert Grey was the driver of the car that killed Bridget

Madden's father," Lawrence said. "And I think he's the lynchpin of this whole case."

He was beaming, actually *beaming* at her. If DiFranco had been inclined to wax poetic, she would have said that he looked ten years younger.

"Okay," she said. "Explain."

He was pleased to do so. "Robert Grey attends Noble College at the same time Emma Gagnon begins working in the music department and Professor Stewart is an associate in the Biology Department. Not only that, but Thomas Atkinson is in his second year and Samantha Harris is in her third year at the college.

"At the end of his first year, Robert Grey hits a pedestrian – James Madden - while DUI, and kills him. Although he initially pleads not guilty, his lawyer, a Boston man no less, changes the plea to guilty. Robert Grey is given a reduced sentence, then paroled after seven years."

"So he was out?" DiFranco asked.

"Only for a short time," Sohm replied. "He hotwired another car and promptly went back."

"Where he stayed," Lawrence added, "for a variety of reasons, until he died two years ago from complications that set in after he was beaten by two fellow inmates. He was buried in Connecticut, where he was imprisoned."

DiFranco started. "Connecticut! But his mother...?"

"His mother was last reported to be living in Florida as of five years ago. We're trying to locate her now."

"Okay... but if she's in Florida and he's in Connecticut...?"

"Who put up a memorial for Robert Grey in Portsmouth?" Sohm finished.

Lawrence grinned. "Good question!"

"And what does any of this have to do with Emma Gagnon?" DiFranco demanded.

"I don't think it had anything to do with her. I think Samantha Harris was the intended victim all along and Emma Gagnon and Sarah Hopper just got caught in the middle."

This caught DiFranco by surprise.

Before she could respond, Sohm went on, "We know that Samantha Harris was from a wealthy family in California and that she was known as the girl all the boys went for. Also, until five days ago, she hasn't been back in Portsmouth since she left."

"When she graduated?"

"She didn't graduate from Noble," Lawrence said. "She transferred in her final year to Breaburn College, in California. *That* was about the same time that Robert Grey went to court, with a fancy lawyer that he couldn't have afforded to hire on his own."

"Meaning..." she said slowly, "that someone else paid for him."

Lawrence nodded. "Right. What's also interesting is the fact that, though she was invited to every alumni and college event, until she arrived five days ago, Samantha Brown Harris never returned to Noble College despite being in Boston frequently. According to her son, she had not stepped foot into the place until she got a tour of the college right before a welcome party on her first night in town."

"Two years *after* Robert Grey's death," Sohm added.

DiFranco held up her hands. "All right, let me get this straight. You think Samantha Harris was involved in the car accident that killed Bridget Madden's father?"

Both men nodded vigorously, eagerly, like two little boys who'd just discovered a way to impress their teacher.

"Both she and Atkinson were questioned by the police at the time, but they had an alibi," Sohm explained.

"Which was?"

"They were together all night," Lawrence said. "But…let's say they weren't. Let's say that Samantha Harris and Thomas Atkinson were in the car with Robert at the time. And let's say that mommy and daddy moneybags didn't want their daughter mixed up with a hit-and-run."

DiFranco nodded thoughtfully. "So they bribe Grey by hiring a fancy-pants lawyer to get him a reduced sentence."

"And Samantha," Sohm tapped her picture on the board, "is shipped back home."

She leaned back in her chair and folded her arms. "So you think that Samantha Harris was killed because of her involvement in a twenty-year-old hit-and-run, and that the other two women were somehow caught in the middle. Okay. So who does that leave us with a motive?"

"Offhand," Sohm said, "I'd say Bridget Madden and Robert Grey's missing mother."

She shook her head. This theory felt better than any other, but there were so many holes in it that she could not see how they could plug them all into a case that would please the DA.

Beverly stood, putting her hands on her hips. "All right,

boys," she said, "that's not bad, but it's a *lot* of supposition. Where are you going to find the evidence to prove any of this?"

To her surprise, Lawrence did not look at all put out. In fact, he leaned back against Sohm's desk with a smug looked, as though she had asked just what he was hoping she would.

"Offhand," he said, grinning, "I'd say from the one person who might know firsthand just what did happen the night Bridget Madden's father died."

46

"I'm so glad you've come. I didn't know what to do."

Max Griffin was wearing the exact same outfit and expression that he had been when Lawrence had met him a few days ago. His movements, as he led Sohm and Lawrence upstairs to Atkinson's office-apartment, were quick and worried. He did not like what he had seen and for a brief moment Lawrence had the panicky thought that once again, he and Sohm had been a little too slow.

His concern was put to rest when the clerk pushed open the door and revealed Atkinson's messy kitchen. It looked much the same as it had the day Lawrence came to question him, with one notable exception; this morning, Thomas Atkinson was not at the kitchen table comforting a beautiful woman. He was on the floor, propped up against the refrigerator, holding a half-empty bottle of Scotch.

Sohm instantly strode forward and crouched down by the man.

Max, hanging back uncertainly by the stairway door, said, "He's been that way since I found him this morning, like, he's catatonic or something."

Lawrence ambled over and looked around. The room was cluttered with books, office equipment and kitchen paraphernalia, the only notable addition being a gray jacket that Atkinson had tossed on top of the pile of yesterday's dishes. Aside from removing his jacket, he had not changed from the night before. A kitchen cabinet door was open, showing a shelf of bottles with an empty space where bottles had been removed—his makeshift liquor cabinet apparently. The smell of liquor was pervasive.

Atkinson shifted and winced, groaning.

Lawrence turned to Max. "Go get him some coffee, will you?"

Relieved, the boy fled downstairs.

Lawrence bent over the man and lowered his voice. "Mr. Atkinson?" Blood-shot, half focused eyes turned toward him. "We need you to come in for questioning, sir."

Atkinson closed his eyes. Then he twisted like a pretzel, rolled towards Sohm, and emptied his stomach on the young detective's shoes.

***

It took them time, coffee, and a full roll of paper towels to bring Atkinson around to a point where he could speak intelligibly. By the time Max returned with a paper cup of coffee from the café down the street, Lawrence already had discovered the bottle of instant grounds on the counter and a clean cup to pour the hot water in.

Finally, when the bookseller's eyes had cleared and his

shakes had subsided, Lawrence sat back in one of Atkinson's kitchen chairs, fingering the bottle of Scotch whiskey.

"How are you feeling?" he asked.

Atkinson leaned forward to rest his face in his hands. "Like I've been hit by a truck, during a hangover."

"I'm not surprised," Sohm said sourly. He was at the kitchen sink, cleaning his shoes, his face white and his teeth gritted. Lawrence felt a flash of sympathy. Sohm took pride in his clothes and especially in his footwear. Atkinson's accident might well have cost him a paycheck or more.

Lawrence kept his attention on Atkinson and pushed the whiskey bottle forward. "We found an empty bottle of this in your trash, Mr. Atkinson. If your stomach hadn't reacted when it did, we'd be taking you to the hospital by now."

"You wouldn't be doing me any favors," the man said bitterly. Then he looked at Lawrence in alarm. "Why are you here? You haven't come to arrest *me* for the murders, have you?"

"Any reason why we should?"

"None at all." Atkinson went on the defensive. "I have nothing but the highest respect for Emma Gagnon. She was like my grandmother."

"And you loved Samantha," Lawrence said.

Atkinson took a long, shuddering breath, then nodded. "Yes. I did."

"That's why you covered for her when she asked you for an alibi twenty years ago, right? When you and she let Robert Grey take the fall for the death of James Madden?"

There was a long moment before Atkinson spoke. When he did his voice came out in a rough whisper. "You know?"

Lawrence nodded slowly. "I know."

With a sigh that seemed to take all the air out of his body, Atkinson sank his head into his hands.

"That," he said, "happened a long time ago."

Lawrence leaned back, too, folding his arms loosely. "Why don't you tell us about it?"

Atkinson did not need much encouragement. A lifetime of secrets and disappointed hopes poured out of him like a fountain. He spoke caressingly, with care and detail, as if by keeping these things pent up in him so long and surrounding himself with books, he had become a storyteller himself.

"She was Samantha Brown then," he said. "A beautiful, intelligent, wild girl. She was from California, some big money family, and I'd never seen anything like her in my life. I fell in love with her, of course. Everyone did. She wasn't in our class, you know? She belonged in the bright lights and glitter. She was 'slumming' at Noble. God knows why, but she took a shine to me, beautiful girl…"

"And Robert Grey?" Sohm asked.

Atkinson shrugged. "He was like me, I guess. Just another kid from the wrong side of the tracks. But unlike me, he was intense, angry, always trying to prove himself. He should have been thrown out several times and would have been too, if someone hadn't stepped in and stopped it. We used to joke that he had a fairy godmother looking after him, because he never was in trouble for long." He paused, took off his glasses, and rubbed the bridge of his nose while squeezing his eyes shut. "We had a rivalry going on, he and I. Always trying to impress Samantha at the expense of the other."

He put his glasses back on and looked at Lawrence. "He knew she liked fancy cars, so he stole one to take her for a ride."

Lawrence nodded. "And was she impressed?"

"Oh yes. She was *very* impressed."

There was bitterness in his tone. Lawrence studied his posture. *Twenty years ago and still it nettles like it was yesterday...*

There was movement at Lawrence's elbow. Sohm was pulling up a chair next to him. He adjusted his own glasses and stepped in where Lawrence had left off. "So she was in the car with him that night, not with you, as you said in your testimony."

"She came to me terrified. She was afraid that they would throw her in jail. Can you imagine a girl like *her* in jail? What they would do to her there? She *needed* protection." Atkinson's finger jabbed at the table to make his point.

Lawrence suggested gently, "She needed *your* protection."

Atkinson sagged in his seat. "Yes. For once, she really needed me."

They sat in silence for a moment, Atkinson defiant and broken, Sohm toying with his glasses and Lawrence drumming his fingers on the table while thinking through his next move.

He decided on a shot in the dark. "When did Samantha tell you the whole truth? That it was she, not Grey, who ran down Bridget Madden's father that night?"

Sohm started and looked at Lawrence in shock.

Their subject, on the other hand, merely snorted and looked at the table again. "Oh, I figured that out really fast."

Lawrence shot Sohm a triumphant look.

Atkinson was absently tracing the wood grain of the table top, speaking thickly, as though through a sore throat. "The night of the accident, Samantha had called her father. He told her to find an alibi and that he'd take care of everything else. She got me to swear that we were together that night. He found Grey and bullied him into taking the rap in exchange for a sum of money, payable upon his release."

"And Grey *accepted* that?" Sohm asked in disgust.

Atkinson shrugged. "He must have. Honestly, it was probably the best deal that a kid like him was ever going to be offered. In any case, he went to jail – and Sam went back to California."

"While you stayed here," Lawrence said.

"While I stayed here." He went back to tracing the wood grain. "Samantha came to see me the day after Emma Gagnon died. She was frightened. She had it into her head that Emma had found out about the accident somehow and was going to blackmail her. She thought that that was why Emma kept pressing her to meet Bridget."

"Did Emma know?" Sohm asked.

He shook his head. "Emma never would have blackmailed Samantha. She wasn't that way. She probably would have told her to come clean. Emma was like that."

"But with Emma dead," Lawrence asked, "why was Samantha frightened?"

"She had given Emma pills during Bridget's rehearsal. Emma didn't take them right away but when she died ,Samantha panicked. She thought that maybe someone had laced them with poison, intending them for her."

Sohm looked sidelong at Lawrence. "Looks like she was correct," he said softly.

"I thought it was ridiculous." Atkinson's voice cracked with the words but he soldiered on, never looking up from the table. "Samantha had bought those pills at some shop while en route to Boston. There was no way anyone could have tampered with them. I told her that. I told her and…" He paused and his mouth tightened. "She couldn't turn them over to you because she was afraid you'd dig and find out about the accident. Then, when Sarah died, she thought she was safe. Only… only she wasn't."

Now he looked up at Lawrence. His eyes were red and he clenched his hand together so tightly that his knuckles showed white. His face was a mask of despair and anguish.

"I couldn't have killed her, Lawrence." He spoke as though he were gasping for words. "I…I loved her. I would have done anything for her, *anything.*"

Lawrence looked into his miserable face, a lonely man surrounded by the remnants of a wasted life, a life that had been constructed around loss and impossible hope. Thomas Atkinson had spent his life waiting for Samantha Brown to pick up where they had left off. He had constructed a wall of books around himself, the battered old stories of other men's lives and deeds, shielding himself from the harsh reality that he had no story of his own because, once upon a time, a long time ago, a girl had cast him in the role of a side character and he had been happy to play the part.

Now Samantha Brown was gone and with her any hope he might have had of becoming the leading man.

Where will you go now? Lawrence thought. *What will you do now?*

Suddenly, the room seemed much too small for the three of them. Lawrence felt the need for air, for space, for movement. He got to his feet abruptly, startling both Atkinson and Sohm.

"I believe you," Lawrence said as he looked down at Atkinson's astonished face. "You would have done anything she asked you to – and Samantha Harris knew it."

Atkinson, the man without a story, swallowed hard and nodded.

"Yes." His voice seemed to resonate, hollow and melancholy, even in that cramped room. "Yes... I guess she did know that."

***

Sohm waited until they were down the stairs and back in the entryway before he tapped on Lawrence's shoulder. "Shouldn't we take him in?"

He looked frustrated and Lawrence felt a pang of sympathy. "No, he didn't do it. He's telling the truth when he says he'd have done anything for Samantha. He couldn't have killed her."

"Are you sure?"

"Aren't you?"

Sohm shuffled his feet and glanced around at his surroundings before looking back at Lawrence. "Where does that leave us, then? Nancy Grey, the boy's mother? Bridget Madden, whose father was killed?"

"You don't really think it was Bridget, do you?"

"With the facts we have, she's as good a bet as anyone else."

"But do *you* think she's capable of murder?"

Now the young man hesitated, his eyes dark with worry. "No. I don't. But I have nothing to support that assumption and if the facts say otherwise..."

He did not finish the thought.

Lawrence looked at him and grinned. *You're dead set against her being the murderer, but you're afraid to say the words 'gut instinct'.*

He did not press Sohm. Someday he would learn that what most people referred to as 'gut instinct' or 'intuition' was really the processing of facts on a level that was too deep for conscious thought. Gut instinct was not admissible in court and could get you into trouble if you followed it blindly. Ignoring it, though, had its own dangers. Sohm would learn, but this was not the place to teach him.

Instead, Lawrence said, "Well, I happen to agree with you. I don't think she had anything to do with any of this."

He turned and pushed out the doorway and into the street. It was a gray, drizzly Saturday morning and Portsmouth was still waking up. The drizzle began to intensify into rain and by the time they got to Lawrence's car, parked a few lengths away down the alley, cool drops were slipping down Lawrence's neck and soaking his collar.

He shivered as he pulled the door open, then stopped and looked at Sohm. "Any word yet on who ordered that stone for Grey?"

Sohm pulled out his ever-present phone and worked with it. After a second, he shook his head. "No word yet. It's Saturday – the place may not even be open today. Is it important?"

"No," Lawrence said. "It's just that I have a hunch that I know who did. Come on, let's go."

"Wait... do you know who the murderer is?"

"I think I do, Sohm. I finally think I do."

47

Little white tablets nestled amongst each other in the little gold and plastic box, glinting as if they were covered in sugar. Samantha Harris never did anything by halves. The pillbox was as pretty as her choice in clothes had been tasteful – gold colored with a curving image of a dancing couple in Louis XVI-era clothing on the cover. A pretty box with pretty pills and it sat inches from his hand on the desk in front of him. His other hand was wrapped around his water bottle. He had brought it with him from the house, thinking, *Wouldn't want to choke on the damn things*

Now he wondered which would be worse, choking or death by affixation, following a torturous twenty minutes or more of back-breaking spasms. He never could stand pain, but though choking might be faster, strychnine was more sure.

His plan was to take a handful, but really, only two pills were needed. Emma was proof of that.

Damn it. He was sweating through his shirt, despite the persistent chills that shook his entire frame. He would look quite the mess when they found him, bottle in hand, confession neatly printed, signed, and dated...

He heard them arrive in the outer room, recognized Lawrence's deep rumble as he asked for admittance. His heart jumped and a panicked thought went through his mind, *I should take them now, before they come in. Now, before I am stopped...*

His hand would not move, though. He was frozen, whether in fear or anticipation, he was uncertain. He could, of course, attempt to swallow a pill now, but they would be on him faster than he could swallow. Rather than the dignified death he had wanted, there would be a hue and cry and a desperate, probably successful, attempt to save his life for the trial. Once in custody, suicide would be next to impossible.

His mind worked swiftly, sifting through probabilities, finding alternatives. He had hoped to avoid this confrontation, but now that it had come, he would play along. It might even work to his advantage.

So when the door opened and the two detectives appeared, he remained as he was: a figure, dressed in black, sitting behind a desk, staring down into a pillbox.

It was Lawrence who spoke first.

"I don't think you want to do that, sir." There was urgency in his voice.

Professor Charles Stewart lifted his head and looked up at the two expectant faces.

"I really should," he said, "but I simply haven't the courage."

He could move then, and he did. He shut Samantha's pillbox and slid it towards the two men.

"I suppose," he said, as Lawrence stepped forward to take

the box, "that you'd like the whole story. You'd best make yourself comfortable. It'll take a little while."

***

They read him the Miranda rights as a matter of course but Stewart waved them away.

"Yes, yes," he said. "I'm going to confess, gentlemen. If you didn't use what I said against me in a court of law, you'd be derelict in your duties."

He offered them a seat and, after a moment, Lawrence sat. The other man followed suit and the stage was Charles's.

He started at the beginning and took his time. "I met Nancy Grey when I was a boy in high school. At the time, people of my... persuasion were persona non grata in the community. She was bright and lively and I thought, 'Why not? Most men go for women.' I was still experimenting, you see."

He stopped there, unexpectedly overwhelmed by memories. Nancy and her floating blonde hair, the way her blue eyes crinkled up in the corner when she smiled, the tingle when she had first kissed him, the way that she had known, almost before he did, that they were over: "I know it's not me, Chuck. It's any woman, right? Well, at least I can say I gave it my best shot..."

Oh, Nancy, Nancy...

Stewart shook his head clear. The detectives were waiting, Lawrence sitting quietly, his young, handsome partner nervously jiggling his leg as he waited for the professor to continue. The young man, Sohm his name was, looked like he would rather be anywhere but here. Lawrence merely looked tired.

Stewart cleared his throat and continued. "It didn't last long. She moved away and I lost contact. I didn't even know I had a son until he was twelve."

"Robert Grey," Lawrence supplied, and Stewart smiled at the name.

"Robert Grey." He drew in a long breath. "It was an odd thing, you know, suddenly discovering you have a son when you've become accustomed to the idea that you'll never have any. Nancy was married at the time and we did not want to confuse things, so we never told him or her husband. I was simply her old classmate, Robert's 'godfather'. He was a good boy at heart, really. His family life wasn't the most stable – the men Nancy chose never stuck around for long."

He remembered sitting in the café, Nancy with her legs crossed on the chair, just as she had done as a student. "I guess you could say you've ruined me, Chuck," she'd said, staring down into her coffee cup, a wry smile on her face. "But it's not like it's a bad thing, you know? Even if you had been... well, I'm not the stable type, if you know what I mean. It doesn't bother me, but a boy like Robert needs someone sturdy. Kevin's many things, but he isn't going to stick around long, I can feel it..."

Lawrence was asking, "You helped him get into this school?"

Stewart nodded. "Yes. I wanted to have him near me. He'd been in trouble and I thought I could help him, give him some stability. Then that dreadful accident happened."

Flashes of memory assaulted him: the long dark night,

Robert's panicking voice on the other end of the line, "It was an accident, an accident, I swear!" The police, the statements, and the car. If only Robert had not taken the car, his car, Stewart's own prized Jaguar, brand new and then crumbled with blood on the bumper, the hood, the steering wheel.

You should have come to me then, Robby. You should have told me then...

"Did you know that Samantha Harris was in the car with him?" Sohm asked.

"No!" His eyes sprang open and he glared at the man. "Robert *told* me he was the one who'd been driving. I believed him. I never would have let him go to prison for something he didn't do, never!"

He broke off suddenly, aware of how he sounded. The two men were watching him warily and he felt that he did not have much more time to tell his story. The truth had to come out now, here, where it could not be denied. Justice had been done but it would not do any good if no one knew about it.

He took a steadying breath and said, deliberately calm, "He really loved her. Sacrificed his life for her."

The two cops exchanged skeptical looks and the younger man said, "Your son was instrumental in James Madden's death."

Stewart leaned forward, anger steeling his voice. "That was Samantha Harris's fault and my son paid the price for it. Do you know what they did to him in prison? A pretty, sensitive boy like my son? They *broke* him, detective. They beat him and they broke him. He never even had ac hance."

They hadn't seen the bruising, the limping, the deepening

lines around the young face. The emotional injuries had been worse than the physical ones. Robby lost his youthful vigor, the light dimming from his eyes, the exuberance beaten out of his spirit. He had grown old in prison, and he never even reached forty.

"You bought a house near where he was imprisoned. Did you visit him regularly?"

Lawrence's voice was gentle, kindly even and Stewart found himself looking at the man's hands. A gold band glistened on the appropriate finger. A family man, probably, and one accustomed to loss and pain. Sohm's hands were bare and he was young. He could not be expected to understand.

"Yes," Stewart said softly. "Nancy visited too, but a boy… a boy needs his father."

I should have told you, son. I should have come clean and let you know that your father hadn't abandoned you as you thought…

"When did he tell you the truth about the accident?" Lawrence probed.

"Not until the very end."

More painful flashes of memory: the sealed off ward in the hospital, the guard who nodded soberly as he passed, the sterile scent of interminable waiting, the steady, reassuring beep of the monitors, the clean drip of the fluid bag. The room was small and cramped with equipment and the bed seemed enormous. The walls were a sad teal color and there were precious few 'Get Well' cards on the table. Robert lay unmoving on the bed, his slight frame barely enough to fill the blankets. His skull gleamed where once dark hair had been so carefully tended. His eyes were both black-rimmed and a piece of tape held his cheek together.

Robert did not stir. He would not, Stewart had known, because of the medication. He couldn't know that Stewart was there, but the big man took his son's hand anyway and squeezed it. "Hello, Robert. How are you feeling tonight?"

Memory receded and he continued. "There'd been a fight. They broke his nose and his ribs. He had fluid in his lungs and he was suffering so… terribly. By then the wardens knew me and they let me visit his bedside. He still had a sick loyalty to that woman, even after all the grief she caused. It was only when he was dying that he told me."

He drew a breath before looking at Lawrence. "He didn't want to die leaving me thinking he was a murderer, you see."

Lawrence nodded, his blue eyes thoughtful but unrevealing. "When did you decide to kill Samantha Harris?"

"When I got the call that Robert was gone. I decided then." He looked at his hands. "But I didn't know how to do it. I was already scheduled to attend a conference in California, so I arranged to meet with her. It was a simple matter – I knew people who knew her and I merely expressed an interest in meeting one of my favorite authors. She was lovely and charming and I remember thinking, *There is no way a court will believe me. She will charm her way past any jury.*

"So I watched her. When I saw her popping those pain pills and heard her complaining about her headaches, I saw how to do it. That was two years ago."

"Two *years?*" Sohm sputtered in disbelief. "Why did you wait so long?

"I couldn't do it then and there, could I?" Stewart said annoyed. "I didn't have the supplies and there was Miles to consider. I didn't want my partner dragged through this." He turned back to Lawrence, the more sympathetic of the two. "That was the hardest thing of all, you know. Driving Miles away, making him think that I..."

Lawrence did not nod, did not blink. He just waited.

Stewart's hands were starting to tremble again and there was a cold sweat on his brow. He had to power through this, stop indulging in so much memory and get the story out before it was too late. The confession he had typed was complete but Stewart realized now how important it was that the confession was not only read, but understood. Somehow, he thought that Lawrence was a man who could truly comprehend.

He pulled himself together and carried on. "I came back here and pulled out my old chemistry books. Making the pills was easy. Arranging for Samantha Harris to come here was harder. I worked for a year to get that lecture series up and going. She had to die here, you see. I wanted her to come back, to be surrounded by memories, and to know, somewhere, why she was dying. I chose strychnine because death was slow enough for the victim to know fear and fast enough that EMTs would likely be too late to help."

That got a reaction. Sohm grunted in disgust.

"As was the case with Emma Gagnon," Lawrence said in a tight voice.

Stewart nodded. "Poor, stupid Emma. That was never supposed to happen."

Sohm cut in harshly, "How did you get the pills into Samantha's pillbox?"

"I had a party the night of her arrival. While she was chatting with Emma, I slipped into my kitchen with her purse and exchanged the pills. She never knew."

"What happened the night of the concert?" Lawrence asked.

He couldn't help the smile that crept over his face. "It couldn't have happened better if I'd planned it," he said softly. "During intermission, I went to look for Samantha. She was outside, trying to escape the clutches of that oaf, Atkinson. I brought some of the pills with me – I always kept a few on me, just in case – and I brought her a coffee after dissolving some of the pills in it. Then I told her I had something to show her and I took her to the memorial that I'd had put up for Robert. As we walked, she told me that she had a headache and had already taken two pills. Then she drank my coffee. No one could have saved her."

"What did she say when she saw the memorial?"

He threw himself back in the chair, annoyed even at the memory. "She launched into her usual act. How much she'd liked Robert, how sorry she was that he couldn't stay out of trouble, how sad it was that Bridget had to grow up without a father. On and on. I let her talk until the stomach cramps started."

"And then?"

Sohm's voice was tight, edged in dangerous temper. But there was nothing he nor Lawrence could do now. Samantha was dead, his goal achieved, so Stewart went on without blinking. If his tone betrayed a touch of satisfaction or glee, well, after years of strain and two years of planning, who could really blame him?

"Then I told her who I really was: Robert's father. I told her what Robert told me, that it was she who'd driven the car, not him. She told me it was a lie, of course and then she realized what was happening to her. She tried to run back to the hall for help. I wouldn't let her. I held her down until she couldn't run anymore."

He could still recall the terrified look on her pretty face, the way her graceful body twisted under the unbearable pressure, the crocodile tears that turned real when she realized the truth, the guttural cries of pain. They were seared into his memory, stored right next to the images of Robert in that hospital bed, wheezing with water-laden lungs.

"It was over quickly," he said. "When she was beyond help, I took her pillbox and slipped back into the hall. No one even noticed me. It was... perfect."

There was a long moment of silence. Lawrence looked remote, as though he had withdrawn into himself, a turtle-like move characteristic of the Irish.

Sohm was a different story. His hands were clenching and unclenching. His jaw worked incessantly, and when he said, "I guess that's it, then," it was with the same steel and relish of a man pronouncing sentence upon one convicted.

Stewart eyed him with interest. *You'd better watch that temper, my boy. It'll lead you to places you don't wish to go.*

Lawrence stood. "You'd better come with us now, sir."

His tone was so remote, so impersonal that Stewart turned on him in frustrated fury.

"He was my *son*, detective, my only son, and she ruined him. She didn't think anything about it. What would you have done? Would you have just let her get away with that? Would you have stood by while justice is trampled on?"

Now it was Lawrence's eyes that flashed. Sohm was not the only one with a temper it seemed.

"The way I see it," he snapped, "your justice was as brutal as her crimes. Samantha Harris could have offered her pain pills to anyone else, her *son*, for instance, and she did offer them to Emma Gagnon." Lawrence leaned forward, hands on the desk, face inches from Stewart's own. "Your brand of justice killed two innocent people, Professor Stewart. I don't call that balancing the scales, do you?"

Two innocents...

Suddenly Stewart was too weary to argue any longer. He had said his piece. What he had forgotten was in the written confession, which he now slid towards the two officers. "I've given you my confession, detective. I've also written it down, so that it would be found with me. Here. You might as well have it."

Lawrence reached for the envelope. It was while the attention of both officers was on the paper that Stewart reached into his drawer and pulled out the pistol. It had been purchased, loaded, and prepared for just this eventuality. He hated to use it, he really did. It was loud and messy, but it had one virtue that even the pills could not provide: certainty.

Cocking the pistol drew Sohm's attention. "Sir!" he warned. He shoved Lawrence out of the way and reached for his own piece.

Stewart had already positioned the barrel against his own head.

"I decided that I couldn't go to prison," he said, pleased that though his hands shook like he had ague, his voice was rock steady. "And I won't."

Lawrence, standing where he had been pushed, said urgently, compassionately, "You really don't want to do that, sir."

For a long, long moment, Stewart hesitated. Like shuffling flash cards, memories of his life assailed him: his student years, the college, his lovely house with his comfortable chair and personal library, his friends and students, the smell of the sea on brisk days, the walks he loved to take to welcome the spring, his café, his office, Cumberbatch, Peter and Arlene, his favorite Merlot, the feeling of a warm fire after a long, cold, winter's walk, the taste of freshly caught Maine, lobster, the gentle pitch of a ship at sea, Nancy, Samantha, Robert… and Miles, poor, dear, gentle, loveable Miles…

All that had made life sweet was lost to him now and long, cold years of isolation, discomfort, and disgrace awaited. If he died today, he would at least preserve the memory of his good name, for, without a trial to drive the crime home, those he knew would remember him as he was. If he went to jail, even that small comfort would be gone. Yet, even realizing that, even knowing that he could never, ever return to the way things were, he found himself unable to pull the trigger. He lacked the courage to do what he had promised himself he would do. Killing Samantha had been easy. Killing himself was impossible.

So was living.

Through the fog of thought, he heard Lawrence speak again: "Sir – put it down."

There was a twitch of movement from Sohm – the young man's hand was on his own gun. He had not drawn it… yet. His hazel eyes were focused only on Stewart. He was outwardly calm, but given half a reason, he would explode.

That was when Stewart realized that he had a plan C.

"Yes," he murmured. "I suppose you're right…"

He turned the gun on Lawrence and the room exploded with sound.

48

They were not able to save him. Sohm's aim, though rapid, had been true, and the bullet entered the chest somewhere around the heart. Lawrence called the paramedics while Sohm, white-faced and shaking, tried to stop the bleeding. They managed to keep Professor Stewart alive until the paramedics arrived, but that was all. He died without ever regaining consciousness.

Sohm, his shirt and jacket stained with Stewart's blood, voluntarily surrendered his pistol and his badge to the officers who arrived on scene. He was pallid and unresponsive to Lawrence or anyone else. He went back to the station under the watchful eye of a patrolman before the media arrived. The last thing anyone wanted was for the press to get a hold of Sohm before DiFranco, the counselor, and the lawyers, did.

After that, there was work to be done. The office was sealed off, the onsite staff quarantined until they could be questioned and released, the lab boys sent for. The body was trussed up and sent to the morgue in an ambulance and it was decided that nothing would be said to the press until

Stewart's family could be located. According to Cumberbatch, he hadn't much family to contact.

"A sister in Florida," he said. He was dressed down from the day before and wore a bewildered expression. "And an aunt in San Diego. I guess someone ought to call Miles."

"Miles?" Lawrence heard the officer inquire.

The assistant nodded and ran a hand through his thinning hair. "He is…was…he was Professor Stewart's ex, but he should be told." He looked around the bustling entry way that was filled with officers and crime scene professionals and shook his head. "Oh God. What will we do without him?"

Lawrence directed everything until his replacement, Richard Matarusso, a senior detective who normally handled the robbery division, arrived. Rich took one look around the room, then focused his attention on Lawrence. "You were present at the shooting, Mike?"

"Yeah, I was."

"You give your statement yet?"

"Yes."

"Good." He jerked his head towards the door. "Get out of here. I've got this and DiFranco's about to have kittens. She's been on the horn with me already, asking where you are."

Lawrence did not argue. He grabbed his coat and keys and was at the door, about to push through it when Rich stopped him.

"Janine called me, Mike," he said. "She heard about the shooting and wanted to check in. She said she tried to reach you but couldn't get through. I told her you were fine. Thought you'd like to know."

Lawrence's throat tightened.

"Thanks, Rich." He shoved his way out of the accursed building and into the light of that awful, rainy day.

***

Lawrence found that he had three missed calls from Janine, only one of which ended in a voicemail. He did not listen to it, neither did he call her back. He did send a reassuring text, though. A text was a poor substitute for a call, he knew well enough, but he had an agonizingly long day ahead of him, very little sleep behind him, and he was not altogether sure how he would react if he heard her voice. Sohm was in trouble and there were still a few pieces of the puzzle that did not fit. He could not afford to fall apart now, so he sent his text and put the phone back in his pocket.

He arrived to find the station in an organized uproar. Sohm was tucked away in one of the interrogation rooms, being debriefed with DiFranco and the lawyers. No one wanted to see Lawrence yet, though he was cautioned against leaving, as he would be required to give another statement and his presence might be required at the press conference.

"Hell of a way to end the case," the desk sergeant commented.

Lawrence could not disagree. "I'll be in my office, if anyone needs me."

"It's probably the only room in the building that you'll find any peace," the sergeant remarked. "Enjoy it while it lasts."

Lawrence nodded and walked away, deep in thought. In the aftermath of Stewart's interview, he had not had any time to think beyond the immediate tasks. Now, in the calm before the real storm, he reviewed Stewart's statement of actions. Something was missing from his confession. He had realized it then, back when he had told Stewart that he was taking him downtown but he had not had time to really consider what it was. In the brief space of time that it took for him to walk from the entryway to the hallway that led to his office, he worked it out.

Falk, dressed in a shirt and tie that looked as though they had been hastily pulled un-ironed from a basket, intercepted him in the hallway.

"Sir," he asked, "is Sohm all right?"

Lawrence shook his head clear. "Yes – well, he will be, thanks."

Falk looked relieved, then jerked his thumb over his shoulder. "I know you're exhausted, sir, but there's someone waiting for you in your office. He heard about your visit to the college and insisted that he needed to speak to you right away."

He did not have to tell Lawrence who it was.

Harry Gagnon didn't give Lawrence a chance to greet him. He hopped out of his chair, fists clenched, eyes on fire, ready for a fight. "They say you've caught my wife's killer!"

Lawrence felt unutterably weary. He dropped his jacket onto his desk and leaned against the desk, rubbing his face. As bad as the morning had been, this afternoon had just taken a turn for the worse.

"Good afternoon, Mr. Gagnon," he said. "Yes, sir, we did catch your wife's killer."

"Not Professor Stewart, surely?" The man's tone was desperate. He flailed his hands around helplessly as he spoke and

Lawrence noted, for the first time, that the right hand was clumsily bandaged. "I called him earlier and his secretary said the police had taken him away. You can't seriously think that Stewart did this. He's known us for years, we've been friends forever. Emma adored him and he-"

Lawrence interrupted. "I'm sorry. He made a full confession."

"No!" Gagnon's voice echoed in the small room. "This is unacceptable! He couldn't have killed Emma, he couldn't!"

"Mr. Gagnon..."

"Damn it, what made you think it was a man! You police-all law keepers are alike, you always get the wrong person! I knew I couldn't rely on you! You're paid to do this and I solved it in a few hours!"

"Oh, you did, did you?" Lawrence nodded towards Gagnon's right hand. "Tell me, how did you hurt your hand?"

Harry Gagnon looked rather like a man who had just run into a brick wall. He gaped at Lawrence, then protectively tucked his hand under his arm.

Lawrence felt a tidal wave of sympathy for the man, but he could not protect him. No one could and no one should. There was only one way for the man to find any peace and that was through facing the truth.

So, while Harry Gagnon stood there, nonplussed, Lawrence told him what the truth was.

"When Sarah Hopper failed to find her backpack in Emma's office, she broke into your house looking for it, didn't she, Mr. Gagnon? Emma had found it and discovered the pocket with the drugs, didn't she? She was as holding on to it, probably hoping to talk Sarah into turning herself in, and when she died, Sarah went looking for the backpack. That's when you found her."

Harry found his voice then, enough for a feeble, "I-I don't know what you're talking about."

Lawrence sighed. "Harry, please. She broke in Thursday night. She'd had a fight with her boyfriend. She was desperate and she was there, rifling through your things, looking for her backpack, the girl you thought killed your wife. You caught her, you lost your temper, and you hit her. I'm guessing that once you started, you just couldn't stop. When you realized that she was dead, you took your boat and dumped her and her purse into the inlet." He tilted his head. "Am I right, Mr. Gagnon?"

Gagnon's eyes were streaming, but when he looked at Lawrence, there was no trace of regret or remorse. Only fury.

"God!" he spat. "It was *so* simple! She'd hounded Emma, threatened her, made her life miserable and that morning that Emma-" He stopped, rubbed his eyes, then roared, "We all saw her running away!"

Falk appeared in the doorway behind Harry, obviously concerned.

"Your duty was to report it to us, Harry," Lawrence said gently and beckoned for Falk to come in. "Not to beat her to death."

Falk placed a hand on Gagnon's shoulder. Gagnon shrugged it off and stepped towards Lawrence, shaking in anger.

"You're arresting *me*? You of all people? That girl *killed* my Emma, the only thing in my life worth having, for a lousy package of pills! You can't tell me you wouldn't have done the same, that you wouldn't see justice done for your daughter if you could! It wasn't murder, it was *justice!*"

The image of Sarah Hopper's body, slight, young, broken, flashed into Lawrence's mind and suddenly he was done with Harry Gagnon. He stepped forward and let some of his anger and exhaustion into his tone.

"It *was* murder, Mr. Gagnon. Sarah Hopper couldn't have killed your wife. The poison was in the pain pills that Samantha Harris took for her migraines."

"No." Gagnon shook his head, desperate and frightened. "You're lying. You must be lying!"

He was crying in earnest now and Lawrence, too exhausted to speak, waved for Falk to take him away. It was done and just in time. Michael Lawrence had reached the very end of his rope.

49

Gagnon did not immediately contest the charges against him. He demanded his lawyer and said nothing after his request was granted.

DiFranco, once briefed of this new event, immediately requested a search warrant for the Gagnon house and assigned Falk to the search team. But before the warrant was even issued, Bridget Madden came walking in, yellow and gray backpack in hand. She had discovered it in the linen closet and recognized it as Sarah Hopper's. She told the desk sergeant that she tried to call her guardian but could not raise him on the phone.

The desk sergeant called Lawrence immediately. "The kid has no idea," he said. "What should I tell her?"

"Nothing," Lawrence replied. "I'll take care of it."

Bridget was shown into Lawrence's office and given coffee and a seat. He broke it to her as gently as possible. Initially, she refused to believe him. After she had calmed down, she came as close to admitting that Harry was capable of killing Sarah as she could without exactly saying so aloud.

"He really did think Sarah killed her," she said softly,

tracing the rim of her cup with her finger. "He thought because she was there, because she had run away – but he didn't know her at all, you see. I knew her a little and Sarah…" She shrugged. "Honestly, she just wasn't smart enough to poison anyone. Not on purpose anyway."

They sat in silence for a time, Lawrence watching her closely. The girl held up well – all those lessons in stage craft and performance were paying off today in a dignified display of self-control and reason in the middle of chaos.

Whether or not the stage is in your future, he thought, *you'll go far, Bridget Madden.*

"What are you going to do?" he asked.

She shrugged. "Harry's the only family I have left. The night of the concert – last night I guess - God, it seems so long ago…"

After a minute, she continued. "We argued again. Last night. He wanted me to stay and finish out my scholarship, like Emma wanted. He volunteered to look after me, to cover things until I was finished." She looked into her untouched coffee. "In his own way, he's been good to me. I know Emma's death… I just can't believe it came to this."

There was genuine anguish in that statement.

"If it helps," Lawrence volunteered, "I don't think he intended to kill her. She'd broken into his house looking for that backpack. When he found her, she probably panicked and he responded in kind. It was, for all practical intents and purposes, an accident."

She gave him a sidelong look and smiled knowingly.

"Yes," she said quietly. "That's a much nicer complexion on the story. Why don't we stick with that?"

****

It took them the rest of the day to process everything that needed immediate attention. Sarah Hopper's backpack contained several packages of pills that bore Sarah's, Emma's, and Rideout's fingerprints. When confronted with this information, Colin Rideout sent for his lawyer again and Jillian Tremblay, of drug enforcement, told Lawrence that she was hopeful of a full confession in return for a deal.

"This could turn out to be a good day's work for you," she said cheerfully when she stopped by his office. "Two murderers and a busted drug ring. The top brass will owe you at least a citation."

She left before Lawrence could respond, which was just as well. No one wanted to be reminded that one of their own was facing suspension and possible criminal charges after the disastrous confrontation with Professor Stewart.

Lawrence had a meeting with the lawyers, several administrators, HR, and PR, and then he retreated into his office to type up his report.

When he was finished, he emailed copies to his superiors and called Sohm. When he got no answer, he left a message and called the front desk.

"What room is Sohm in?"

"He's gone home for the day," the desk sergeant said. "Want me to call him?"

Lawrence checked his watch. It was after six now. It occurred to him that he had not eaten lunch today.

"No," he said. "Let the man have some peace."

He hung up, leaned back in his chair, and closed his eyes. He felt the world begin to swim and spin and wondered if he was capable of driving. If not, it looked like he was spending another night in the office.

Hell of a way to celebrate the end of a case, he thought. *I hope Sohm can find some peace.*

He did not have much time to sit and wonder. His intercom buzzed. DiFranco was on the other end: could Lawrence come to her office? There was no reason not to, so he took his jacket and made his way down to the hall.

***

She was waiting for him with a cup of coffee and a plastic wrapped sandwich from the cafeteria.

"Eat," she ordered and he did, though the bread stuck to the roof of his mouth and the tuna tasted like wallpaper paste.

While he forced the food down, she told him that Sohm had given his statement like a trooper and that all the evidence found on the scene proved his statement out.

"Of *course* it did," Lawrence muttered.

She ignored his foul temper. "According to the lawyers and the DA, Sohm can look forward to a couple weeks off at the state's expense but he'll be back, reputation and badge intact." She paused. "I know you two are close. I thought you'd want to know."

He nodded his thanks, swallowed a mouthful, and asked, "Does Sohm know?"

"It wouldn't be appropriate for me to tell him," she said lightly and looked at her hands. "Look, Lawrence, I know he hasn't any family around here and I don't know what his social life is like and I can't inquire, but he considers you a friend at least. You'll keep an eye him for me?"

Lawrence thought of Sohm's white face, the panic in his eyes when he realized what he had done.

"He shot the man thinking he was protecting me," Lawrence said. "He was provoked."

"I know that," DiFranco said. "*You* know that and the evidence is on your side. Just make sure Sohm knows it too, will you?"

"You can count on it, ma'am."

"Excellent. Now, detective, you've had a busy day. Mind filling me in on what's been going on?"

He gave her the rundown on their interview with Atkinson and Stewart and his own interviews with Harry Gagnon and Bridget Madden. Colin Rideout's decision to cooperate she already knew, so he told her about Bridget's surrendering the backpack and her own concerns about Harry.

"She's all alone now," DiFranco said, her voice unexpectedly soft. "What will she do?"

"She's standing by him. She was offered a part in an off-Broadway show, but she turned it down. She said she thought Harry had lost enough and that since he'd been her family when she had none, the least she could do was return the favor. For his sake and for Emma's." He stopped and drew in a long breath. "She's going to be okay. They both are."

"What about Matthew, Samantha's son?"

Another difficult call that he had to make. "I talked with Jonathan St. Jean, Matt's step-father. He's coming here to claim the body and to bring Matt back with him to California as soon as they can. He told me that he never had much of an opportunity to bond with the boy before, but maybe he can make up for lost time now. As for Atkinson, I turned every-thing over to the DA. He can decide what to do with him."

"Poor man. What a mess." She looked down at the sea of paperwork that had washed over her desk, plucked up a sheet of paper and handed it to him, "A copy of Stewart's confession. It tallies with the statements you and Sohm gave. I've got people looking for Nancy Grey now."

He took the statement. It was a printed on Noble College stationary, with the date and time at the top and Stewart's flourishing signature at the bottom. The man thought of everything and he had had enough iron-willed resolution to carry out his revenge. In the end, though, he lacked the courage to actually pull the trigger for his own suicide. He had to force someone else do it for him. By taking justice into his own hands, he had left Matthew without a mother, widowed Jonathan, killed Emma, set up the scenario that lead to Harry's breakdown and Sarah's death and nearly ruined Sohm, both personally and professionally.

Samantha Brown Harris had been directly responsible for one man's death and another's ruination. One crime might have been avoided if she had had the courage to come for-ward at once, but she had not. In the end, she hadn't any more real courage than Stewart had and between the pair of them, how much damage had been done?

Anger washed over Lawrence and he pushed the page back towards DiFranco with an abrupt motion. "It's a pity so many had to die for his private satisfaction."

She raised her eyebrows at the bitterness in his tone but did not directly address it. Instead, she leaned back in her chair and took her reading glasses off.

"So," she said, "tell me the truth now, Lawrence. Was it really Dickens that led you to Stewart?"

"When Sohm read the quote on the bench it reminded me of a poster I'd seen in his office." He shrugged, but could not resist adding, "It was elementary."

"And circumstantial." She bit the end of her glasses, musing. "I think Professor Stewart was a romantic at heart."

He snorted. "They all were. Emma risked her life to save Sarah's soul. Atkinson and Grey lied to protect Samantha, the woman *neither* could have, and loss drove Stewart and Gagnon to kill. The whole thing was so – melodramatic. All this mad sacrifice for love."

DiFranco was watching him, her eyes glittering. "Or what they *call* love. It all comes down to choices. We have to make them every day and this case was series of different people making very bad choices."

That, Lawrence thought, *is the understatement of the century.*

"There seems to be a very fine line between good and evil sometimes," he said aloud.

She was unmoved by his melancholy. "It may be fine, but it's clear."

There was a moment of silence. Then Lawrence burst out, "All these grand gestures. Makes me wonder if they were living in the real world and not some Dickens novel."

They disgusted him. They sickened him. And they frightened him, because these people had experienced tragedy and done something about it, all of them, while he, the lawman, the head of the household, the father and the husband, had been sitting on his hands for the past six months, doing nothing. But while he longed to take action, look at where action had got Gagnon and Stewart. They had broken the law and lost their families. Lawrence had not but he was losing anyway. He was losing Lizzy…and he was losing Janine. Not just losing her, driving her away.

If there was a line, where was it?

There is no difference. You can't make a difference. There is nothing to be done.

But that could not be the answer either. It just couldn't be.

DiFranco sat leaning back in her chair, studying Lawrence as he fought against despair, hopelessness, and his own weariness. Only when he finally had enough strength to lift his eyes and really look at her did she speak.

"People make grand gestures every day, but not everyone is called to be Sydney Carton, Michael." She leaned forward and rested her arms on the desk, looking as if she were talking to her own brother rather than her subordinate. "Some people are asked to die for the ones they love. But most of us are asked to live for them, to walk with them through the everyday grind and hardships and to stand with them when the going gets tough. It's easy to die for love. Living for it is harder."

Then, as he was processing that, she tilted her head and fixed him with a firm look. "You look tired, Michael. Don't you think it's time you went home?"

50

I f there was one place left on the planet that felt like home to Portsmouth Police Detective Michael Lawrence, it was Meadowbrook Hospice. He still hated the size, smell, and look of it. The food still tasted like someone purposefully processed all the taste and texture out of everything that passed over their counters and he could hardly bear the idea that he had a reason to come, but when it came right down to it, there was no place he would rather be. Visitors come to comfort the sick and remind them that they were not forgotten. Sometimes they came because they were the ones in need of the reminder.

Meadowbrook Hospice was not forever, but for the moment, it was where he was needed. More than that, it was where Lizzy and Janine were and where they were was home.

It was late when he arrived and Candace was off duty. He did not recognize the girl at the desk, but then he barely spared her a glance before hustling by, down the hall towards the familiar door where the little girl in the great big room was silently waiting.

She was not alone. Janine lay half asleep in the recliner,

her cell phone in one hand, the other hand wrapped in a rosary and covering her eyes. The pile of used tissues on the table beside her testified to the kind of day that she had had, the kind of day that every policeman's wife had at one point in her existence.

Janine did not stir. Michael stood in the doorway, watching her, taking in every familiar line and curve. Only then did it occur to him…how many times was she unable to help and had to stand by and wait for him to come home? How many times had she cried herself to sleep on his account?

Oh, Lord…

Janine shifted suddenly. Her hand came away and she blinked twice before recognizing him. Expressions of relief, happiness, and sorrow crossed her face in rapid succession before the mask of separation settled over her features. She rose and began to gather her things to leave. He stood there, in the doorway, watching her, his hands growing cold.

Don't leave, he wanted to say. *I'm back. I'm back for* you. *I'm not leaving. I won't ever leave.*

But his mouth was dry and the words would not come.

Janine had her purse and her jacket. She paused to stroke Lizzy's face, smiling as she bent to kiss her and whisper in her ear.

Janine, don't leave…

She pulled back and moved around the bed towards the doorway where he stood, carefully keeping her eyes on the floor so to avoid eye contact. When she came to the door she had to stop, for he was in the way. When she tried to step around him, to slip past him into the hallway, he put out his arm and stopped her.

Then he found his voice.

"Janine," he whispered.

She looked at him with watering eyes.

He wanted to tell her so many things. He wanted to apologize, to explain that he understood what he had done, what his distance had done. He wanted to tell her that he was back if she wanted, to stay by her side until the ordeal was over. He wanted to say that he did not blame her, could not blame her, but could only regret that he could not remove the burden from her shoulders. He wanted to hold her. He wanted to just *be* with her. But in the echoing silence, their last conversation rang loud and clear in his head and he just could not speak over it. Janine reached up and gently stroked away the tears that he had not realized were pouring down his face.

He took her hand and pressed it to his chest. "Janine, I…"

He choked and then, suddenly, she was in his arms, holding him tight, her head pressing against his chest. He responded in kind, bending over her, and then the words came freely, apologies, inadequate but the best he could do, poured out in a whispered torrent. She did not respond to any of them. She just nestled deeper into his arms, sighing.

"Oh, Michael," she said, "how I've missed you."

Michael Lawrence should have been immune to emotion by this time, but that night, he was overwhelmed. He held onto his wife, leaned his cheek on the top of her head and let her warmth melt away his cold loneliness. He had not expected this – had not expected her to take him back, but he had come anyway.

Hope is a stubborn thing.

So is faith.

As he stood in that dark room, holding his wife and basking in her acceptance, it occurred to him that where there was life there was hope of a full recovery. Hospices were supposed to be places where you came to die or to visit the dying. But that night, Michael knew differently.

Lizzy Lawrence would live to walk again…and both he and Janine would be there to see it.

About the Author

Killarney Traynor is a New England-born novelist, director, actress, history buff, and martial artist. She has published seven books, including 3 co-written with her sister, Margaret Traynor.

Killarney also works as a writer, director, and producer. She's written and directed two feature films, *Michael Lawrence* and *The Dinner Party*, as well as a several short films.

When she isn't writing, she can usually be found rummaging through used bookstores, scouring the internet for little-known Scifi shows, getting lost in Boston, or searching for the perfect cup of tea.

You can learn more about Killarney and her books on www.killarneytraynor.com.

More books by Killarney Traynor

Jenny Goodnight

The Mysteries Next-Door series
Summer Shadows
Necessary Evil
Michael Lawrence: the Season of Darkness

The Encounter Series (with Margaret Traynor)
Tale Half Told: 1971
Universal Threat: 1985
The Monster of Deep Water Lake: 1934

www.ingramcontent.com/pod-product-compliance
Lightning Source LLC
Chambersburg PA
CBHW070619300726

48975CB00006B/1862